NEIGHBORHOOD
GIRLS

NEIGHBORHOOD GIRLS

JESSIE ANN FOLEY

HARPERTEEN

For Mom and Dad, with love, for everything

HarperTeen is an imprint of HarperCollins Publishers.

Neighborhood Girls
Copyright © 2017 by Jessie Ann Foley
For information address HarperCollins Children's Books, a division
of HarperCollins Publishers, 195 Broadway, New York, NY 10007.
www.epicreads.com

Library of Congress Control Number: 2017939014
ISBN 978-0-06-257186-1

19 20 21 22 23 PC/LSCH 10 9 8 7 6 5 4 3 2 1

First paperback edition, 2019

The world breaks every one and afterward
many are strong at the broken places.

            —**ERNEST HEMINGWAY**, *A Farewell to Arms*

PART ONE

THE CREATOR, THE REDEEMER, AND THE SPIRIT WHO MAKES US FREE

1

IT WAS A WARM FRIDAY AFTERNOON in late September, and I was sitting in Ms. Lee's Honors Brit Lit class doing that thing where my hand moves my pen across the page, taking perfectly coherent notes, but my brain is somewhere else entirely. It's a bad habit, but one that even a straight-A student like me can't resist when the clock is forty minutes away from the weekend and the sun is filtering golden light through the third-floor classroom windows and my week of being a bored girl in a plaid skirt surrounded by other bored girls in plaid skirts is about to give way to the wild possibilities of a late summer weekend, when Saint Mike's is playing a home game against Notre Dame Prep under their new stadium lights, and the weekend is like a juicy peach I'm holding in my hand, just waiting to be bitten into and devoured, pit and all.

I uncapped my pink highlighter and was beginning to color in my nails while I half listened to Ms. Lee's well-worn lecture about the importance of thesis statements when the

PA clicked on. There were a few seconds of dead noise, and then a throat cleared.

"Excuse me, young women," Sister Dorothy began. "Please pardon the interruption." We all looked up expectantly at the ancient speaker system, like it was a TV or something. "Teachers, please escort your classes down to the auditorium for an important assembly. Thank you."

"What's *this* about?" Marlo Guthrie demanded from the front row. Marlo's GPA trailed her best friend, Ola Kaminski's, by a hundredth of a point, and she didn't like these kinds of disruptions throwing her off her valedictorian game. Besides, we were a month into our junior year, and we'd never been called to an unscheduled assembly before.

"Your guess is as good as mine," Ms. Lee answered, gathering up her keys and gradebook and herding us toward the door. "I guess we'll soon find out." She smiled then and began nervously twisting her engagement ring around her finger, and everyone knew that she was lying. And that's when we knew it was something bad.

Down in the auditorium, I found Kenzie, Sapphire, and Emily sitting in the last row, passing a bag of Skittles back and forth. When they saw me, Kenzie lifted her backpack from the seat she'd been saving for me.

"First week of school and I already got a fucking JUG," she complained, waving the telltale pink slip of paper at me before crumpling it up and stuffing it into the front pocket of her backpack among the various tubes of lipstick and frosted eye shadow. Other schools call this kind of punishment a detention. But at Academy of the Sacred Heart, where everything is God-ified, we call it JUG: Justice Under God. I shoved my backpack under the sagging velvet seat and sat down.

"I told you your skirt was too short," Em said through a mouthful of candy.

"Well, you know what? I'm not always going to have legs like this." Kenzie stuck them out for us to admire. They were as long and lean as a waterbird's, still deeply tanned from her summer lifeguarding job, and glistening with jasmine-scented, shimmer-flecked body lotion. "These things are a national treasure. Why would I ever want to cover them up? I should be like one of those supermodels and get them insured for a million dollars. Sister Hairy Penis is just jealous."

"I believe her name is pronounced Sister Mary Eunice," Sapphire giggled, "and I doubt some eighty-five-year-old nun is jealous of your hot legs."

"Yeah, Kenz," I laughed. "Don't be such a narcissist."

I glanced around for teachers, then pulled a can of contraband Dr Pepper from the front pocket of my backpack. I burst into a fit of fake coughing to cover up the *ka-chhh* as I cracked it open.

"Don't use your honors-class words on me, Wendy," Kenzie said. "So, what do you think this assembly is about, anyway? Like every nun in the school is up onstage." She raised her clasped hands to the high gilded ceiling of the old auditorium. "Please, please, *please*, oh Lord: please let us be going coed!"

Sister Dorothy, dressed in the signature dull gray of the Sacred Heart nuns, glided up to the mic at the center of the stage. One thing eleven years of Catholic schooling has taught me is that nuns don't walk; they *glide*. I guess this could be an optical illusion of their floor-length habits, but I've always thought it's because they're so much holier than the rest of us that they practically float. Come to think of it, that might be why I'm such a good student: it's kind of hard to cut class or blow off a homework assignment when you have to answer to somebody whose best friend is literally Jesus Christ Himself.

"Let's begin our assembly today, as we begin whenever we gather together," Sister Dorothy began, "with a prayer."

We all sat up a little straighter—Mr. Winters was patrolling the aisle—and made the sign of the cross. "In the name of the Creator, the Redeemer, and the Spirit Who Makes Us Free," we murmured, and it didn't even sound weird anymore because we've been saying it the Sister Dorothy way since freshman year, when, during orientation, she taught us about gender-inclusive language and how God transcends our ideas of male and female and therefore it's inaccurate to say "in the name of the Father, the Son, and the Holy Spirit." I guess the cardinal had gotten wind of it and had a disapproving little chat with her, but Sister Dorothy, who has been principal of ASH for approximately a hundred years, isn't exactly used to having people tell her what to do.

"I look out at this gathering of intelligent, compassionate young women on the brink of adulthood, and the sight of it fills me with peace." She opened her mouth to continue, then closed it. She tried again: opened her mouth, shaped it around a word, and clamped it shut again. That's when we realized that she was gulping back tears. And then we knew that whatever she was about to tell us must be *really* bad. After all, this was a woman who, according to school legend, had been arrested over thirty times, for protesting deforestation by chaining herself to trees or spray-painting peace signs on nuclear cooling towers or throwing overripe tomatoes at politicians who supported military strikes in the Middle East.

She worked as a Red Cross nurse during the Vietnam War and made us all watch *Apocalypse Now* during Teach-ings in Catholic Social Justice class, even that horrible water buffalo slaughter scene that made Veronica the Vegan barf into the recycled paper bin. And instead of apologizing for making Veronica so upset, Sister Dorothy yelled at her for a) throwing up all over the paper, rendering it unrecyclable, and b) being more affected by the portrayal of animal slaugh-ter than of human slaughter.

She was a tough lady.

"It's been a rough few years for Academy of the Sacred Heart," Sister Dorothy finally continued, her voice still wobbling. "In the past ten years alone, our enrollment has dropped by fifty percent. Our graduates move away and lose touch. The city public schools are improving. People don't believe in single-sex education anymore. Or in religious education at all, for that matter. Meanwhile, the costs of maintaining our school in this crumbling old building keep going up."

As if on cue, a little piece of plaster broke loose from the gilded ceiling and landed with a small puff of dust on the stage behind her.

"I have prayed over this matter a great deal," she resumed. "And one thing I am quite sure of is that God always answers our prayers, but not always in the way we'd like God to." I heard a stifled snort and looked over, stunned, to see that Mr. Winters, ASH's basketball coach and sole male teacher, was standing in the aisle beside us. He had removed his bifocals and was wiping his eyes with a handkerchief he'd fished out of his pocket.

"The Board of Trustees made the decision last night that Academy of the Sacred Heart is no longer a financially viable institution. And that's why I've called you here today: because I believe you, our students, should be the first to know that at the end of this school year, ASH will be closing its doors forever."

A collective gasp swept through the auditorium, followed by several shrill screams, loud protests of "no!" and, of course, a smattering of applause from Veronica the Vegan and her friends, as if their boycott of the crispy chicken patty special was somehow the thing to bring down this institution for good. Emily immediately whipped out her phone and began tweeting about it; Sapphire held her hands over her open mouth and was, for possibly the first time ever, speechless; while Kenzie sat perfectly still, the bag of Skittles crumpled in her hand.

"This," Kenzie finally said, a slow smile spreading across her beautiful face, "may just be the greatest day of my life."

I can't say I was all that surprised by her reaction. Kenzie had never made a secret of her resentment at having been forced to attend ASH. She'd been all set to go to Lincoln, our neighborhood public high school, until she came home from her eighth-grade graduation dance with a neck ringed in hickeys. Her dad sent her transcripts to Sister Dorothy the next day.

"If anybody can straighten you out," he told her, "it's the Sacred Heart nuns."

He'd been wrong about that, of course.

Sister Dorothy rapped the microphone, and we quieted down instantly.

"To our seniors," she continued, "this means you will have the bittersweet distinction of being our last-ever graduating class. And for our underclasswomen: I know that it was your intent to cross this stage at graduation in your cardinal-red cap and gown. I know that is what you wanted, what your families expected, and what you deserve. And I am so sorry that we failed you." She stopped to wipe her eyes. "But please know that this decision was made after much discernment and prayer, and that we would not be closing this school—a place that, for the women up here on this stage, is not just our life's work but our *home*—unless there was simply no other option. I'm so sorry, girls. We tried our very hardest."

And then, without responding to the waving hands and shouted questions that filled the echo-y expanse of the auditorium, a space that was built to accommodate twelve hundred girls and now held a population of barely two hundred, Sister Dorothy walked off the stage. Sister Mary Eunice, Sister Gertrude, and Sister Mary-of-the-Snows, all of whom were weeping, followed suit. The lay teachers standing in the aisles and at the exits were bum-rushed with angry girls demanding answers.

"Let's get out of here," Kenzie said, throwing her empty Skittles bag on the floor. "There's twenty minutes till last bell but it looks like Mr. Winters has his hands full."

We ducked past the crowds of yelling, crying girls, out the auditorium doors, and down the Saints Corridor toward our lockers. My head was spinning. Given ASH's half-empty hallways, the class sizes of nine or ten girls, the pathetically outdated computer labs, the cuts in sports teams and academic clubs and the near-constant fundraisers, you would think that we would have seen this coming. We hadn't. Academy of the Sacred Heart had stood on the same Chicago corner since ladies wore corsets and men took the streetcar to jobs in the stockyards. Our mothers went here, and so did our grandmothers. So did our *great*-grandmothers. ASH was an essential and immortal piece of our city; saying it was closing was like telling us that Lake Michigan was drying up. No matter how many signs there might have been, we hadn't seen them, because we hadn't believed that ASH was a thing capable of dying.

And how could this timing be any worse? It meant that next year, my *senior year*, I'd be at some other high school, walking to some other locker, without the saints watching over me as I gathered my books. I don't mean that last part in a religious, God-watching-over-me sense. When you go to ASH, you actually have saints watching over you because their faces are painted all over the walls and ceiling of the main hallway. Back in 1902, the school's principal, Sister Xavieria Schmidt, commissioned a group of art students from our first graduating class to paint a mural of the Virgin Mary on the east wall outside the auditorium. In over a hundred years, the paint hasn't faded a bit, and now, on bright mornings, when the sun shines through the glass front entrance, it hits the gold of Mary's halo in such a way that she actually glows with divine light. The painting was such a success that the next year, Sister Xavieria Schmidt commissioned the class of 1903 to create another mural—this time, to Saint Anne, the mother of Mary. A tradition was begun, and every year since then, the art students from each graduating class have added another female saint to what has come to be called the Saints Corridor, and now these images cover every inch of space in the main hallway that isn't taken up by a locker, a light fixture, or a door frame.

The artists, who always sign their names and their class year somewhere on their painting, include my mom, whose name is scrawled in the grass at Our Lady of Lourdes's feet; my grandma, whose name snakes up a fold in Saint Margaret of Scotland's purple robes; and my Aunt Colleen, whose looping signature is painted like a wedding ring around Saint Attracta's finger. In fact, the only woman in my family whose name doesn't appear anywhere is my Aunt Kathy, the youngest of my mom's two sisters and our family's resident black sheep, and that's only because, as she once explained, "The only extracurricular I did was the smoking-cigs-in-the-locker-room club."

The Saints Corridor is also the source of much of our school lore. Saint Agnes of Bohemia, painted in 1968, the era of free love, has big curving boobs and a sexy red, open mouth. You're supposed to kiss her feet before prom night if you're hoping to lose your V card. Saint Maria Goretti has the words *I LOVE BRAD* painted faintly within the folds of the sheep that she's holding. And Saint Catherine of Alexandria's red robes have been rubbed away to a splotchy, faded pink, from three decades of ASH girls touching them for good luck before a big exam, hoping that the patron saint of learning will help them remember the formula for ammonium phosphate or how the Seven Years' War helped lead to the American Revolution.

The corridor is even said to be the site of a religious miracle. Back in 1988, two popular seniors named Tiffany Maldonado and Sandy DiSanto were driving home from a homecoming party, dressed in neon taffeta and drunk out of their minds. When they reached the railroad crossing at Avondale Avenue, they miscalculated the distance of the oncoming headlight and were creamed by a California-bound freight train carrying three thousand tons of coal and limestone. School lore has it that my mom's painting, Our Lady of Lourdes, who reigns over the wall across the way from the science lab and directly above my locker, wept for the entire week of their funerals. At the end of the week, after people had come from miles around to venerate the painting and news crews had reported on the phenomenon and my mom dug out her old paintbrushes and brought them to Queen of Heaven church to have them blessed, the janitor discovered a leaky air-conditioning unit on the second floor directly above Our Lady's head, and suddenly Academy of the Sacred Heart went from site of holy miracle to citywide laughingstock.

Here's the thing, though: I'm not crazy and I'm not superstitious. I've totally outgrown that simple, unquestioning religious faith I had as a kid at my First Holy Communion, decked out in a white lace dress and matching tiara from David's Bridal and kneeling for the Body of Christ for the very first time. I don't believe the people who claim they see the Virgin Mary in their grilled cheese sandwiches. But there's something special about Our Lady of Lourdes. Maybe it's just the connection I feel because my own mother helped to paint her, back when she was carefree enough to care about things like art and beauty. Maybe it's because my locker stands right beneath her and I feel like she's been watching over me—literally—since day one of my high school career. But whatever it is, I can *feel* her, like a peaceful presence pressing down on me, whenever I get my books from my locker. I talk to her sometimes in my head, which I guess is the same thing as praying. *Hey, Our Lady. Please let me pass my precalc test. Hi, Our Lady. Please let my mom get enough hours this week to pay our gas bill. Hey. It's me. Can you help me work on not hating my dad so much?* I'd never tell anyone I do this, of course. If you knew my friends, you'd understand why.

On this particular afternoon, Our Lady gazed down at me and Kenzie as she always did, smiling her lonely smile as we gathered our stuff.

"Don't tell me you're seriously gonna do homework this weekend," Kenzie said as she watched me load my backpack with my physics textbook and my precalc notebook.

"Why wouldn't I?"

"Um, because our school is closing? And therefore

homework is pointless from now on?" She leaned over me, dabbing her lip gloss into place in the small magnet mirror on the inside of my locker door.

"Oh really? And what was your excuse before today?"

"I'm philosophically opposed to homework. You know that." She smacked her lips together, satisfied, and began vigorously finger-combing her impossibly shiny waist-length hair. "Young girls like us should spend our free time *freely*. We have the rest of our lives to shrivel away in a library reading"—she picked up the novel I was reading by its spine, with her thumb and forefinger, like it was a rotting banana peel—"*Pride and Prejudice*."

"You know," I said, "you'd actually really *like* that book."

"'It is a truth universally acknowledged, that a single man in possession of a good fortune must be in want of a wife,'" she read. "Oh, *I* see. You think I'd like it just because it's about a rich single guy? I have other interests, you know, Wendy."

"Name one."

"Well, poor single guys, for one. And rich married guys. And emotionally unavailable middle-class guys—"

I snatched the book away and zipped up my bag. "Look, you can spend all the time you want being free, but I, for one, need to get a full ride to a college that is far away from this city, and in order to do that, I need an A average. The stuff with my dad completely wiped out my college savings, in case you forgot."

"You and your 'dad stuff'," she sighed, slinging her empty

bag over her shoulder. "You think *I* have any college savings? Or, for that matter, an A average? Do I look worried to you?"

"It's easier not to worry," I retorted, "when you've never cared about going to college in the first place. But what exactly *do* you plan on doing for the rest of your life?"

"Me? I don't know. Model. Act. Bartend. Move to New York and play the guitar in smoky little clubs."

"You don't even know how to play the guitar, Kenz."

"Well, I'll have plenty of time to learn, won't I? Since I won't be wasting my time in college."

"You're insane."

"But you love me." She leaned over then and planted a wet, sticky-glossy kiss on the tip of my nose.

Out in the school parking lot, I climbed into Red Rocket, the heap of rusted metal my Aunt Colleen had bequeathed to me on my sixteenth birthday. I wasn't wild about the fact that Kenzie had nicknamed my car after a dog's penis, even if it *did* feel like sort of an apt description. I took the wire hanger from the glove compartment and jiggered open the passenger side door, whose handle had long since fallen off. Kenzie hopped into shotgun, put on her sunglasses, kicked off her shoes, and dangled her bare feet out the rolled-down window, the better to show off the shooting star tattoo across her right ankle. Kenzie has four tattoos: the shooting star, a small heart on the soft swell of the top of her right breast, the American flag on the inside of one wrist, and the Chicago flag on the inside of the other. For two years now, she's been trying to convince me to get one with her, but every time I think I've worked up the nerve, I can't bring myself to do it. The idea of permanence scares me, you know? Like, what do I love now that I'll still love in ten or twenty years? For Kenzie, it's different. To her, *nothing* is permanent. With her makeup-smudged eyes, her straight black hair ombréd into bleached tips, her electric-pink-painted lips, and her wool scrap of a uniform skirt, Kenzie is like a poster girl for the Now. People, ideas, clothes, art, music, love: according to her, none of it lasts, all of it is replaceable, and this includes everything from hair color to body art to Catholic high schools with a century-old tradition of academic excellence in a single-sex setting.

I revved the ignition, and finally, reluctantly, Red Rocket came to life, spraying gouts of foul-smelling smoke from its exhaust pipe.

"You have *got* to get a new car," Kenzie sniffed, waving the smoke away and scanning the parking lot for Saint Mike's boys, who sometimes wander over here from their school across the street.

"You're right," I said. "With all the piles of cash I'm making as a part-time ham slicer, I don't know *why* I haven't treated myself to a new Mercedes yet."

"You and that boring-ass job," she sighed.

"I *like* working at the deli," I said.

"I know. That's what I find so tragic. So, what do you

think about the big announcement? Your mom is going to freak out. She went here, didn't she?"

"Yep." I nodded. "I'm, like, a third generation ASH girl. I can't believe it. I mean, it's kind of sad. Don't you think?" *Kind of sad.* This was such an understatement that it was almost a lie. I loved Academy of the Sacred Heart. When Sister Dorothy had made the announcement, I immediately felt hot tears pricking the backs of my eyes. But I had blinked them away, because I knew that if my friends saw, they would laugh.

Now Kenzie shoved her sunglasses up, pushing back her dark bangs. "You expect *me* to be sad about Academy of the Acrid Fart? Wendy, haven't you ever noticed that ASH is the school that time left behind? Did you know that Lincoln has an open-campus lunch? And a pool that's not covered with mold spores? And *iPads*? Not to mention, of course, *boys go there*? Living, breathing, XY-chromosome *males*? The day they take a wrecking ball to this place, I'm throwing a party. I'll even invite you, if you're lucky."

"Gee, thanks."

"Can we still go to the Saint Mike's game tonight?" she demanded now. "Or are you too emotionally distraught?"

"No," I laughed, steering Red Rocket toward the school gate in a belching haze of gray smoke. "I'm fine."

"Good. Because I promised Evan I'd go and I need you to be there to explain what's going on to me. Why the hell does football have to be so complicated anyway?"

"Why don't you ask Evan that?"

"I did, once! And his explanation was so boring I had to give him a hand job just to shut him up."

She gave the radio a tremendous slap and it burst into life. Then she plugged her phone into the adaptor and turned the music all the way up, effectively ending the conversation. Which was cool with me, because I didn't feel like arguing with her or pretending like I didn't care that my whole world had just been turned upside down for the second time since I started high school. What I felt like doing was relishing this Friday afternoon and its lingering summer weather. As we pulled out of the parking lot of our dying school and into the blue September afternoon, the two of us fell silent, alone with the music and our weekend thoughts, content to trade our worries about the rest of high school for the much more manageable worries about the next forty-eight hours.

2

WHEN I ARRIVED HOME FROM SCHOOL, I found
my mom and my Aunt Colleen basking in the sun on our
apartment balcony, their eyes shaded by the fake Chanel
sunglasses my brother had sent them from his shore leave in
Dubai. A half-empty bottle of 7-Eleven chardonnay sat on
the glass table next to a mostly empty pack of Virginia Slims
Luxury Lights. When they saw me coming through the slid-
ing doors, they both leaped up.

"It's not true, is it?" Aunt Col said, attacking me with one
of her breasty, perfume-y hugs. "It *can't* be true!"

"It can," I said, my words muffled by her cleavage.

My mom pulled on her cigarette and exhaled with a sigh.
"As if you haven't already been through enough. What are
we going to *do*?"

"Well, she'll have to go to Lincoln, I guess," said Aunt
Col. The two of them exchanged a look. They do that a
lot—have silent conversations with their eyes. My mom and
Col are eleven months apart and could pass for twins. Same

dark-brown-almost-black, wavy-just-short-of-curly hair, same squinty blue eyes, same bump in the middle of their noses. Aunt Col lives a block down from us, and she might as well be my second mom, especially because she and Uncle Jimbo were never able to have kids of their own so Stevie Junior and me are the sole targets of her maternal smothering.

"You guys say that," I said, leaning against the railing and looking down at the parking lot below, "as if it's the worst thing in the world."

"Well, it *certainly* isn't *ideal*, now, is it?"

Both my mother and Aunt Col have this perception that public high schools are places where a bunch of kids dressed in skimpy outfits spend the day buying drugs and being atheists. It's like they've totally forgotten that their own Catholic-school experiences were steeped in misery. When she was a kid, my mom's punishment for slouching in theology class was to spend the rest of the day kneeling next to her desk on grains of dry rice. And Aunt Col is only right-handed because her first-grade teacher, who believed that left-handedness was a sign of the devil, had taped the fingers on her left hand together every day until she learned to write legibly with her Christian hand. And yet, the two of them both act like those were their glory days. I guess that kind of brainwashing never really goes away.

Aunt Col was now gazing into her wineglass, searching for something positive to say about the situation. "Well," she finally said, "Lincoln *does* have that new fine arts complex, doesn't it?"

"Yeah," said my mom, "but is *that* the measure of a good school? A goddamn pottery studio? What about *moral* education?" I put my head down and stifled a laugh. Given what's happened in our family over the last two years, I don't think the Boychucks are the most qualified people to be making decisions about *moral education.*

"Bernie, times have changed," Aunt Col responded. "People don't respect old-fashioned Catholic values the way they used to." She leaned over to flick her cigarette butt onto the asphalt below, and they sat for a while, sipping their wine sullenly.

"My daughter going to a coed public high school." My mom shook her head finally and poured the last of the chardonnay into her glass. "Can you imagine what Ma would say about that if she were alive?"

"Can you imagine what Ma would say if she found out ASH was closing?"

They were silent again, ruminating on this possibility. My grandma had been the president of ASH's class of 1958, and, until she got sick, chairwoman of the annual alumnae fundraiser. Just outside the journalism room, there's a big black-and-white yearbook photo of her and two of her friends hanging on the wall, with these amazing gravity-defying bouffants. At seventeen, Grandma was beautiful, which is hard to square with my final memory of her: skeletal, sour-smelling, two inches of white at the roots of her black hair, staring at all of us from sunken, milky eyes and wheezing through that horrible throat machine thing with uncomprehending, unspeakable rage. Throat cancer: and here were two of her daughters—who are both, by the way, *nurses*—smoking. It amazes me how stupid adults can be sometimes.

I left my mom and Aunt Colleen to their cocktail hour and spent the rest of the afternoon lounging on my bed, scrolling through my various social media accounts and halfheartedly plodding my way through *Pride and Prejudice*. When the cicadas began to buzz outside my open bedroom window, I finally got up and went to take a shower.

Not to sound like a total princess, but every time I get ready to go out in our tiny, moldy apartment bathroom, with its vertical coffin of a shower, all I can think about is my old house. I know that thinking about that kind of stuff is both pointless and dangerous, but I can't help it. I've gotten used to nearly everything about our new life, but God, it would just be so nice to have a shower with good water pressure and a bathtub where you could spread around some scented bath salts and just hang out for a while. And maybe a hallway that doesn't always smell like cat piss. And hey, if we're dreaming big here, how about some air-conditioning and a front room carpet that doesn't have a gigantic mysterious black stain in the shape of Australia? Not that I ever appreciated this kind of stuff when we actually *had* a house. I grew up thinking that big houses with dishwashers and bathtubs and a big oak tree in the backyard were, like, constitutional rights. It's only now that we've lost everything that I realize how lucky I was.

After my shower, I pulled a towel around myself and cracked the window to release the fog of steam. In the parking lot below, my downstairs neighbor, Sonny, was chivalrously opening the door to his Jeep for a bleached blonde in one of those bandage dresses generally worn by women half her age. If their date went well, chances are I would hear about it later that night, when pornographic sounds began emanating from his bedroom, which was situated, tragically, directly under mine. Gagging at the possibility, I put on shorts, a tank top, and my espadrille wedges. As I globbed my eyelashes with mascara, I could hear the music drifting from the open windows of Emily's Ford Focus before it had even pulled around the corner. I slicked my tongue over my teeth and smiled fiercely in the mirror. I stuck my phone in my pocket, called good-bye to my mom and Aunt Col, and headed down the stairs and out into the purpling night. Before I climbed into Emily's car, I took a deep breath, steeling myself for the onslaught of deafening club music and peach body splash that awaited me.

When I opened the car door, Kenzie immediately whipped around in her seat to give me that big, glittering smile that had already paralyzed the hearts of so many Saint Mike's boys.

"You look hot," she said approvingly, arching a penciled eyebrow. "I have a feeling about tonight. A good one."

"Your hair looks adorable," Sapphire said with a pout, shoving over to make room for me. "Mine looks disgusting. I wish I had *your* hair."

"No," I said, reciting my lines. "*My* hair looks disgusting. *Your* hair is gorgeous."

She began teasing the crown of her hair with her fingers, using the mirror on the back of her iPhone case to make adjustments. Sapphire's beautiful, thick curls were her greatest vanity, so in the strange, inverted world of popularity, it meant that she had to spend as much time as possible ridiculing them.

"I love your top," Emily shouted over the music as she eyed me from the rearview mirror.

"This?" I snapped the shoulder strap dismissively. "This stupid thing was like three bucks." Which, of course, was a lie. The top was from the Young Contemporary section at Bloomingdale's, a gift from my rich aunt Kathy, and it was my favorite piece of clothing.

But this is the ritual of my friends: we pick each other over like preening monkeys, exchanging compliments and insulting ourselves with machine-gun quickness. I'm not sure why we do it, exactly, but I suspect it's a combination of envy and insecurity. Whatever the reason, the nice things my friends say to me have long since ceased to mean anything. I remember once, at the end of sophomore year, when Ms. Lee handed back my *Grapes of Wrath* research paper, she told me that I had a fresh way of looking at things, and that I was one of the best writers she'd come across in eight years of teaching. To this day, I still smile to myself whenever I remember that compliment, because I could tell that Ms. Lee had actually meant it, and because it wasn't about my outfit.

The thing is, even though it's been two years now, I'm still not quite used to being popular. I hadn't counted on how exhausting it would be, how much pretending it involved. Being an honors student, I learned early on, is an embarrassment that I have to downplay, which is why I've started reading novels the way other kids my age probably watch porn: sweaty-handed and in secret, hoping that no one will walk in on me. I also have to pretend I'm attracted to a revolving cast of douchebags and meatheads, because the quiet, bookish boys I usually like don't attend parties in the woods that flow with foamy kegs of lukewarm beer and are populated mainly by barfing football players. Evan Munro, for example, is Kenzie's boy of the moment, and we're all expected to swoon over him because, I guess, he's the star quarterback at Saint Mike's with Division 3 colleges scouting him and he's built like a brick shithouse. It doesn't matter that I once watched him sit in a chair at a party, drunkenly squeezing at a huge zit on his shoulder with two pudgy fingers until it ruptured and he wiped a streak of bloody pus onto the wallpaper, concluding this activity with an earth-shattering belch.

Our complimenting ritual now complete, Emily floored it, and we were off, speeding past the Dairy Hut, where families lined up in the warm night for what would probably be one of the last cones of the season, and turning down Avondale Avenue along the train tracks. Someone had put fresh flowers at the memorial crosses that marked the place where Tiffany Maldonado and Sandy DiSanto were killed in the crash that, if you believe such things, had made Our Lady of Lourdes cry.

We slowed past the night-darkened windows of Academy of the Sacred Heart and pulled into the parking lot of Saint Michael's High School for Boys, threading our way past tailgating parents who were gathered around portable grills drinking beer from coffee mugs, and found one of the last open spaces near the chain-link fence butting up against the soccer fields. When we got out of the car and headed for the ticket line, which was already snaking out from the stadium and into the parking lot, Kenzie stopped short.

"Wait a second," she said, closing her eyes and sniffing the air. "Do you smell that?"

"Smell what?" Sapphire took a panicked whiff of her own armpit.

"*Testosterone.*" Kenzie's eyes darted around the hordes of

boys standing around in groups, drinking them in from head to toe as shamelessly as any catcalling construction worker. "*God*, how I've missed that smell. We've been locked up in that estrogen cave for a week!"

"I don't know how you're even going to handle public school next year." Emily laughed. "You're going to be going around humping desks or something." In response to that, Kenzie wiggled her eyebrows at us, jumped into a basketball player's defensive stance, arms and legs spread wide, and began thrusting her hips in Emily's direction, slowly inching toward her with her pelvis in the lead. Emily, thrilled to be receiving such attention from the queen bee, squealed with delight, until suddenly Kenzie stopped midthrust. "Oh my God," she said, grabbing both Emily and me by the arm. "That's *Christian*."

"Who?"

"Where?"

She pointed to a tall kid standing in the ticket line about ten people in front of us, kicking around a hacky sack and laughing loudly with his friends.

"Which one is he again?" I asked. It was hard to keep track of the men in Kenzie's life.

"*You* know! The guy who started stalking my Instagram after he met me at that party in the forest preserve for Sami's birthday," she said. "And he's been, like, professing his love for me to everybody at Saint Mike's ever since."

From the looks of him, Christian was just the kind of obnoxious boy-toy sort Kenzie often went for: a baby face partially obscured by a flat-brimmed hat, fake diamond earrings in both ears, and wrists weighted down with neon bracelets. His flip-flops were plastered with designer logos, the kind of shoes you buy at Marshalls when you don't have a ton of money but you want people to think you do.

"If he's so madly in love with you," Sapphire said, shading her eyes from the setting sun, "why don't you see if he'll let us cut the line?"

"I was *just* thinking that." Kenzie pulled down her tank top to expose the trim of her paisley-patterned bra and flounced in the boys' direction while the rest of us followed in her wake.

"Hey, Insta-Stalker," she said, brushing her hand against his bare arm. "Mind if we budge the line?"

Kenzie was such a child of the digital age that even her spoken words were like text messages: the tone was impossible to interpret. Christian didn't seem to even notice that she'd just insulted him. "Hi, Kenzie!" he said, gazing at her like a slobbering golden retriever who just saw a piece of steak fall to the kitchen floor. "Yeah, totally squeeze in!"

As we shuffled into the line, ignoring the halfhearted protests of the kids behind us, Christian nodded toward a dark-haired, lanky boy standing next to him. "Hey," he said, "do you guys know my buddy Darry?" Before any of us could answer, the boy reached across the cloud of Christian's cologne and shook each of our hands. This might be a normal thing to do in the adult world, but I couldn't remember there ever being a time when a boy my own age *shook my hand*. I was used to guys who might glance up from their phones to give me the up-and-down and then mumble hey before returning to their mindless tapping. I wondered if Darry was one of those weird boy-men who wears blazers to parties and plays the stock market, but other than the handshake, he was dressed like, and looked like, a normal kid. Except for one thing. His *eyes*. They were a light copper brown, almost golden, and they were resting on my face, and they were not looking away.

"These are my girls," Kenzie said, pointing at each of us one by one. "That's Sapphire, that's Emily, and that's Wendy."

"*Wendy?*" Christian snorted. "Your parents named you after a fast food joint?"

"No." I glared. "They named me for a girl in a Bruce Springsteen song."

"'Born to Run'?"

"Yeah." I turned to Darry, surprised. "How'd you know?"

"Because it's one of the greatest rocks songs ever, and I know all the lyrics by heart." His eyes rested on me in a kaleidoscope of soft browns and golds. "My parents named me after a book. *The Outsiders*."

"Darry Curtis," I said, nodding. "I love that book."

We smiled at each other, and for just a second, it felt like the whole world was holding its breath.

"Tickets, please." The bored voice of the ticket taker broke the spell—we'd finally reached the front of the line. When Darry turned to hand off his ticket and we entered the stadium, Kenzie kicked me and bugged her eyes at me while Emily declared that she had to use the bathroom.

"I'm having a few people over later," Christian said, gazing hopefully at Kenzie and her peeking paisley bra. "We're going to head there after the game. You guys should come."

"You really should." Darry said. He was speaking to all of us, but he was only looking at me. "Corner of Strong and Melvina."

"Hey," called Christian, grinning stupidly, "there are only three streets in Chicago that rhyme with a part of the female body. Know what they are?"

Darry rolled his eyes at me, flattering me with the realization that he saw in me a person who was about to be as bored as he was with the immature comment that was sure to follow.

"Melvina, Paulina, and Lunt," Christian cackled. Kenzie graced him with only the slightest hint of a smile.

"We'll try to stop by," she said, glancing over his shoulder to scan the crowd for people more interesting than him.

"Come in through the alley," Darry said, and when he

turned to follow Christian toward the bleachers, I caught the faintest scent of piney soap, and then the world rearranged itself back into the infinitely less interesting place it had been before I knew he lived in it.

"Christian's *hot*, Kenz," Emily observed. "And he's totally into you."

"He's pathetic." Kenzie picked a long black hair from the strap of her tank top and rubbed it between her delicate fingers until it sifted to the ground. "I could practically *see* his boner rising when I came within ten feet of him. Does he even know that me and Evan are kind of a thing now? Evan would beat his ass if he saw Christian ogling my boobs like that."

"Yeah," Emily said, quickly reevaluating her opinion. "I guess he *is* kind of sad."

"His party should be good, though," Kenzie said. She took out her phone. "I'm going to tell Evan to meet us there after the game."

"What about that other guy?" Sapphire said. "Wendy, he was *staring* at you."

"He wasn't *staring* at me," I objected. "I mean, he just likes Springsteen."

"*Staring*. Like a stalker."

"He seemed cool," I ventured.

"Code for 'I want to bang him,'" laughed Emily.

"Well, you'll get your chance," Kenzie said. "Christian's

parties are always out of control. Come on. Let's go find a seat."

At the risk of sounding like a shallow, superficial asshole, here's why all the pretending and the fakeness of popularity is worth it: for that one moment when you and your clique climb the bleachers at a crowded football game. The four of us, dressed in our uniforms of tiny cutoffs and tinier tank tops, push-up bras thrusting our breasts up and out, sunglasses shading our eyes from the setting sun still warm on our bare, smooth legs, *this* was why I had made it my business to be popular when I started high school. This is the moment when everybody is watching you even if they pretend like they're not, and everybody knows who you are even if they pretend like they don't. It's this crazy, intoxicating power, a power that I never had in elementary school, that makes me feel totally secure and completely unafraid. I knew that if I broke away from the group to go use the bathroom or buy a Dr Pepper at the concession stand, then all the magic would die and I'd just be me again. But surrounded by these girls, it's different. It's like no one can touch me. No one would say a word about my father; no one would post something awful about my family on social media. They wouldn't dare. Being part of our clique makes me untouchable and admired, feared and respected. I'm not dumb enough to believe that everybody genuinely *likes* us, but they all do a good job at pretending, because they all know what happens when you piss off Kenzie Quintana. It's an airtight kind of protection, and if it means that I have to dumb myself down a little bit and trade fake compliments and fawn over pimple-popping jocks, I figure it's a small price to pay.

We found an open spot near the top row, up against the protective fence that ran along the back of the bleachers. There had been other, closer spots on the way up, but this one allowed for maximum visibility.

"Okay, everybody," Kenzie said, leaning against the fence seductively and posing for a rapid series of selfies, "you guys need to help me pay attention to this stupid game. Evan is gonna be asking me about it afterward, and I have to pretend like I was on the edge of my seat, watching him tackle the shit out of people, okay?"

"He's a quarterback, Kenz," I reminded her. "Quarterbacks don't tackle."

She patted the open space on the bleachers next to her.

"And *that*," she said, "is why Wendy gets to sit next to me tonight."

Saint Mike's kicked off, and the first quarter was underway. I was in the middle of explaining to Kenzie the concept of a first down for the hundredth time when I saw Ola Kaminski, Marlo Guthrie, and Alexis Nichols, the three smartest girls at Academy of the Sacred Heart, climbing the bleachers. They stopped for a moment, looking around for an open spot. Kenzie cupped her hands around her pink mouth and called, "Sit down, losers! I'm *trying* to watch a football game here!" The three of them looked up, in the direction of the insult, and Alexis's eyes rested on me for just a moment. In that moment, I saw her taking in my carefully styled blond waves, my minuscule jean shorts, the sticky sheen of my lip gloss, the cotton candy–colored straps of my padded bra. When she finally looked away, I couldn't tell if she was only squinting from the setting sun, or if she was smirking. Whatever it was, I felt a small crack in the armor of my popularity. I turned back to Kenzie and resumed my football tutorial as if nothing had happened. But I felt self-conscious for the rest of the game. Alexis Nichols was the only girl at ASH who could make me feel that way, because she was the only one who really knew me.

3

CHRISTIAN'S HOUSE WAS A BEIGE BRICK ranch on a block of identical beige brick ranches, the parkways lined with those wimpy little trees the city plants each spring. We followed Kenzie down his gangway toward the drifting smell of cheap beer and the shouts of teenagers, through a small square of neatly mowed backyard, and out into the alley where the garage was packed from wall to wall with about two dozen kids, the door standing open to the warm night. Before we had a chance to even step inside, a burly kid with a patchy brown beard, a backward Cubs hat, and a Kris Bryant jersey blocked us from going any farther.

"Five bucks each," he said, thrusting a Solo cup in front of us that was already stuffed with money.

"Christian invited us," Kenzie said importantly.

"So? It's still five bucks. Or do you think kegs grow on trees?" He smiled, pleased with his display of figurative language.

"Can you break a hundred?" Kenzie sighed, reaching into the pocket of her cutoffs and casually producing a crumpled bill. Her family had no more money than the rest of ours did, but she liked to carry around large bills to give the impression that she was rich. The boy was clearly impressed, though he tried not to show it. He plucked the money from her outstretched hand and made a big production of holding it up to inspect for counterfeit currency while we rolled our eyes at one other. Finally, when he was satisfied, he slowly counted out eighty bucks in change and handed us four Solo cups.

"Wait a second," Emily piped. "I'm the designated driver. You're making me pay, too?"

He looked her up and down, assessing her. Finally he said, "Consider it a tax for letting you hang out with us."

Emily shrank back, embarrassed, while Kenzie reached forward and neatly plucked a five-dollar bill back from the wad in his hand.

"Why don't *you* consider *this*?" she asked, leaning toward him on a jutting hip. "Your sandals are a fashion tragedy, and boys who haven't finished going through puberty shouldn't try growing beards. Now where's the keg?"

"Over there," he muttered, pointing toward a big bucket near the edge of the garage. While the four of us collapsed into laughter, he sauntered away with his eyes downcast on his generic Birkenstocks and his fingers moving self-consciously across the patches of hair on his chin and cheeks.

We filled our cups with watery light beer and stepped into the close, sweaty air of the party. Most of the space was taken up by a large Ping-Pong table, where a group of Saint Mike's guys and some girls we didn't know were playing a raucous game of beer pong. Just past them, in a clearing of space near a bunch of fishing rods, I spotted Darry. He was squatting down over a plastic milk crate, his dark, shiny head cocked to the side, and he was fiddling with a laptop that was connected to a pair of large black speakers. When he saw me, he winked at me—he actually *winked* at me, like some pervy old man. Except, of course, it didn't seem quite so pervy coming from him. It felt, I don't know, *sexy.* My face went hot.

"Kenzie!" Christian, who was standing at one end of the Ping-Pong table, flagged her down with an eager hand. "Be my beer pong partner?"

"Ugh," Kenzie whispered to us, rolling her mascara-spiked eyes. "Could he be any more *obsessed*? Evan is gonna kill him." But she accepted his invitation with a nod and sashayed over to the table, cozying up beside him as he beamed. The rest of us arranged ourselves against the wall and tried to look cool. Sapphire picked at her nails between slugs of beer while Emily took little sips from a can of Red Bull, her searchlight eyes sweeping across the party and filing the faces and actions of everybody there away in the gossip chamber that was her brain. Meanwhile, I tried to get drunk, hoping that it would help me feel like I fit in, help to loosen the spring inside me that tightened every time I went to parties like this. But the beer tasted so awful that I had trouble keeping it down. The last thing I needed was to puke all over Christian's family's collection of fishing rods. So I just sort of stood there and watched as Kenzie played beer pong with her new friends, tossing the little white ball with a graceful flick of her wrist so that it landed perfectly into the Solo cup of the opposing team and she curtsied gracefully to their applause.

We heard the arrival of Evan Munro and his teammates before we actually saw them. They'd destroyed Notre Dame 31–0, and Evan had thrown for a career-high 365 yards. They came careening down the alley—Josh Gonzalez, Derrick Dunn, and a guy who was known only as Sully—in Sully's beat-up Chrysler convertible, wearing their jerseys, chanting the Saint Mike's fight song and waving white-and-green flags. It was like they were throwing a parade for themselves, and everybody at the party went nuts. Sully came screeching to a stop in the middle of the alley and they all hopped out, 1980s-movie style, without opening the car doors. As soon as Christian saw them, I could see the conflicted look on his face: excited that the coolest kids in his class had shown up at his party, disappointed that Kenzie, who he thought he might have a shot with, had now detached herself from his side and was jumping into Evan's arms, wrapping her long, tan legs around his waist and pouring her beer directly into his open mouth.

Seeing how everyone was now distracted, I took advantage of the moment and stepped out into the alley to dump out the warm remains of my own beer. When I returned to my station against the wall, Darry was once again squatting before the speakers, laptop balanced on his knees, and finally the music kicked on, guitar chords as familiar to me as the sound of my father's voice.

> *In the day we sweat it out on the streets*
> *of a runaway American dream,*
> *At night we ride through mansions*
> *of glory in suicide machines*

It was the opening lines of "Born to Run," and suddenly, I was transported away from this party, even away from Darry, who was smiling at me now over the glow of the laptop, and I was remembering a late-summer night like this one, up on the shores of Crooked Lake, with all of us: Stevie Junior, Aunt Col and Uncle Jimbo, Aunt Kathy and one of her weird hipster boyfriends, Mom and Dad and me sitting on the pontoon boat that was docked, bobbing, in the harbor, and in the middle of the lake the fireworks were exploding against a black sky, reflecting in trembling mirrors of light on the surface of the water, and my dad turned on his portable boom box, while I perched on his lap in perfect happiness, hoping that the song would never end.

> *Together, Wendy, we can live with the sadness*
> *I'll love you with all the madness in my soul*

I felt my stomach go sour, detached myself from the wall, stumbled past Darry and the fishing rods, past the beer pong table, out into the dark alley, and found a spot between a trash can and the neighbor's backyard. I leaned over the chain-link fence, waiting to puke. But the cooling night air calmed my nausea, and instead of vomit, what came instead were tears. I didn't know that I was going to cry—the sadness had come from somewhere deep inside of me, from a place I thought I had buried because I knew better than to dwell on pointless scenes from the past.

"Hey. You okay?"

The dark figure coming toward me was carrying a giant garbage bag full of crushed cups and empty cans. He stepped beneath the streetlight and I saw those copper eyes and died a little inside now that I realized my new crush had found me crouching behind a trash can like some complete head case.

"Sorry," I mumbled. "It was sort of hot in there."

Darry smiled and adjusted the clanging bag over his shoulder.

"Open the lid for me?"

I lifted the top of the blue recycling bin and he heaved the bag inside.

"Hey," he said, closing the lid and looking at me, his face pale and serious. "I didn't mean to upset you. I thought you'd like it if I played your song."

"I'm fine," I said quickly. "It just reminds me of something, that's all."

"What does it remind you of?"

"My dad."

"Oh. Did he die?"

I was sort of thrown off by this question. People weren't supposed to go around *asking* you this sort of stuff directly. They were *supposed* to say something vague, change the subject, and then Google your name later in the privacy of their own homes.

"No."

He waited a second, expecting me to elaborate, but I didn't. Sergeant Stephen Boychuck was a conversation topic that, for the past two years, I had declared officially off limits—even for tall boys with golden eyes who thought "Born to Run" was the greatest rock song ever made. I took the opportunity of the awkward silence to dig a tin of Altoids from my bag. I offered him one, and he took it.

"Thanks." His fingers, warm, brushed my palm.

Just then, a crash came from inside the garage, a beer bottle smashed to pieces, and two blond boys locked in some sort of wresting stance came tumbling out into the alley, fists flailing, while the rest of the party followed, yelling encouragement.

"Oh, shit." Darry shifted his gaze to the boys as they fell onto the pavement and proceeded to pummel each other.

"Those are the O'Donnell twins. They do this every weekend. Hey, Wendy, I should get your—"

"*Cops!*" someone screamed, just as the warning *blat!* of a siren ripped through the night and the alley lit up in flashing swirls of blue and red. Kids began streaming from the garage like ants from a kicked anthill, tossing their beer cups and scattering down the alley, over fences, and through yards.

"*Shit!*" Darry said again, grabbing my hand. "Come on!"

He braced his arms on the top of the gate behind the garbage cans and launched himself into a neighbor's yard, then turned around and held out his hand while I hooked my feet into the laths of the fence. As I toppled over the edge he caught me, his body a wall of summer heat, still smelling faintly of the soap I'd first noticed when he'd stirred the air around me in the ticket line at Saint Mike's. I felt dizzy, unsure of whether it was the siren lights flashing through the yard, pitching it from red to blue to dark again, or being there with him, so close that his sweat was dampening my clothes. We took off running hand in hand, hopping the low chain-link fences that bordered identical squares of Chicago backyards, our hearts pumping with that glorious mix of adrenaline and fear where you know you might get caught but you think you probably won't and your night is unfolding into a story that will be worth telling Monday morning at school. We kept running at full speed, even when the sirens had long disappeared and our legs ached and the whispers and drunken laughter of the other running, hiding kids had faded away. We kept running for so long that I started to think that maybe this is what we'd wanted all along—to be alone together—and finally, after we'd hopped our hundredth fence and I could feel the blood on my heels rubbed raw against the backs of my espadrilles, I stopped in front of a wall of high bushes threaded with browning lilacs and pulled Darry to a halt by the back of his shirt.

"You can slow down now," I gasped. "I'm pretty sure we're in the clear."

"Sorry," Darry laughed, leaning with his hands against his knees and wiping the sweat off his forehead on the sleeve of his T-shirt. "It's just that my dad's a cop. If I got caught, the arresting officers would tell him they caught me drinking, and he'd kick my ass."

I nodded, grateful that I was still catching my breath so that I didn't have to respond. After all, my dad was once a cop, too.

I slumped down into the grass, my back pressed up against the vines, and he sat next to me.

"Hey," he said, turning to me, and before I could say "hey" back, he was leaning over to kiss me. *I guess he isn't big on small talk*, I thought, as his tongue wormed its way into my mouth.

A word about kissing: I secretly think it's overrated. It's not like I'm frigid or anything. I think cuddling, for example, is adorable. And hugging is like crack for the soul. But kissing? The tongues, the drool, the paranoia about bad breath? No, thanks. My theory is that the only reason people kiss is because if your mouth is occupied, you don't have to talk. And who wants to chitchat when they're touching another person's body for the first time? That would be incredibly awkward. Which is why you never see old married couples making out. They still hug. They still hold hands. And if I had to guess, they still probably have sex (ew). They've just dropped the drooling, pawing makeout sessions, because when you've been smelling someone's farts for decades, awkward silences are no longer much of a concern.

I know what you're going to say: if you kiss the *right* person, you're supposed to feel electrified. Weak in the knees. Dizzy. And maybe that's true. But the thing is, I knew I was attracted to Darry. I wanted to touch his hair and feel the soft skin of his neck and the worn cotton of his Saint Mike's Wrestling T-shirt. I *wanted* him to kiss me. But then when he did, my mind went to the same place it always went every time I'd kissed a boy: I wondered when it was going to be over. So when a floodlight snapped on and the owner of the house stepped onto the deck and yelled, "Hey! What do you kids think you're doing back there?" I was embarrassed and startled, but not really all that disappointed.

Maybe the next time he kissed me, I thought, as he grabbed my hand and we went flying back over fences and through manicured yards, *then* I'd feel something. Because that was the other weird part about kissing: even though I didn't enjoy it, I still wanted to do it again.

As we climbed our last fence and emerged back into the world hand in hand, I saw that we were standing by the train tracks, at the place were Tiffany and Sandy's whitewashed crosses stood still and crooked beside the railroad ties.

"My dad told me that when they died," Darry said, stooping down to pick an empty Cheetos bag from the tangle of carnations someone had left there, "their bodies were so messed up that their parents had to identify them by their high heels."

"There's this painting of Our Lady of Lourdes in the hallway at ASH," I said. "Legend has it that she wept for a week after they died."

"You really believe that?"

"Well, I mean, I don't know. Afterward, the janitor found a leaky air-conditioning unit on the floor just above the painting. But still. The timing kind of creeps me out."

"All right," he said, "if you believe that, then I've got another one for you."

"Okay."

"Did you know that if you come here at midnight when there's a full moon, and you say their names out loud, the streetlights explode?"

"I never heard that one." I looked up at the streetlamp above us, which beamed a halo of white light onto the street.

The moon, I noticed with some relief, was only a sliver in the clear September sky. "Do you believe *that*?"

"Not really," he said, then turned and smiled at me so that my heart squeezed a little tighter. "But maybe we should try it for ourselves sometime."

"I don't really feel like disturbing the dead, if it's okay with you."

"My grandma used to say that we shouldn't fear the dead—it's the living we should be afraid of."

This made me shiver.

"Hey," he said suddenly. "You ever gonna answer my question?"

"What question?"

"The one I asked about your dad."

"Oh. That."

"Yeah."

"He lives in Nebraska. And I haven't seen him in a while. So I was just thinking about him, that's all."

"Oh," he said. "*Now* I get it. I mean, it sucks that you don't get to see him much, but trust me, there's an upside to it. My parents tried the whole let's-get-divorced-but-live-in-the-same-neighborhood-for-our-kids'-sake thing. It's weird how, now that I have two houses, I feel like I have less than one. And it seems like whatever I need at Mom's house, I left at Dad's. And vice versa. I leave my history book at my dad's house *literally* every Sunday. My teacher is starting to think it's bullshit."

"No." I shook my head. "My parents aren't divorced. They're . . ."

I looked down the empty train tracks to where they disappeared into the hazy Chicago skyline. If this was going to go anywhere, he would eventually have to find out somehow.

"My last name," I said "is Boychuck."

I saw a tremor, the tiniest frowny movement, in the corner of his smile. His fingers slackened in mine.

"Boychuck as in Sergeant Stephen Boychuck?"

I nodded. "Is that a problem?"

"No, not a problem," he said quickly, but something in his voice had gone cold. He let go of my hand.

"Good." I smiled, trying to fake our way back to flirty. "Because, you know, I'm not like him, if that's what you're worried about."

Darry cleared his throat.

"No, I don't think that," he said. He shoved his hands in his pockets. "So, which way to your house?"

I pointed down the sidewalk. "Just a couple blocks that way."

"Are you okay to get home by yourself?" He pulled out his phone and held its glowing shape to me. "It's getting late. I gotta get going. My mom is going to kill me enough as it is."

"Sure," I said quickly. "It's no problem."

We stood there across from each other before the crosses of the dead ASH girls. "So," I said, "should I give you my phone number or something?"

Darry's hand hovered over his cell.

"The thing is," he said finally, "my dad just made commander." He looked at me, waiting for me, I guess, to tell him that I understood. But the words were jammed up at the base of my throat, and I couldn't say anything. "I mean," he continued, "it's not that *I* care, but I think it would look bad. For my dad. If, you know, you and me were hanging out. Because, you know, people still—cops, I mean—he made the whole department look bad. You know?"

I nodded woodenly. My eyes burned, but I blinked fiercely until the tears went away. It's not that I was, like, in *love* with Darry. I'd only known him for a couple hours! But here it was again, this curse that would trail me all my life. The curse that struck every time someone figured out who I was.

"You understand, right?"

"Totally. It's cool." My heart had dried up like salt, but my two years of popularity had skilled me in the art of pretending to be happy. I smiled. *Never let them know how much you care, and then they can't hurt you.* This was my Aunt Colleen's advice in the days after my father's arrest when reporters were camped out on the lawn and #boychuck was trending on Twitter. I stood on the sidewalk, trying so hard not to care, and watched Darry disappear around the corner, the piney smell of his skin still hanging on my clothes.

When I got home, I was so close to calling Alexis Nichols. I'd long ago erased her number from my phone, but of course I still knew it by heart—she *had* been my best friend for nine years, after all. I knew that she would give me good advice, and more importantly, that she would *listen*. She wouldn't say something like, "you're so much hotter than he is anyway," or "Who cares? Just find someone else!" or "Are you seriously upset by this? You met the dude once, psycho," all of which were pieces of advice I'd heard Kenzie dole out to our brokenhearted friends at one time or another. Alexis would understand that it wasn't even about Darry at all. She would understand everything.

Which was exactly why I'd abandoned her.

4

IT WAS JUNE, ONE WEEK AFTER my eighth-grade graduation, when my father was arrested. I had just helped him digitize his CD collection, and we were out in the garage together, blasting Bruce Springsteen and Turtle Waxing his '72 Mustang.

"If these speakers got any louder," he shouted to me approvingly from across the cherry-red hood, "we could be fined for a noise violation." At that moment, as if on cue, the first police car came down the alley. Dad straightened up, grinning. His cop buddies sometimes stopped by to shoot the breeze when they were cruising down our alley on neighborhood detail, because in the summers, my dad spent a lot of time in the garage doing typical Dad things—babying the Mustang, drinking beer, watching the Cubs on the little black-and-white TV he had mounted above his tool bench. Inside our house, my mom and Aunt Colleen were arranging big foil trays of macaroni salad and fried chicken for my graduation party, while Stevie Junior and Uncle Jimbo played beanbags beneath the big oak tree in the backyard.

The smile faded from my dad's face, though, as another police car came down the alley, and then another, and, from the other direction, an unmarked squad. Something was about to go down.

"The hell's going on out here?" Dad put down his rag and walked out to the alley. He turned to me. "Wendy, turn that music down."

The two cops who got out of the first car didn't look like they'd come to chat: their faces were hard and their hands rested on their guns. One of them, Terry Ryan, was an old friend of my dad's, a guy I'd known all my life, a guy who came to our family parties and whose two young daughters I sometimes babysat. But I almost didn't recognize him, because the Terry I knew had pale, laughing eyes and some-times let his little girls paint his toenails pink, and today his face was set in these firm, cold lines that made him look like an entirely different man. His eyes were like gray stones, and they seemed to hover just above my dad—at his forehead, sort of, as if they were unwilling or unable to make direct eye contact. Lots of kids my age think it's cool to hate cops, but being from a cop family, I could never understand why you'd despise the people whose job it is to save your life if you're ever in trouble. Looking at Terry Ryan now, though, my stomach dropped. I could see how a person could fear—could even hate—the police.

Terry said something quietly to my dad, while the other

cops got out of their cars, hands hovering near guns, and then my dad said, "not in front of my kid." And they all looked over at me, standing in my bare feet in front of the speakers with the stupid laptop in my hands, which were shaking so hard I could barely hold on to it.

"Terry?" My voice was small. I heard footsteps behind me and then my mom was standing there, too, still wearing oven mitts on both hands, with Aunt Col trailing through the yard behind her.

"Terry!" she said sharply. "What's going on?"

He wouldn't look at her. Instead, he put his hands on my dad's shoulders—almost gently, the way a coach might calm down a player before an important free throw—and turned him around so he could click the handcuffs closed around his wrists.

"Wait!" I screamed. "You don't need to arrest him! We'll pay the fine! How much can it be for a noise violation? I've got a bunch of graduation money coming—" I stopped talking when I saw the faces of Terry and the other cops, tight and self-conscious with pity. It's funny, when I look back on it now, how unbelievably naïve I was.

Terry opened the door of the squad, and just like they do on TV, he put his hand on the top of my dad's head and guided him into the back seat.

"This is all a big misunderstanding," my dad told my mom, who was covering her open mouth with an oven mitt. Stevie Junior and Uncle Jimbo were standing behind her now, dumbly holding the sets of beanbags in their hands. "I'll call you."

"Now just what the hell—" Uncle Jimbo took a step toward the alley, but Terry ignored him, closed the car door, and got into the driver's seat. One by one, the police returned to their cars, leaving us standing in the garage with "The River" playing faintly in the background and one half of a Mustang waxed to a mirror shine. And then, like a funeral procession, they took off down the alley, turning out of sight down McVicker Avenue.

It was the story of the summer. Reporters actually camped out on our front lawn until Uncle Jimbo tried to run them off with his riding mower. This made things even worse, because one of my dickhead neighbors recorded the incident and posted it on YouTube, where it racked up three hundred thousand views by the end of the weekend. I sat in my room alone and punished myself by reading all the user comments.

Overnight, the name Boychuck became the new Capone, the new Dillinger, and my father became the most hated man in Chicago. In a city of rival baseball teams, machine politics, and gang warfare, hating Sergeant Stephen Boychuck was the one thing that everyone—black, white, rich, poor, north siders, south siders—could agree on.

They said that he tortured confessions out of nearly a hundred suspects—electrocuting them, beating them, shoving loaded shotguns in their mouths, whipping them with power cords. They said he harassed and intimidated suspects and witnesses and neighborhood activists, some of them women, some of them old, some of them only fourteen or fifteen. They said he had no heart, that he was a sadist, and that he had single-handedly destroyed the credibility of an entire department of twelve thousand officers.

How was it possible? My dad was one of the good guys. All my life, he'd painted a picture for us of the twenty-sixth district, where he worked, as a world that was less than ten miles from our house but might as well be on a different planet. According to him, his beat was a battleground of good and evil, and there was no in-between. In my dad's stories, he was the great force that strode through the neighborhood, protecting the hardworking normal people and destroying the gangbangers and thugs. When he worked the night shift, he'd often come home as me and Stevie Junior were getting ready for school. He'd greet us with barely a grunt, the purple bags like weights under his eyes, and go straight to bed. He wouldn't come out until we were eating dinner, when it was time for him to leave for work again. And I'd always thought that's what saving the world did to a person—it sapped you of your energy and your ability to show your family that you loved them. I resented everybody in the twenty-sixth for the sins they committed that weighed so heavily on my poor, heroic father.

❧ ❧ ❧

We had to borrow money from my aunt Kathy, who'd never liked my dad in the first place, to bond him out. The night before his bench trial began, we had a family meeting in the kitchen—me, Stevie Junior, and my parents.

"I want everyone to be prepared," my dad said. His voice was quiet and neutral. "I'm going to be found guilty, and I'm going to go to jail."

"But that's bullshit!" Stevie Junior exploded. Ever since my dad's arrest, he'd been out with his friends or his girlfriend nearly all the time. When he was at home, he'd go straight to his room, shut the door, and blast heavy metal until the house shook. It was shitty, the way he gave me no choice but to make me deal with it by myself. And even shittier when, the day after my dad went to prison, he dropped out of college and took off to join the navy. "You were only doing your job!" Stevie was insisting now. "You were trying to get those scumbags off the streets. You didn't even do anything *wrong*!"

"I know." My dad took a long sip from his bottle of beer.

"It's so unfair," Stevie said bitterly. "So fucking unfair."

Mom gave Stevie a look for cursing at the dinner table, but she didn't reprimand him.

"Look, guys," my dad said, running a thick finger across the drops of condensation that had gathered on the neck of his beer bottle, "the people who are outside of this, who don't see what I see every day, they have no clue. You think the mayor gets it? Or the judge? You think the rich people living large up on the Gold Coast, in Lincoln Park, you think *they* get it? They act like they know this city, but they don't. They don't *want* to know."

Stevie Junior nodded furiously in agreement, his eyes narrowed, his shoulders hunched forward.

"I don't care what those nuns have taught you, kids. Not everybody in this world is a 'child of God.' There are some people who don't have even a flicker of God within them at all."

"Stephen," my mom protested gently.

"I'm sorry, Bernie, but it's true," he said. "I've seen it. I know. And to let that evil continue to live among us, free, is a threat to our city. A threat to *my children*. Wendy could run into one of these people on the train, on the street. Then what?" He took a long drink and slammed his beer back down, suddenly angry. "I'm not sorry about what I did. I won't apologize." He looked at each of us in turn. "And neither should any of you. Don't ever let anyone make you ashamed of being a Boychuck. Understand?"

I nodded, chewing the inside of my lip to keep from crying.

"All we can do now is pray," my mom said softly. "It's out of our hands." She got up and walked to the windowsill above the kitchen sink, where she kept all her holy candles. She pulled her lighter from her pocket and lit them one by one. My mom was always lighting one holy candle or another. But the only other time I'd seen her light them all at once was the day my grandma went into hospice care. Two days later, grandma was dead.

In the dim flicker of the candlelit kitchen, we sat in a circle around the table and held hands while we listened to my mom recite the prayer to Our Lady of Lourdes, a prayer we'd heard uttered a thousand times, a prayer that every one of us believed in, even my cynical, blaspheming father. "O ever Immaculate Virgin, Mother of mercy, health of the sick, refuge of sinners, comfort of the afflicted, you know my wants, my troubles, my sufferings; deign to cast upon me a look of mercy. . . ."

"Stephen Boychuck," the prosecutor said in her opening statement at the trial, "is a very, very bad man. I'd call him a monster, really. Or, if that's too dramatic for you, a sociopath." Her name was Stephanie Zot, and she had beady eyes and a huge purple-painted mouth, and throughout the trial, while she strode up and down the courtroom, berating my father while dressed in suits that were tight over her wide thighs and showcased the lines of her giant underpants, I sat there and prayed that she'd split a seam and have to feel, for just a moment, a shred of the humiliation she so clearly enjoyed inflicting on my family. If I thought about it logically, I knew that she was just doing her job, but it was easier to focus my energy on hating Stephanie Zot than on watching the grainy video footage of my father electrocuting a suspect's balls with a cattle prod.

Even taking into account the videos the prosecution claimed my dad destroyed, there was a lot of evidence like that. The video that upset me the most still returns to me in my dreams sometimes. My dad was in this interrogation room with this guy. A boy, really. He honestly looked about my age. And in the video, my dad takes a plastic garbage bag and holds it over the kid's head, tightening it until the kid is kicking and flailing and gasping like a fish flipping around at the bottom of a boat. Finally he goes limp. My dad takes the plastic bag off. Kicks the kid in the stomach. Leans down and spits in his face.

As Stephanie Zot played the video, on regular speed, in slow motion, sometimes zooming in on my dad's face twisted up in this awful way I'd never seen before, I had to keep reminding myself that the kid he was interrogating was not a kid at all. He was a killer. A cold-blooded murderer. But sometimes convincing myself was hard to do. It's one thing when you're told things. It's another when you're forced to watch them for yourself.

By the end of the trial, I had begun to feel it: the black seed of disloyalty flowering within me. It was like everything I ever believed about my life, about goodness and badness and fairness and the way of the world, was being washed away. How could the man in those videos be my father? My laughing, big-hearted, Mustang-polishing, Bruce Springsteen–bellowing dad? I almost began to hope that he'd be found guilty, so that I wouldn't have to live alongside him anymore, watching him drink his morning coffee or make his famous steak marinade as if he *hadn't* just spent his evening with his gun shoved down some sixteen-year-old's throat. I never told anyone I felt this way, though. My heart was twisted up like a pretzel. I mean, it was definitely wrong to turn against your own father, right? But what about all those victims? How could I feel compassion for them and still want their torturer to be free? Forced confessions, Stephanie Zot had pointed out during the trial, often end up being false confessions. How many of those "scumbags" weren't scumbags at all, just innocent people who confessed to crimes just so my father would lift his boot from their neck? I was the product of nine years of Catholic schooling, of religion classes and retreats and soup-kitchen Sundays and service trips, yet here I was, facing a real-life moral dilemma instead of a hypothetical essay question on a theology test, and I had no clue how to handle it.

As the summer went on, I avoided turning on the TV or reading the newspaper headlines or, God forbid, looking at Twitter or the comment sections of news websites. The Boychucks were the most famous family in Chicago, and for all the wrong reasons. A city of three million people had never felt so small. Every time I left the house I was gripped with paranoia that someone would recognize me. I couldn't think straight. I could barely breathe.

Alexis Nichols had been my best friend since kindergarten, and in late July, the night before my dad's sentencing, I showed up at her front door. In the kitchen, her little sister was helping her mom wash the dinner dishes, and a lingering scent of grilled chicken and boiled corn hung in the air. Her dad was sitting on the back porch, smoking a cigar and reading a fishing magazine. It was all so beautifully normal, so calm and ordinary, and so far from what my own family's life had become, that before we could even make it up to her room I crumpled into tears.

"Come on," Alexis said, putting her arm around me and steering me around and right back out the front door. "I'm taking you somewhere."

Alexis was normally so quiet and passive that her sudden determination stunned me into following her, quickly and without asking any questions, out the door, down to Jefferson Park el station and onto a westbound blue-line train. We rode all the way through that weird depressing blend of land that isn't quite city and isn't quite airport, the gray industrial parks and the planes that roared above us at intervals like giant silver albatrosses, all the way to the end of the line, where the train burrowed underground and came to rest deep in the underbelly of O'Hare airport.

"Follow me," she said.

I did as I was told, up the escalator, through enormous hallways that echoed with the electronic hum of the moving walkways and the clatter of suitcase wheels. A solitary busker played the saxophone for loose change beneath a painting of the late Mayor Richard J. Daley. Alexis stopped walking and stood in front of him, listening carefully, her head cocked to one side. Then she turned to me, grinning.

"That's Rachmaninoff!"

"*Who?*"

"This ridiculously amazing Russian composer. I'm giving him a dollar."

She opened her purse, found a folded bill, and placed it in the velvet lining of the saxophonist's open case. He winked at her, never breaking his rhythm.

"Is that what we came here for?" I asked.

"No."

We continued on our way. Three moving walkways later, when we had reached the international terminal, Alexis finally stopped walking and sat down in a plastic chair in front of a large digital flight board.

"We're here," she said.

"We're *where*?" I looked around. "Are you proposing I run away? Even if I had the money for a plane ticket, I don't even own a passport."

"Neither do I."

"Okay." I sat down next to her. "I'm probably gonna need an explanation at this point."

"So," Alexis said, turning to face me. Her eyes were bright in a way I'd never seen them before. "Sometimes, I feel like

I just want my life to *begin*, you know? Not high school, I mean. High school's not real life. It's just the place where you do stuff to *get* you to real life. I mean college. Beyond college. Going to see *Carmen* at the Royal Opera House in London. Or seeing a symphony at the Vienna Philharmonic. Or, maybe," she added softly, "*playing* in a symphony at the Vienna Philharmonic."

She shook her head, her ears turning pink.

"I mean, that last thing, that's obviously a ridiculous dream. But that's why I come here. To dream ridiculous dreams."

She pointed up at the flight board above our heads, where the names of faraway cities flashed across the screen like titles of dreams: *Abu Dhabi, boarding in ten minutes. Bangkok, final boarding. Berlin, on time. Karachi, at the gate.*

"Whenever I'm feeling lonely or stuck, or like my real life is never going to get here," she went on, "I remember that I'm a fifteen-minute train ride from the busiest airport on earth. The best thing about Chicago is that there's no place in the world that's easier to leave."

"Sounds like you've given this some thought."

"I come here all the time," she said, her eyes never leaving the frenetic glow of the sign. "But I've never been on a plane. Never been to a different time zone. Never seen a mountain, or an ocean, or a weird-looking bird hanging out in a tree."

"Don't feel bad." I shrugged. "I've been to California. Once. And Wisconsin. That's about it."

"But we *will* see the world," she said fiercely. "Both of us. We may just be neighborhood girls now, but we don't *always* have to be neighborhood girls." She turned to me, and her eyes reflected the lit names of unfathomable cities: *Shanghai. Amman. Mexico City.* "Wendy," she said, "we are going to have the *best* lives. I know it."

She nestled into her chair, folded her hands behind her head, and began to read. "Try it. You'll see what I mean."

"Try *what*?"

"Tonight," she said, "I go to Paris. My flight leaves in twenty minutes."

"Paris, huh?" I smiled in spite of myself. Just the word made me think of delicate crepes bubbling on the griddle and people drinking coffee hunched together under green-and-white awnings and cobblestone streets that smelled like fresh bread and rain.

"*Oui.*"

"Well, I'm going to . . ." I looked at the sign, searching. "Kuala Lumpur."

"Malaysia, huh?"

"Is that where it is?"

"Yes. Learn your capitals."

"What are the chances that your average Kuala Lumpurian has heard of Sergeant Stephen Boychuck?"

"Slim to none."

"Good. Kuala Lumpur it is."

🦢 🦢 🦢

The following morning, my dad was found guilty of three counts of perjury, two counts of obstruction of justice, and twenty-six counts of torture and aggravated battery. When the verdict was read, he turned to look at us, his mouth straight and defiant. My mom crumpled to the courtroom floor, crying out like a wounded animal, but I was grateful for the distraction—it gave me an excuse, as I leaned down to help her to her feet, not to meet my father's eyes. Out in the parking lot, Stevie Junior punched the car door, splitting open his knuckles and bleeding all over his brand-new suit. He held his broken hand to his chest, wrapped in a wad of McDonald's napkins my mom kept stashed in the glove compartment, as we drove home in stunned silence. My father had been sentenced to seventeen years in a federal prison in Clay County, Nebraska. Seventeen years: three years longer than I had been alive.

For the rest of that summer, whenever we had nothing better to do, Alexis and I rode the blue line out to the airport, sitting in front of the international terminal's flight boards and trading dreams. Tegucigalpa. Florence. Dusseldorf. Ulan Bator. Names like flowers and unknown spices we'd never tasted. At night, we wandered the quieting terminals and traded facts about the far-flung places on the screens that we'd filed away in memory in order to impress each other: In a cave near Happurg, Germany, archeologists have recently discovered the world's oldest instrument, a forty-thousand-year-old flute made from a vulture's bone. In Caracas,

Venezuela, a forty-five-story half-finished skyscraper stands in the middle of the city, occupied by over three thousand squatters complete with barber shops, security guards, and day care centers for their kids. Reykjavik, Iceland, is home to the Icelandic Phallological Museum, which displays over 280 preserved penises, belonging to whales, seals, and yes, even human beings. At last, when our eyes were like paperweights and the sharp edge of the night was dulled by our fantasies and our exhaustion, we finally turned around and got back on the downtown-bound blue-line train. Fifteen minutes later we were standing again at Jefferson Park station, but it didn't feel so claustrophobic anymore. The world felt bigger. The stranglehold my dad's crimes had put on my life seemed to loosen, just a little bit, and I thanked God for a best friend like Alexis.

But then something happened that changed everything. It was at the end of August, just before we were about to start high school. David Schmidt had a graduation party and he invited every single person from our eighth grade class, even the nobodies like Alexis and me. This act of kindness was a very David Schmidt thing to do: he wasn't like the rest of the kids at Queen of Heaven Elementary School. He could afford to be nice to everyone, even the dorks, because it didn't cost him anything socially. There was something mature about David, even cosmopolitan. Maybe it was the fact that his parents were divorced, and on weekends he lived in his dad's condo in River North where he did things like go to brunch and hang out at the skateboard park with a mysterious gang of public school friends, many of whom were already in high school and weren't even Catholic. Or maybe it was the fact that outside of school, all the other boys in our class wore backward hats and jerseys and listened to hip-hop, while David dressed in crisp button-down shirts and fitted jeans and listened to EDM. Whatever. It doesn't matter: The point is, he wasn't like the rest of us, and because you could tell that he didn't *want* to be like the rest of us, he got to play by his own rules. When I got the invitation to the party on the rooftop of his dad's building, I was beyond thrilled.

Once Alexis and I had gotten over the shock of being invited, we spent the ensuing days agonizing about what we were going to wear. Well, that's not exactly true. Alexis never really cared about clothes. *I* agonized about what I was going to wear, furiously scrolling through fashion blogs for inspiration and fretting about the size of my ass in front of her bedroom mirror while she sat on the window seat that overlooked the sour cherry tree in her front yard, the breeze stirring her hair, and drew the bow lovingly across the strings of her beloved violin, or lay on the carpet with her eyes closed and her hands conducting in the air, her giant headphones blaring Beethoven's symphonies.

The night of David's party finally arrived, a gloriously hot, clear, end-of-summer night. I wore a two-piece white dress that showed off my midriff. I'd chosen it because I knew that my dad would never let me out of the house wearing something like that. But he wasn't around, and neither was my mom, who'd been working at the hospital around the clock to earn extra money for all of our legal bills. I had become, all of a sudden, the type of kid who could dress and act however I wanted, but it didn't feel nearly as good as I thought it would.

Alexis and I took the el downtown together, and as soon as we got on the train I began to feel self-conscious. I felt like everyone from my graduating class was going to think that I was slutty or, worse, conceited, thinking I could pull off a hot outfit when everybody knew I was a loser with a criminal for a father. I wished I had worn something more like what Alexis had on—the same dress she'd worn to our eighth-grade graduation dance. It was floral and modest and vaguely dorky, way too young-looking for a soon-to-be high schooler. But at least she wasn't trying to be anything more than what she was.

"Or *maybe*," she said when I began to express my anxiety, "they're just meaningless pieces of cloth and you should try to forget about them and just have fun tonight."

When we walked into the party, David's stepmom, who was younger and shorter-skirted than any other mom I knew, handed each of us a name tag with a photo of our first-grade picture that she had tracked down from an old Queen of Heaven yearbook. It was a perfect icebreaker, with all of us leaning in close to one another to compare our old chubby, baby-teethed faces with the ones they'd grown into eight years later.

There were massive trays of appetizers arranged in neat little rows: dates wrapped in crisp bacon, fresh cherry tomatoes skewered on toothpicks between smooth balls of fresh mozzarella and deep green basil, flaky pastries folded over thin slices of salty ham. Every other graduation party I'd ever been to had been fried chicken and Italian beef congealing with hunks of white fat. A waiter walked around with a big tray, handing out flutes of sparkling grape juice. There was even a DJ, one of David's skateboard park friends, and he spun mixes of all the big pop songs of the summer, and it was all so crazy and glamorous that I forgot to be self-conscious about my outfit or my last name or anything at all. Alexis and I talked to kids who had ignored us since kindergarten as if it was no big deal. That night, I wasn't a loser, and I wasn't the daughter of Chicago's most ruthless cop, either. I was just a person, you know? An actual person with three dimensions.

Later in the night, Josh Gonzalez, who was the best dancer in our class, tried to teach everybody how to salsa. He was all hips and feet and sweat seeping through his blue dress shirt. His joy and his confidence were sort of infectious, and before I knew it Alexis and I found ourselves folded up into the crowded dance floor, and just before it was time to go home Josh came up behind me and put his hands on my waist, on the bare skin between my top and skirt, and whirled me around and danced with me until I was sweating, too, and laughing, and moving my hips for all they were worth.

At the end of the night Alexis and I thanked David's father and stepmom and promised everyone that we'd keep in touch in high school, and we took the elevator down to the waiting city and the train back to Jefferson Park. We walked home together as far as Alexis's house, and then I headed the rest of the way by myself, hunched over the glow of my phone screen, scrolling through all the pictures I'd taken and already feeling nostalgic for that giddy, happy final night as a grade schooler. I was breaking my dad's first rule of personal safety—phone away, stay aware of your surroundings—but honestly, even if I had been paying attention, I'm not sure that I would have been able to stop what happened next.

"Hey, Boychuck."

The voice was close behind me—too close. When I turned around they were standing there, five girls across, on the sidewalk behind me. They were older than me, and they looked tough.

"Wendy Boychuck?"

The tallest one was pointing at my name tag, the one that I'd forgotten to take off before leaving the party, the one with my first and last name typed in large capital letters and the little black-and-white photo of a blond, pigtailed, six-year-old me.

"Yeah." My voice came out smaller than I meant it to.

"We followed you all the way from Logan Square."

"Followed me?" I was repeating her words to buy myself time, though I wasn't quite sure what I was even buying time *for*. I just knew it was going to be bad, and I wanted to hold on to the last remaining moments of the best night of my life before these girls, whoever they were, ruined it forever.

"Yeah. We followed you. To ask you one question. You're *his* kid, aren't you?"

"Whose kid?"

"*You* know. Stephen Boychuck. Are you his kid or not?"

"Yeah," I said. I was scared, but I looked her straight in the eye, drawing on the reserves of courage I had gained so unexpectedly on the dance floor of David Schmidt's party, the happiness of the night still glowing around me like a force field.

"I knew it." She crossed her arms. "I hope someone murders him in prison. I hope someone guts him like the pig that he is." The molten hatred of her words struck me like the first blast of heat when you walk out of an air-conditioned building into the hottest day of the summer.

"I love my father." I knew, even as I said it, that it was the wrong thing to say. It just sort of came out. The girl stepped toward me. She was queenly, tall and muscular, with pale eyes like broken glass.

"I love my father, too," she said calmly. "Only *my* father can't walk, can't talk, can't remember his own name or the names of his children. Want to know why?" Her eyes glittered in the streetlight like some nighttime animal's while her friends fanned out, surrounding me. "Because *your* father put him in a chokehold five years ago. Which gave *my* father a stroke and nearly killed him."

She took another step toward me, and that's when I tried to run, but found myself instead slamming directly into the immoveable chest of one of her friends.

"*Get her*," I heard, as my arms were twisted behind my back and the Our Lady of Lourdes scapular I wore for protection was ripped off my neck. Somebody's arm was around my neck, lifting me off the ground, cutting off my air supply. A thought bubbled up in my mind, terrifyingly clear and assured. *She's going to crush my windpipe.*

"*Where's my lighter?*" I heard. Then, a sickly smell of burning flesh—*my flesh?*—as she flicked it on and held it to the exposed skin on my back. Sucking in a scream, I tried to squirm away, and somebody kicked me between the legs. I dry heaved, tasting bacon-wrapped dates and blood, then felt a hot, gravelly pain as my face scraped the concrete. There was more kicking and punching once I was on the ground, but I don't know how long it lasted, because that's when my memory goes sort of blank.

I do remember limping home, unlocking the door to our empty house, and looking in the mirror. My neck was swollen. A blood vessel had burst in my eye, leaving the round gray iris to float in a smear of red. My knees were open wounds. A blister as wide and long as a dollar bill had bubbled up over the burn across my back. The attack had left me terrified, aching, and scarred, but not surprised. Ever since my dad's arrest, I could not leave the house without feeling naked and exposed, held hostage by my own name in my own city. I had always known this was coming. This was Chicago, after all—there could be no sin without retribution.

The next morning, as I stood in front of the bathroom mirror and gingerly blotted concealer across the bruises on my neck before my mom came home from work and started asking questions, my phone rattled on the sink. It was Alexis, calling me for our usual morning chat. I didn't answer. Nor did I respond to her follow-up calls, texts, Snapchats, her ringing of my doorbell, or the pebbles she threw up at my bedroom window every day for the rest of the summer. And on our first day of freshman orientation at Academy of the Sacred Heart, when she came running up to me in her pressed uniform skirt, her violin held under her arm and a panicked question on her face, I didn't even give her the chance to ask me why. I just walked right past her as if I'd never seen her in my life, as if our nine years of best friendship had never happened. Looking back on it now, I don't really even know why I did it. I knew that nothing was her fault. I knew that those visits to the airport were the only thing that saved me from going crazy that summer. I knew that she was the only real friend I'd ever had. I guess maybe I figured now that I was in high school, I could remake myself somehow, into someone tougher and harder and cooler. I was finished with kindness and loyalty. What I needed now were the kind of friends who laughed loud and threw the first punch, who could give as good as they got.

Girls like Kenzie Quintana.

5

ONE SATURDAY AFTERNOON IN LATE OCTOBER, I was at work when Kenzie swung open the tinkling glass door of the Europa Deli and looked around with contempt.

"Hi, I'd like some large wieners," she said loudly, ringing the service bell so that Alice looked up from the egg salad she was mixing to glare at her. Alice and Maria had learned to tolerate Kenzie's occasional visits, even though they made no secret of their disapproval of her.

"Free sample?" I held up a plate lined with slices of cured meat and she waved me away, gagging theatrically.

"How do you *stand* it here?" she demanded. "Not only do they force you to stick your hands in, like, *mayonnaise* all day, it *smells* in here." She looked up at the fat brown links of sausage coiled from the ceiling and wrinkled her nose.

"Yeah," I said, popping a bite-size piece of sausage into my mouth, "but the free knockwurst makes it all worth it!"

"Don't make me vomit." Kenzie squatted down to get a better look at the trays of salads and meats behind the counter. "Hey, what *is* that? Blood?"

"It's borscht. Beet soup."

"*Sick.*"

I had tasted it earlier that morning and liked it, but I certainly wasn't going to admit that now. Seeing it through Kenzie's eyes, it *did* look like blood, and it bobbed with bald-peeled vegetables like dead white fingers. She held out her phone and took a picture of the tub of borscht. Later, during my lunch break, when I was sitting in the storeroom eating a ham and potato salad sandwich, I would see Kenzie's picture on my Instagram feed with the caption:

Beet soup or murder scene? #EuropaDeli #nasty #worstjobever

"If I worked here," she announced, strumming her French-manicured nails on the glass counter, "I'd kill myself."

Kenzie's tendency for hyperbole aside, she did have a point: working at Europa Deli isn't exactly a teenager's dream job. Sure, mixing drinks at the smoothie bar at the Harlem Irving Plaza would be a lot more fun, but Maria and Alice pay me twelve bucks an hour and I can't afford to waste my time working somewhere else for minimum wage. I'm trying to save up for college. Some months, I'm even just trying to help pay for groceries.

See, after my dad went to jail, at the end of my first semester freshman year, my homeroom teacher, Sister Pauline, handed around everybody's report cards, and girls started excitedly comparing grades and GPAs. But all I got was a note ordering me to go downstairs and see Sister Dorothy immediately. I sat across from her desk in the principal's office, beneath the mournful eyes of an enormous framed painting of Jesus, his Sacred Heart bursting from his chest surrounded by jagged rays of light, while she told me in her gentle voice that the school couldn't release my semester grades.

"Why not?" I demanded.

"That's a conversation you'll need to have with your mother," the old nun said.

I confronted my mom as soon as I got home from school, while she was in her bedroom, packing her suitcase to go visit my dad in Nebraska. She admitted that our tuition check had bounced and, even worse, that we'd spent all of our money, including every dime of my college savings, on my dad's legal fees. In order for me to continue at ASH, my mom had to swallow her pride and borrow money from my aunt Kathy to cover the payment. Although she's never said anything to me about it, I have a feeling my crazy aunt has been paying my tuition ever since.

The following month, the bank foreclosed on our house. After my royal ass beating on the way home from David Schmidt's party, my anger toward my father had mutated into a simmering rage, and now, with this latest setback, it solidified into full-blown hatred. Watching my mom deal with the loss of our house wasn't exactly a party, either. She dropped thirty pounds. Her hair started falling out in clumps. Every time she took a shower I could hear her trying to muffle her sobs under the hiss of the water. The doctor put her on anti-depressants, which as far as I could tell didn't actually make her feel better so much as make her feel nothing at all. I think there was a good six months that went by where she didn't smile, or cry, or laugh, or sing. It was like living with a dead person. And still, every other month, like a loyal lapdog, she made the long, lonely drive across the Great Plains to visit the man who had destroyed her life. Worst of all, she always tried to talk me into going with her and couldn't understand why I kept refusing.

By this time, Stevie Junior was already floating around on some aircraft carrier in the Indian Ocean. It was just me and the emaciated zombie who vaguely resembled my mom. For a couple months we set up camp in my uncle Jimbo and aunt Col's drafty, half-finished basement. My mom slept on the couch and I slept in a sleeping bag on the floor. But eventually we found the cat-piss-smelling apartment where we still live today, and even though most of my mom's hair has grown back, she's still on the antidepressants, and sleeping pills, and something for anxiety, too. She works so much, mostly at night, that sometimes a whole week will go by and I won't even see her. And even with all that overtime, we're still broke.

When I first started at the deli, I found myself surrounded by a bunch of middle-aged ladies who were always clucking at me in a rapid-fire mix of Polish and English. According to them, I didn't wipe down the cutting board properly after cutting up chicken. I overstuffed the *nalesniki*. I put too much vinegar in the red cabbage salad. I was four generations removed from my Eastern European ancestors, which made me, in their eyes, hopeless.

I was all set to quit, but one paycheck gradually became two, and then a month had gone by and then a season. Eventually, either because they felt sorry for me or because I started complying with food code when dealing with raw poultry, the ladies' criticism softened into affectionate sniping. Soon they began to treat me like a beloved (if not very intelligent) family pet. I grew to sort of enjoy the quiet walks to the deli as the sun rose pink over the bungalows of my sleeping neighborhood, the nosy questions the ladies asked me about boys and school, the lunch breaks where I'd sit in the cool, quiet storeroom on an overturned packing crate and eat a piece of fresh-baked bread smeared with butter and homemade plum jam. Two years later, I still work every Saturday and Sunday morning shift, more in the summers and on holiday breaks. And even though over the course of those two years I've only been able to save enough for about two weeks of college tuition, not including room and board, I still feel like I'm contributing in some way to our decimated family. I guess in life you have to look on the bright side, right? I mean, yeah, we've lost everything and my brother's on a ship on the other side of the planet and my mom's depressed and my dad's a criminal and sometimes I have to hear the horrifying sounds of Sonny's porno channels drifting up into my bedroom, but I have $2,496.54 in my savings account and I can whip up the best batch of pork meatballs in dill sauce you've ever tasted.

That's not nothing, right?

"Hey," Kenzie said. She was standing on the other side of the counter from me, snapping her long fingers in my face. "Are you alive in there?"

"Uh, yeah." I shook away my thoughts, leaning down to adjust a spoon in the horseradish beets while I waited for the heat to burn away from my face. "Sorry."

"Whatever. What are you doing when you get off?"

I shrugged. "No plans."

"Do you have Red Rocket with you?"

I pointed outside at the candy-red Ford Taurus, laced along the bottom with a fine sifting of rust.

"Cool. You want to take me to get a tattoo?"

"You say this," I laughed, "like it's a typical Saturday afternoon errand. Oh, I'm just gonna pick up my dry cleaning, go to the post office, and pay some guy to draw a picture on my skin that will remain there until the day I die."

"It *is* a typical errand for me," she said. "Over fifty percent of Americans have tattoos, Wendy. You and my grandma are the only people left on earth who still think they're a big deal."

"I *don't* think they're a big deal," I protested. "I just think—"

"Look, can you take me or not?"

With Kenzie, if you want to have any hope of being allowed to finish your sentences, you better talk fast.

"Fine. I'll pick you up at four."

"So, what's it gonna be this time?" We were stuck in Saturday afternoon traffic on our way to see Jayden, Kenzie's tattoo guy.

She pulled out her phone and held a picture up in front of my face while I tried to navigate into the left turn lane. It was a round pink heart, and inside, in bubble letters, it said I LUV BOYS.

"Isn't that amazing?"

"I LUV BOYS? Seriously?"

"What?"

"I mean, aside from the misspelling, don't you think that's a little general? There are, like, three point five billion boys in the world. I'm pretty sure you don't 'luv' all of them."

"You're *completely* missing the point," she sighed, propping her booted feet up on my dashboard. "It's supposed to be *ironic*."

"But how is it ironic?"

"Because it's funny!"

"But funny isn't the same thing as ironic," I ventured.

"It's *ironic*, then, because I'm totally boy crazy. And it's funny."

"But it would only be *ironic* if you *didn't* like boys. Like, if you were a lesbian, *then* it might be ironic."

"Ew!" She reached over and smacked my shoulder. "I'm not a fucking lesbo, okay? I love boys! That's the *point!*"

"How about those boys?" I pointed to a pair of pale, skinny kids with wispy mustaches, glasses, and *Star Wars* T-shirts, in line outside the Portage Theater for a sci-fi film festival. "Those are boys. Are they included?"

"*Those* boys are repulsive losers," she snapped, "and you know it. You're just being a bitch, and trying to act like you understand irony more than I do just because you're in honors fucking English."

"*Evan Munro pops his own pimples in public and wipes the pus on other people's wallpaper!*" The outburst exploded from me before I could stop it, like a wayward belch. In the shocked silence that followed, I braced myself for the withering wrath of Kenzie Quintana, for the guillotine to come down, for my official banishment from the cool group and the commencement of my life as a lonely loser.

Instead, she began laughing hysterically.

"I know," she gasped. "He is *so* disgusting. But his abs are insane and he's amazing at football." She flipped down the sun visor and examined her lipstick in the mirror. Pleased with what she saw, she snapped the visor back into place. "You're hilarious, Wendy," she said, shaking her head. "For a minute there I thought you were actually pissed."

Jayden's "studio" turned out to be nothing more than a

corner of his mother's garage. It smelled like spilled paint and stale weed, and the ceiling was strung with red and green Christmas lights. On one end of the garage stood a sagging velveteen couch where his cousin, who he introduced to us as Tino, sat slumped beneath a Sox hat, sipping an energy drink and glowering into a paperback novel. On the other end was an old pleather office chair next to a workman's bench lined with little jars of colored dyes and needles in plastic wrapping. The walls were covered with construction tools hanging from nails and faded classic movie posters: *Taxi Driver, Scarface, Boyz n the Hood,* and *Goodfellas*—which was, I remembered with a painful twinge, my dad's all-time favorite movie.

While Jayden directed Kenzie to a folding chair for her "consultation," I went and sat opposite Tino on the velveteen couch. He glanced up at me before returning to his book. I tried to catch a glimpse at the cover—it was so rare to see somebody reading an actual book instead of staring into a phone—but he had it folded over so I couldn't see what it was.

On the other side of the room, Kenzie was showing Jayden the picture of the tattoo she wanted.

"*I LUV BOYS?*" Jayden handed the phone back to her. "Seriously?"

Kenzie sighed loudly. "Is *everybody* fucking stupid today? I just had to explain why it's ironic to Wendy in the car, and I don't feel like doing it again, okay?"

"But why *is* it ironic?" Tino had put his book down and was looking at Kenzie. I saw the title: *The Collected Stories of Anton Chekhov.* "Are you a lesbian?"

"*No*, I am not a lesbian, dumbass," she snapped. "Do I *look* like a lesbian to you?"

"Sexual orientation isn't, like, a skin color. You can't know just by looking at someone whether they're gay or not."

"Yeah, well, girls who look like me?" She flicked her hair and posed for him. "*Not lesbians,* okay?"

Tino shrugged, half smiling. "Okay."

I was sort of astounded. He was maybe the first boy I'd ever seen who didn't turn into a pile of mush in Kenzie's presence. He seemed sort of amused by her more than anything else.

"Okay," Jayden said. "So where are we putting this *ironic* tattoo anyway?" Kenzie lifted up her shirt, showing off the narrow plank of her perfect abdomen, accented with a twinkling teardrop-shaped belly-button piercing.

"Here." She pointed to the small hollow beneath her rib cage.

"The definition of irony is when what you say and what you mean are completely opposite," said Tino, stretching out on the couch. "So you could describe the tattoo as campy, maybe. But it's not ironic."

Kenzie stared at him for a long time.

"Yeah, well, the definition of ghetto is *you*," she finally declared.

"Good one."

I stared down at my phone, fighting the sudden urge to laugh while Kenzie huffed over to the old office chair. She took off her leather jacket, draped it over the chair, and pulled her shirt over her head, lying back so that when she breathed, the two swells beneath her blue lace bra heaved up and down. After Jayden finished tracing the image onto her stomach, the needle buzzed to life. He leaned over and began boring into her skin with it, and I had to look away, unzipping my backpack and pulling out my homework.

"What are you reading?"

Tino had closed his book and was looking over at me expectantly. He was dressed in a fleece hoodie and track pants, and had sleepy brown eyes and skin the color of sun-warmed clay. His teeth were sort of crooked, but not in a bad way. He was, all in all, sort of disarmingly cute.

"Oh," I said, "just a book for my English class."

"*What* book?"

"*Othello.*"

"Nice." He nodded approvingly.

"Boring," I said. "Have you read it?"

"'It is the cause, it is the cause, my soul!'" He sat up dramatically on the couch. "'Let me not name it to you, you chaste stars, it is the cause.'" He flopped back down, stretched one leg across the other and grinned at me. "Act five, scene two. You look surprised."

"A little," I laughed.

"Not so ghetto after all, am I?" He stood up, then, and lifted up his sweatshirt. Tattooed across one smooth pectoral muscle was Michael Jordan's face. On the other was William Shakespeare's.

"Wow," I said. "I guess you're a fan."

"Basketball and literature are my passions. Hey, have you read any of the history plays?"

"The history plays?"

"Yeah. *Henry the Fifth. Henry the Fourth. Richard the Third.* The history plays."

"No. Where'd you learn so much about Shakespeare, anyway?"

"I read some of his plays in school—I go to Lincoln. You know, that scary public school that all you ASH girls are freaking out about having to go to next year. But I read the rest on my own. I'm something of an autodidact."

I knew he was using that word to impress me, or to make me feel stupid for not knowing what it meant. I decided he was arrogant and that it was best to ignore him, although the image of his broad, tattooed chest was going to prove sort of difficult to stop thinking about. I purposefully turned to a new page and furrowed my brow in an attempt to look like I was engrossed in my Shakespeare. After a while, he got the hint. He picked up *The Collected Stories of Anton Chekhov* and turned to the page where he'd left off.

"Hey, Wendy," Kenzie demanded from the other side of the room above the dull buzzing sound of the needle, "Jayden doesn't believe me. About your dad. Is he, or is he *not* Stephen Boychuck, aka Chicago's most notorious police officer, aka the guy who shoved guns up people's asses and Tasered people's balls, aka the guy who's in jail for, like, fifteen years?"

I felt the blood rush to my face, remembering the moment when my arms were twisted behind my back, my scapular was ripped off my neck, and a girl whose father couldn't walk or talk said *Gut him like the pig he is.*

"Well?"

"He's Stephen Boychuck. Yeah."

"*See?*" She hit Jayden playfully on the arm. "I told you. You owe me five bucks."

I opened *Othello*, which had fallen closed in my lap, and paged absently, pretending to concentrate, but really just reading the same underlined line over and over again:

> *Reputation, reputation, reputation! O, I have lost my reputation! I have lost the immortal part of myself, and what remains is bestial.*

"Hey." Tino's voice was gentle. He'd moved down the couch and was sitting next to me. "You okay?"

"I'm fine." I didn't look up.

"Why are you *friends* with that girl? She's awful."

"No, she's not."

"She just *humiliated* you."

"Yeah, well, she didn't say anything that wasn't true."

"But that's so shitty!"

"And you're making it worse!" I moved away from him. "I don't even know you. Just drop it, okay?"

"Sorry." He was quiet for a minute, while we both listened to the buzzing of the needle. "But seriously. I'm asking. Why are you friends with her? You don't seem evil. So what do you two have in common?"

I sighed, and tented my book on my lap. "Even if I *wanted* to explain it to you, you probably wouldn't understand."

"Try me."

"Maybe some other time."

"*Wendy!*" Kenzie's voice, queenly and demanding, beckoned from the other side of the garage. "Come check it out!"

Dutifully, I put away my homework and went over to the chair, where Jayden was wiping the fresh tattoo with a soapy cloth. Kenzie's skin beneath the pink and blue ink was flaming and red, like someone had held an iron to it.

"Well?" she said. "What do you think?"

"It's exactly like the picture," I said, which was neutral without being a compliment.

She held her phone above her bare belly and began snapping pictures. When she was satisfied, she handed Jayden a wad of cash, then leaned up and kissed him on the cheek.

"You're a master, Jay. I love it."

"Do you L-O-V-E it or do you L-U-V it?" Tino asked.

"Shut up, weirdo." She turned to me. "Let's go."

❧ ❧ ❧

It was only late afternoon but already getting dark as we walked to the car. The leaves were still hanging on to the trees, and the small saplings planted along the parkway of Fullerton Avenue were a spindly riot of reds and oranges. They made the whole street look festive, despite its dreary façade of brick strip malls and auto body shops lined with stolen tires. A cold threat hung in the air, whispering at the long Chicago winter ahead.

"What's the story with that Tino loser?" Kenzie said when we got in the car. "I saw him pulling up his shirt like he thinks he's got a hot body or something."

"He was showing me his tattoos," I said. "He's got one of Michael Jordan and one of William Shakespeare."

"William Shakespeare, like that old-ass writer?"

"No, Kenz. William Shakespeare, the starting point guard on the Chicago Bulls."

"There's a William Shakespeare on the Bulls?"

"No. I was just— Never mind."

While Kenzie proceeded to call Emily and Sapphire and babble on and on about her latest ink, I drove back to our neighborhood slowly, absently, thinking about Tino's question and the conscious choices I'd made after David Schmidt's graduation party that had led me to where I was today: totally popular and totally miserable.

6

A LITTLE OVER TWO YEARS EARLIER, on my first day of high school, I was sitting in my assigned seat in the front row of Sacramental Journeys class, and this girl strolled in a full five minutes after the bell rang. You knew by the way she walked that she wasn't late because she was just another clueless freshman who'd gotten lost on the way to seventh period, but because being on time was not a priority that she valued. She was wearing a pair of black spike-heel ankle boots paired with a uniform skirt that had been tailored to butt-skimming shortness. She clacked into the room, the heels making her stand just over six feet tall, and every single girl in that room, myself included, took a look at the dimensions of those never-ending legs and felt like a sucker and an unforgiveable dork for following the handbook rules with skirts no more than one inch above the knee. She had black hair and black eyes lined in black eyeliner and she was carrying a purse on a fake gold chain, holding her books and her pencil case under her arm, and when Sister Mary-of-the-Snows took a long, disapproving look at her skirt before directing her to her seat, then turned back to the syllabus she was reading off of, I saw the girl reach into her pencil case, pull out her phone, and check her lipstick—a shade of fuchsia that would have looked ridiculous on me, but on her looked perfect. By the time Sister Mary-of-the-Snows looked up, the girl had already put her phone back in her pencil case, but she hadn't been rushing or secretive about it: she either didn't know or didn't care that, in the space of three minutes, she'd broken nearly every classroom rule the old nun had listed on the syllabus.

Kenzie Quintana was the type of girl who couldn't be invisible if she tried—but don't worry, she didn't try. And I knew right then that if I was going to remake myself in the image I had in mind, I had to become her friend.

It took me a while. Girls like Kenzie Quintana don't exactly roll out the red carpet for the nobodies of the world. But that's the thing: I wasn't exactly a nobody anymore. I was a somebody, even if it was for all the wrong reasons. A couple days into the school year, Kenzie fell into step next to me as I walked down the hallway to Sacramental Journeys.

"You're the girl, right?" she said.

"What girl?"

"The girl with the dad who's in jail."

"I'm sure there's more than one of us," I said.

"At this place?" she laughed, waving an arm at the wall of

saints curving over our heads on either side. "Please. Everybody here is a nun in training."

I didn't say anything, but kept walking. I desperately wanted to talk to her. Just not about this.

"So is it true he singed off some guy's pubes with a curling iron?"

"No," I said.

"Waterboarded?"

"No."

"Chopped off fingers?"

"No."

"Cattle prodded a guy in the balls?"

I hesitated.

"No."

She smiled at me. "I see how it is," she said. "You still believe he's a good guy just because he's your dad. Don't worry, you'll figure out the truth sooner or later. Like me. I haven't seen my mom since I was eleven. She ran off to the Florida Keys with a real estate developer named Luciano."

"Oh," I said. "I'm sorry."

"Don't be." She threw herself into her seat and adjusted her knee-high socks into place. "After she abandoned us, me, my sisters, and my dad moved in with my grandma. She's crazy and senile and she doesn't even speak English. I do whatever I want now."

I thought, now that we had commiserated over our

messed-up lives, that we were on our way to becoming friends. But Kenzie didn't acknowledge my existence again until October, when Sister Mary-of-the-Snows, bless her heart, paired us up for a project about sacramental rites, and Kenzie invited me over one Saturday to work on it.

Whenever guests used to come over to our house, my mom always apologized for the "mess," meaning, usually, a neat stack of mail on the little end table in the foyer that hadn't been put away. When Kenzie's grandma opened the door, wearing a stained velour tracksuit and one of those baseball hats with a big fake ponytail tumbling out the back, she didn't apologize for anything—not the cat hair sifted in piles on the stairs, the tangle of shoes piled up in the hallway, the gallon of milk that someone had forgotten to put away dripping sweat on the kitchen table still covered with breakfast dishes. She just smiled at me, gestured up the stairs, and padded away in her pink fuzzy slippers.

The bedroom Kenzie shared with her three younger sisters was a loft that took up the entire top floor of the bungalow where they lived. The room was an absolute disaster—mountains of clothes exploding from the closet; a jumble of bras hanging on the doorknob; hair dryers, belts, headbands, books, and magazines strewn across the matted, stained carpet; and a giant vanity table scattered with paper plates of mummified pizza crusts and every makeup product Cover Girl has produced in the last ten years. The walls were covered in tie-dyed blankets and boy-band posters, the kind you fold out of teenybopper magazines, and the unmade beds were piled with faded, mismatched sheets and pillows so old they were practically flat. I'd always been happy to have my own room, and content with my one brother, but standing here in the middle of this girl zone, I wanted a sister so badly that it ached.

We didn't make much headway on our project. For one thing, Kenzie's ten-year-old sister, Gloria, had just mastered the art of fishtail braiding and wanted to practice on me over and over again. For another, Kenzie discovered that twelve-year-old Dalia had been "borrowing" her thong underwear, an argument that began with a screaming match and ended with Kenzie using her gym lock to padlock her underwear drawer shut. The TV was on, music was blaring, and seven-year-old Marissa was flying around the room, maniacally turning cartwheels. Not exactly optimal study conditions. We created our title page and changed the font around a few times until it looked pretty, but then Kenzie's dad called up the stairs that he had ordered pizza, and the project was forgotten.

We ended up finishing in the computer lab at lunchtime, an hour before it was due. It was total crap, and we got an F (the first and last F for me, the first of many Fs for Kenzie). That made us feel persecuted, and persecution can form an instant bond: our friendship was sealed.

During the first semester of their freshman year, girls change lunch tables more often than they wash their uniform skirts. Up until my Sacramental Journeys project with Kenzie, I had been sitting with a couple bland, studious girls from my honors English seminar who, by some strange miracle, seemed not to have any clue who my father was. Alexis, I had noticed, sat alone. It made me feel horrible, watching her sit there bowed over her turkey sandwich, knowing that her mom had peeled the skin off the edges of the turkey and sliced the bread in a diagonal because that made it feel fancier than straight across. And I understood that she saw *me*, knowing that I drank my Dr Pepper with a straw because I'd heard it would prevent my teeth from getting stained, and that the only sandwich cheese I could stand to eat unmelted was provolone. Even though I had cut her out of my life, the intimate details of Alexis's Alexis-ness remained with me, like an aftershock from the earthquake of what I'd done to her.

One fall afternoon a couple days after our disastrous sacramental rites project, Kenzie stopped me on the way out of seventh period.

"I saw you at lunch today," she said.

"Oh," I said. "I saw you, too." Which was sort of stating the obvious, because our school population was so tiny that sometimes there'd only be twenty or thirty girls to a lunch period; everybody saw everybody all day long, which was the best part of ASH or the worst, depending on your perspective.

"Who were those girls you were sitting with?"

"Um, Mary Bridget Kearns and Lisette Crawford?"

"Lisette *who*?"

"Craw—"

She waved a French-manicured hand. "Never mind. It doesn't matter. *They* don't matter, and you should be eating lunch with people who do. Come sit with me and my friends tomorrow. You'll have a lot more fun. Cool?"

"Cool."

I didn't even hesitate. It was what I'd been waiting for.

The next day, as I put my lunch tray down at the table with Kenzie and Emily and Sapphire, I could feel Alexis watching me. Kenzie, who was slurping a Diet Coke and pawing through a giant bag of cheese puffs, held court at the table, talking about *this* fucking guy and *that* fucking bitch and did you ever notice that when Mr. Winters sits on his desk you can see the outline of his ball sack and *God*, I wish there were boys here and who *cares* if you didn't read *A Raisin in the Sun*, there's only, like, twenty different movie versions on Netflix and it's not like you couldn't bullshit your way through Ms. Lee's tests *anyway*, while the rest of us laughed and agreed.

When Alexis finally leaned down to her backpack and pulled out her headphones, I was relieved. Part of me wanted to ask her for forgiveness while the other part just wanted to punch her. *Find some new friends!* I imagined myself screaming. *It's not that hard!* But then, a couple weeks later, when she finally gave up waiting for me to come back to her and found some, I felt irrationally jealous. Now it was Marlo Guthrie and Ola Kaminski's turn to know about Alexis, about her diagonal-cut sandwiches and the way she listened to music with her eyes closed and pulled on her earlobes when she was nervous. Maybe she'd even take them to O'Hare Airport and tell them about her dream to play at the Vienna Philharmonic. *Like I even care,* I thought to myself, turning back to my new friends, all the while knowing that's exactly what you say to yourself when you still care.

7

A COUPLE WEEKS AFTER THE I LUV BOYS tattoo, my mom had the night off for once, so we made plans to hang out on the couch and watch movies. But then word got out that Evan Munro's cousin's parents were out of town. I tried to say I didn't really feel like partying, but my friends were having none of it.

You're hanging out with your MOM? Kenzie wrote in our group text. *What are you, five?*

Seriously! Sapphire added. *Do you have your period? Take a Midol! This is a PARTY we're talking about here!*

Until I met my current group of friends, I never believed that peer pressure was an actual thing. I always thought it was something adults made up so they would have someone else to blame when their kid got drunk or came home with a piercing in their face. Turns out, peer pressure is real, and it is powerful. I knew my friends didn't want me to come out with them because they just couldn't get enough of my sparkling personality; they really just wanted a designated driver. And yet, despite this knowledge, there I was at seven o'clock, yelling excuses to my mom over the roar of the hair dryer, and then I was clicking out the door in my high-heeled boots, while she sat alone on the couch with a big bowl of popcorn on her lap, trying not to act like I'd totally crushed her feelings.

Evan's cousin Ned lived about a half hour from us, in a ritzy suburb on the North Shore. When we turned off the expressway exit, I saw that we had entered not just a different zip code but a completely different life. The streets were paved with cobblestones; the stunning, pristine homes were protected from ogling onlookers by enormous, rambling trees; even the street signs were tasteful and expensive-looking. Purebred dogs pranced along the sidewalks on leashes held by beautiful, well-dressed owners, while young, vibrant couples pushed their heirs in strollers that were almost certainly worth more than my car. This, I understood, was a neighborhood reserved strictly for people whose dreams had come true.

Ned's house, at the end of one such block, floated out of the falling darkness like an enormous white yacht. Just beyond, in his backyard, you could make out the shores of Lake Michigan undulating calmly.

"These people are *loaded*," whispered Sapphire, her voice shrill with envy, as Red Rocket, belching smoke, came to a hissing stop in the circular drive behind a glittering row of sixteenth-birthday presents.

"So?" Kenzie spritzed her wrists with the body splash she kept in my glove compartment. "Just because we don't live in Winnetka doesn't mean we're trailer trash. When we get in there, act like you belong."

We stepped up the manicured brick walkway and stood on the front stoop between two large urns filled with red and yellow mums. From inside, we could hear laughter and the thrum of hip-hop.

"Hey, Saph," Kenzie said, reaching out and pressing the doorbell. "I dare you to steal something from this place."

"No way." Sapphire hung her head between her knees and began furiously scrunching the underside of her hair. "I dared you to sneak a boy into school *last year*, and we're all still waiting for that to happen." She flipped her hair back into position.

"Okay, let's make a deal," Kenzie said. "You steal something from this house tonight, I'll sneak a boy into school next week. Deal?"

Sapphire grinned that pretty cat smile of hers, showing both rows of her pearly teeth.

"Deal."

They shook on it.

When the door opened, I was momentarily confused. I'd been expecting the Great Gatsby, or at least some hot variation of a football jock. What I saw instead was a small, gangly kid with a shock of wiry orange hair standing wildly atop his head, a face as red and shiny as a boiled apple, and a complicated, gleaming set of braces. I couldn't figure out which was harder to believe: that he lived in this palace or that he and Evan Munro were first cousins.

"Hi," he said shyly, looking at Kenzie. "You're Evan's girl-friend, right?"

"*Hi*, Ned!" She threw her arms around him and his face deepened from its natural apple red to a painful-looking burgundy. "Evan's told me *all* about you!"

In the foyer, a glass chandelier bathed the marble floors in soft pink light. A large table stood before us, displaying a crystal vase of fall flowers and a few abandoned beer cans. To the left of the table was a spiral staircase covered in plush peach-colored carpet, disappearing up to the second floor.

"You can hang your coats up in the closet if you want." Ned led us to a door with a ceramic knob painted delicately with green vines. Inside, we hung our jackets on a couple of empty hangers we found sandwiched between a bunch of lavish fur coats.

"Jesus, Ned, are these *real*?" Kenzie held out the sleeve of a gorgeous silver stole, her fingers disappearing into the soft pile.

"They're my mom's," Ned said, not answering the question. Kenzie glanced at Sapphire, then let go of the sleeve and shut the closet door.

Evan, who must have heard Kenzie's voice in the echo chamber of the foyer, came loping down the stairs with a can of beer in each hand. She squealed when she saw him, and he swooped her up with a war whoop and slung her over his shoulder, carrying her off into the party with her perfect little ass swaying in the air. The rest of us followed, trying to remember to act like we belonged.

The gleaming white kitchen, which was approximately the size of an airplane hangar, featured at least four separate ovens and a refrigerator that was only slightly smaller than the walk-in cooler at Europa Deli. Kids in various states of drunkenness milled about, helping themselves to the food in the pantry and fridge. There was a large sectional leather couch in front of the biggest TV I'd seen outside of a professional basketball game, and a few kids were playing Mortal Kombat X, ripping each other's heads off in 3D. Everybody there was good-looking and they all had nicer clothes than we did—this was no Saint Mike's backyard garage party. Sapphire, Emily, and I stuck together, scuttling around like a six-legged bug. Only Kenzie, who would always be the most beautiful girl in any room regardless of socioeconomic status, carried on as normal, allowing herself to be herded over to the beer pong table under the iron weight of Evan's shoulder, and handing off her cup to be filled with beer.

"This house is sick," Sapphire said breathlessly, staring up through a giant skylight at a night faint with stars. "Is that a refrigerator just for wine?" She squatted down to examine the digital thermostat.

"My cousin has a house like this, too," Emily said in her high, annoying voice. "I mean, actually, it's even bigger. It has a theater in the basement." When no one responded, she added, "With a popcorn machine."

"Shut up, Em," Sapphire said absently. We had now drifted down a luxuriously wallpapered hallway that was lined with gold-framed paintings, a couple tribal masks, a painting of a naked woman sprawled across a red couch, and a plastic case containing a row of delicate silver knives and forks with a small plaque at the bottom that read: "Official state silverware, Abraham Lincoln White House. 1864." There were pictures of a tall white guy with faded orange hair—Ned's dad, I guessed—posing with various super famous people: George W. Bush, Elton John, Al Pacino, Mike Ditka. There was another photograph of this same man dressed in khaki safari clothes, holding a rifle and kneeling happily next to a dead cheetah.

"Holy *crap*," said Emily, her voice tremulous with awe. "I guess that's where the mom gets her fur coats from."

"Bet your cousin with the popcorn machine never shot a cheetah," Sapphire said.

"He *might* have."

"Shut up, Emily."

While Kenzie and Evan dominated at the beer pong table, the three of us wandered around together, staring. Sapphire even took pictures when she thought no one was looking. The only other person who seemed as self-conscious as us was Ned himself, who clearly had only been invited to this party because it happened to be at his house. He hovered around the three of us for a while, looking for an opportunity to start a conversation, but we ignored him until he lurked off, nervously sipping a vodka and cranberry.

At some point, Kenzie detached herself from the game and grabbed me by the arm.

"Come pee with me," she demanded, and dragged me down another hallway, teetering on her high heels, to a bathroom that had a steam shower, a regular shower, a hot tub, and a regular tub. Ned might not be the coolest guy on the planet, I thought, but he had to be the cleanest.

"I'm *so* drunk," Kenzie said proudly, unbuckling her jeans and shimmying them down her legs, followed by her red lace thong. She crash-landed on the toilet seat. "Aren't you having the best time ever?"

"Definitely." I smiled, sprawling myself across a love seat that I guess Ned's parents had put there just in case you needed a short rest between brushing your teeth and using the toilet.

"I love peeing," Kenzie declared, hanging her head between her long legs. "It feels *awesome*." She laughed, spun the toilet paper roll a few times, wiped, then stumbled back to her feet.

"Fucking high fucking heels," she muttered.

"Kenz, maybe it's time to switch to water," I counseled. She buttoned her jeans, slowly, carefully, like she was threading a needle, then marched over to me. She reached out, gently, and cupped my chin in her hand.

"Wendy, darling, I love you, but you are *so* boring," she said, then strode out the door and back into the party.

Alone in the cavernous bathroom now, I looked at myself in the mirror. What did people see when they looked at me? A pretty girl, I guessed, but with too much makeup, huddled inside a red peacoat that looked cheap because it was. I looked like a girl waiting at a train station in a foreign country, not knowing the language, not knowing if the ticket she'd bought was even going to the right place.

I opened a crystal-knobbed cabinet in the vanity and came upon a stockpile of makeup. I chose a lipstick, a deep, creamy shade of fuchsia, and slicked it over my lips.

"Darling," I said to myself in the mirror, "I love you, but you are *so* boring."

Then I wiped off the lipstick and went back out to the party.

I was just turning the corner into the kitchen when Emily grabbed me tightly by the arm.

"Wendy, we've gotta go. Like, *now*." Sapphire hovered behind her, shifting nervously from foot to foot.

"Okay," I said. "Where's Kenzie?"

"She's saying good-bye to Evan by your car."

As soon as we got outside, Evan and Kenzie, who had been drunkenly tonguing against Red Rocket's hood, untangled themselves from each other.

"I'll call you, baby!" She trailed a finger down his muscle-bound chest.

"Are you sure you gotta leave?"

"You know Emily and her parents' pathetic rules about curfew." She put her palms out, as if it was all beyond her control. She kissed Evan good-bye one last time, and as soon as he had disappeared into the house she got in the car, propped her feet on the dashboard, and said, "Hey, guys, I'm *starving*. Should we go get some burritos?"

Emily and Sapphire began to giggle helplessly.

"Oh yes," Emily finally managed. "I would *love* some burritos. Is TBQ cool with you, Wendy?"

I shrugged, feeling that this was some sort of trap but not knowing how. And besides, I did kind of crave some chicken nachos with extra sour cream and a large Dr Pepper.

On the expressway, I white-knuckled it all the way back to the city on Red Rocket's balding tires and screeching brakes as my friends danced in their seats and screamed along to Kenzie's *PARTYPARTYPARTY* playlist. At Taco Burrito Queen, the dingy spot where all the high school and college kids line up for good greasy drunk food into the early hours of the morning, as we sat waiting for our order to come up, Sapphire, Em, and Kenzie kept exchanging smirky looks and stifling their conspiratorial giggles.

"Okay," I sighed. "What is it?"

"Nothing." Emily snickered, then exploded into hysterics.

Our food arrived on a big tray, and we all began reaching for our orders.

"Hey," Sapphire said, unwrapping her steak taco, "do you guys need some silverware?"

"Yes," gasped Emily. "This burrito is *huge* and I can't eat it without a knife and fork!"

I rolled my eyes and stood up. "I'll get them."

"No need, Wendy!" Kenzie grabbed my arm and pulled me back into the booth. "We brought our own!"

And the three of them, eyes glittering, watched my reaction as Sapphire slowly reached into her big, slouchy fake-leather bag and dragged out the large plastic case containing the engraved silverware from Abraham Lincoln's White House.

"Are you guys kidding me?"

I watched them laughing helplessly as Sapphire opened the back of the case and began removing the delicate pieces from their satin displays, handing them around the table.

"Thank *you* very *much*, my dear," Emily said. She took out her phone and began taking pictures of herself posing with the stolen heirlooms, then sawed into her burrito, the silver pieces of our nation's history clinking together expensively. Sapphire tried to give me a fork, but I batted her hand away.

"Oh, relax," Emily giggled. "It's just some silverware, Wendy."

"It's Ned's silverware," I said. "It doesn't belong to you." I shook my head. "No. Scratch that. It's Abraham *Lincoln's* silverware. You know, the man who saved the union. Four score and seven years ago? The Emancipation Proclamation? The man who *freed the slaves*?"

"Yawn," said Sapphire, stabbing at a fried onion and stuffing it in her mouth.

"Why do you even care?" Kenzie dipped a chip into a plastic cup of salsa. "It's not like he freed the slaves with a bunch of *forks*. You probably just want to fuck Ned. Is that it?"

The very idea of *anyone* being attracted to poor Ned sent the three of them dissolving again into peals of laughter.

"Kenzie's right," Emily finally said, two words that pretty much could have been the motto of her life. "I mean, maybe you should be more angry at the fact that some guy spends more money on some crap to hang on his wall than your dad makes in a year." She stopped herself. "I mean, not *your* dad. Like, people's dads in general. Like, *normal* people whose dads aren't . . . I mean, not that your dad's not normal. More that he's just sort of . . ."

"Shut up, Emily," sighed Kenzie. She pointed her chip at

me. "Wendy, what's your deal lately? You've become such a buzzkill. You know, you don't *have* to be friends with us, okay? And, more importantly, we don't *have* to be friends with you. So if I were you, I'd just watch it, okay?" She lifted one of the forks from Emily's plate, never taking her eyes off me, and with a quick, violent motion, bent it in half. She tossed it across the table and it landed in my lap. I picked it up, stunned, and tried to bend it back into shape. But it was already ruined.

"I mean," she went on, "who are *you* to get all up in arms about some missing silverware? At least nobody got electrocuted. At least nobody got suffocated. Or burned. Or beaten, like certain victims of certain disgraced cops who shall go unnamed. Know what I mean?"

Emily, who had a dollop of guacamole smeared across her lower lip, emitted a nervous giggle. Sapphire had commenced using a fork as a tool to fluff her hair and pretended not to have heard.

"I do know what you mean," I said, standing up. "Thanks for giving me some perspective, Kenz. I'll see you guys in school." And, boiling with rage, I put on my red peacoat, pushed away my untouched chicken nachos, and walked out of Taco Burrito Queen.

8

MY AUNT COLLEEN ONCE TOLD ME a story about her first job out of high school. She was waitressing at this all-night diner in Albany Park, run by a short, hairy guy named Wally whose two favorite pastimes were doing the crossword and ogling women's breasts. Aunt Col was blessed with both a big brain and a big rack, so she quickly became one of Wally's favorites. According to Col, he was icky but harmless, until one night in the middle of winter when the place was so dead even the cook had gone to take a nap in the store room, Wally, seeing his chance, came up behind her as she was pouring herself a cup of coffee. He pinned her up against the machine, nuzzled his face into her neck, then reached around and put a red, meaty hand on each of her breasts, whispering something in Greek. "In my country," he murmured, his oniony breath hot on her neck, "that's what I would call you when I took you into my bed." Aunt Col whirled around, spilling hot coffee all over her hand. "And in *my* country," she said, ripping off her apron and throwing it in his face, "I'd call that sexual harassment!"

After ducking past him and out into the snow, she told me how exhilarated she'd felt: It was the first time she'd really stood up for herself, and she knew she was going to be just fine making her way in the real world. But two weeks later, when she realized that February was the slowest season of the year for restaurants and couldn't find another gig, she had to go back to Wally and ask for her job back. "I never went so quick from being that proud of myself to hating my own guts," she told me.

Walking into chapel that Monday morning, I kind of knew what she meant.

After the incident in TBQ, I'd spent the rest of the weekend mentally high-fiving myself for finally growing a spine, but by the time Sunday night came around, it began to dawn on me that if I didn't have Sapphire, Emily, and Kenzie, I didn't have anyone. There were forty-two girls in the junior class at ASH; I'd spent the last three years ignoring thirty-nine of them. Where did that leave me? I thought about Alexis, sitting with her head bowed and her ears burning, alone at that lunch table for the first two months of freshman year. Was I really prepared for that to be me? Did I really have the guts?

So when I arrived at chapel, I was both relieved and disgusted with myself when Kenzie waved me over to our usual spot in the back row and Sapphire shoved over to make room for me.

"So *there's* our supposed best friend who just *ditches* us in the middle of TBQ on a Saturday night."

"I just—" I looked at my lap. "I don't think you guys should have taken the silverware."

"Don't worry!" Kenzie put an arm around me, bathing me in the sickly sweet smell of her peach body splash. "It was just a harmless prank. I'll give it back to Evan tonight, okay?"

"Okay."

"Good. Glad we've got that cleared up." She planted a glossy kiss on my cheek.

"More importantly," said Sapphire, unwrapping a low-fat granola bar, "I filled my end of the deal, Kenz. Now it's your turn."

"It's impossible," Emily sniffed. "You might as well just give up. Sister Dorothy has special nun senses that can detect testosterone from a mile away. You could *never* sneak a boy past her."

"It's not impossible," Kenzie declared. "Because I've already figured out how to do it. I just needed to find the right boy to agree. And now, I have."

"Evan?" Sapphire shot forward in her seat. "He actually agreed? I thought he was too scared of getting caught!"

Kenzie smiled triumphantly. "It's amazing what with-holding sex will do to a guy who's basically one big walking erection." She licked a swath of pink frosting from her donut. "I told him that I wouldn't sleep with him unless he agreed to let me sneak him into school. *That* changed his mind pretty quick."

"But *how*?"

"Gym class. Soon. That's all you need to know."

9

I'M SURE THERE ARE SOME GIRLS out there—perky, athletic types with perfectly proportioned bodies absent of moles, birthmarks, and body hair—who actually look forward to the swimming unit in PE class. Then there's the other 99.99 percent of the female population. For two weeks each year, a collective dread fills the ASH locker room as we are forced to trade in our knee-length cotton gym shorts and oversize red T-shirts for the exponentially more heinous school-issued bathing suits. These Lycra nightmares, with their weirdly thick straps and chokingly high necklines, are the most unflattering swimsuits known to womankind. If you get assigned one of the newer ones, the leg holes squeeze so tightly that your thighs ooze out like sausage casings. Get one of the older ones, and the leg holes are stretched out to the same size as the head hole, so that every time you jump into the water you run the risk of exposing your vag for all your classmates to see. The suits are all the same color—maroon faded to a dull pink by years of boiling in between units—but despite these sterilization measures, there's always a couple unlucky girls who inherit a suit whose white cotton crotch bears a faded streak of a stranger's menstrual blood.

As an added layer of cruelty, Ms. Lally always begins the swimming unit in December. Snow is already on the ground, the sun sets at five o'clock, and here we were in the dank basement of Academy of the Sacred Heart, drifting around a sad net that sagged across the middle of the barely heated depths of the Sister Xavieria Schmidt Memorial Swimming Facility, pretending to play water polo. I say pretending because one of the worst-kept secrets at ASH is that Ms. Lally is a barely functioning alcoholic. Four days out of five, she's either hungover to the point of being half brain-dead or flat-out drunk. She chomps on gum and wears heavy blasts of old lady perfume to mask the beery smell of her skin, but there are plenty of girls at ASH with alcoholics in their families, and we all know the signs. If she's drunk, she's usually pleasant enough, and can muster up the energy to organize us into squads or lead us, in warmer weather, out to the muddy softball fields for a pickup game. If she's hungover, we usually receive some form of two-word instructions: "play dodgeball," "run laps," "shoot free-throws," before she disappears into the athletic office, her track pants swishing sadly, and closes the door until the bell rings, where I imagine her sitting behind her little desk lined with its dusty softball trophies from the eighties, lapping away at her vodka, washing it down with a Tums, and praying for the three o'clock bell.

According to my aunt Col, who was in Ms. Lally's graduating class, she hasn't always been like this. The drinking started fairly recently, when her only child, a daughter, went with her sorority sisters down to Fort Lauderdale for her college spring break and broke her neck falling off the third-floor balcony of a Holiday Inn. Sometimes I wonder what's going to happen to Ms. Lally next year when ASH closes. Who's going to want a depressed alcoholic gym teacher near retirement age who doesn't know even the most basic rules of water polo? It wouldn't surprise me if we started seeing her among the homeless people who drift around the outskirts of the Jefferson Park el station, shuffling through flocks of pigeons, wearing skirts over pants, talking softly with far-away eyes.

But anyway.

Since Ms. Lally doesn't exactly have her eye on the ball, gym class is the one place at ASH where it's easy to get away with stuff. It's where girls text, sell weed, copy each other's homework, pierce each other's ears, and blast music with filthy lyrics without worrying about getting a JUG. So it only made sense that this was the class where Kenzie was going to carry out her dare, though none of us had the slightest clue how she was going to pull it off.

That Friday, as usual, we changed into our hideous suits and put on our white swim caps so that when we stepped out of the locker room and into the dark, chlorinated reek of the Sister Xavieria Schmidt Memorial Swimming Facility, we looked like a gathering of large red penises. Rays of afternoon light spilled from the small, rectangular windows near the ceiling, illuminating the small square tiles etched in a thin layer of green fungus at the bottom of the pool. A filter gurgled quietly. Hanging on the cinder-block walls, among the swim team conference banners from ASH's athletic heydays in the 1950s and '60s, was a large painting of Saint Adjutor, patron saint of swimmers, boaters, and drowning victims. The severe expression on his bearded face and the large silver anchor he gripped in his fist like a dagger didn't give the impression that he'd be much help if you were ever thrown into the deep end and couldn't swim. The edges of the painting crept with lacy black mold spores, threatening to take over the whole canvas. Even if you *liked* swimming, this place would give you the creeps.

As we climbed into the pool and awaited our instructions, I looked around for Kenzie. She wasn't there, but luckily for her, Ms. Lally never bothered to take attendance. "Divide yourself into teams of seven," barked our haggard gym teacher, peering down at us with bloodshot eyes while we hung on the sides in the water and shivered uncontrollably.

"Um, Ms. Lally?" Gretchen Giddings raised her hand timidly. "There are only ten girls here."

Ms. Lally looked down at us with vague surprise. We were

eye level with her squat, muscular legs.

"Okay, teams of five, then." She lifted the whistle to her lips and bleated on it halfheartedly. "Gretchen, you keep score. And if I catch any of you without a swim cap, it's an automatic JUG—I found a hairball in the filter yesterday." With a weak underhand, she heaved a water polo ball into the pool, sauntered back into the athletic office, and closed the door behind her.

Gretchen, Marlo Guthrie, Ola Kaminski, and Alexis were the only ones who even attempted to follow Ms. Lally's instructions. Veronica the Vegan, who'd had her mom write a note excusing her from the entire water polo unit because she could not, in good conscience, play a game that required the use of a cow-leather ball, did her homework in the bleachers. Imani Jenkins and Lisette Crawford watched YouTube videos. Me, Emily, and Sapphire floated on our backs and traded gossip.

It was shaping up to be another dull, leisurely gym class, and Emily and I had just decided that we might join in on the water polo game just to pass the time when we heard a knock at one of the small, snow-covered windows near the ceiling that looked out onto ASH's front lawn. Just as we realized it was Evan Munro's face, red from the cold, smushed up against the glass, Kenzie emerged from the locker room. She was dressed not in her school-issued swimsuit but in a minuscule white string bikini. She tossed her long, black hair—Ms. Lally's warning about swim caps be damned—winked at me and Emily, then jogged across the tiles, bouncing in all the right places. She stopped at the diving board, unhooked the metal ladder, and wheeled it over to the window. The girls who had been trying to play water polo had stopped what they were doing, and now everyone stared.

"Kenzie, what are you doing?" Marlo Guthrie demanded. Her voice, all shrill with valedictorian authority, echoed off the cinder-block walls.

"What does it *look* like I'm doing?"

"You can't let that guy in. Don't even *think* about it."

"Oh, shut up, Marlo," Kenzie laughed lightly. "Live a little. It would be good for you." She minced over to the window and lifted the long hooked pole. After a couple failed attempts, she caught the hook into the hole and the window creaked open, bringing a cold blast of winter air. Evan Munro peered inside.

"Come on, Wendy!" Kenzie waved to me. "Help me sneak him in, okay?"

I glanced first at the closed door of the athletic office, then at the goody-two-shoes girls who were looking at one another nervously.

"You need to stop her," Alexis hissed at me, holding the water polo ball tightly under one arm. "We could all get in a lot of trouble."

"I don't know what you think," I hissed back, "but Kenzie doesn't listen to *anyone*, me included."

"Squeeze through, baby!" Kenzie was calling up at Evan, who had turned his body around and was now reaching with one leg, then the other, to the top rung of the ladder.

"Where's the teacher?" He twisted around to scan the pool for authority figures.

"I told you," Kenzie laughed. "She isn't around! Now get down here!" Apparently satisfied with this explanation, Evan slowly made his way down until he was three rungs from the floor. He jumped the rest of the way, and just like that, there he was: the first boy in 113 years to ever set foot inside Academy of the Sacred Heart. Kenzie lifted her phone from where she'd stowed it beneath the strap of her bikini top and took a picture to commemorate the moment. Meanwhile, Evan looked around nervously at the hanging banners, the dour painting of Saint Adjutor, the crowd of anxious girls floating around the pool in tight swim caps and thick, sexless maroon bathing suits. He was wearing a crisp white dress shirt and a green Saint Mike's tie, and he looked uneasy and a little bit embarrassed. His eyes cut to the athletic office doors. I think it was dawning on him just how much trouble he could get in if he got caught.

"Now what?" he asked.

"Now," Kenzie said, "we go swimming." She placed her phone on the pool's edge, wheeled the ladder back to the diving board, climbed it, took a delicate hop, then dove with perfect form and barely a splash into the deep end. That was what broke him of his nervousness. Evan, staring at Kenzie in her white bathing suit that was now see-through and showed the faint outline of her brown nipples, yanked his tie loose and pulled his shirt, still buttoned, over his head. When he unbelted his khakis and dropped them around his ankles, so that he was standing there in nothing but a *very* tight pair of boxer briefs, Alexis gasped audibly. She, Ola, and Marlo swam off to a corner of the pool to consult.

"Wendy!" Kenzie, who'd surfaced and was now treading water, beckoned me over with a windmilling of her mani-cured hand. "Come on over here!" I could feel my swim cap cutting into the skin of my forehead, the maroon swimsuit pressing down my already unimpressive breasts. But it wasn't even that I looked and felt gross. It was that having a guy see me in the middle of the day at my all-girls school somehow felt like an invasion. Everyone felt that way, I could tell. Sure, Sapphire had dared Kenzie to sneak a boy into school, but no one had believed she'd actually do it. Now that she had, it was like pulling up the curtains and letting a stranger spy into our secret, dying world. I stared at the door of the athletic office, not knowing whether I wanted it to stay closed or to swing open.

"Kenzie, we could all get in trouble," I called weakly.

"Oh, don't be a pussy!" She flipped over to float on her

back, her hair fanned out across the top of the water like a big black lily pad. It was only when Evan climbed the ladder, and, with a joyful shout, cannonballed into the pool, that Alexis took action. She climbed out of the pool and walked quickly toward Ms. Lally's office, her doughy legs trembling with every step.

"Where do you think you're going?" Kenzie's voice was quiet, but it carried over the echo-y expanse of the Sister Xavieria Schmidt Memorial Swimming Facility.

Alexis turned to face Kenzie. She straightened her slopey shoulders. I could almost feel her gathering nerve as she lifted a hand and flipped Kenzie off.

"You knock on that door," Kenzie warned, "and you're dead, bitch."

It was too late—Alexis was already pounding, the thump of her fists echoing across the tiles. And just as Evan had swum to the surface, grabbing Kenzie by the waist and spinning her through the water, laughing and beautiful, Ms. Lally, looking more sober than I'd seen her in my life, threw open the door.

10

HOLY CRAP. THE TEXT FROM EMILY came in at seven a.m., early for a Saturday morning gossip session, even for her. *Did you hear what happened to Evan?*

What? I rubbed my eyes and curled up under the flannel sheets with my phone on the pillow next to me.

He got suspended.

So? I wrote. *Saint Mike's suspends people for tying their ties crooked.*

My phone rang.

"You don't understand," Emily exploded the second I picked up. "Saint Mike's is playing Mount Carmel next weekend in the Catholic League playoffs, and all these college scouts are supposed to be there, and since Evan's suspended he can't play!"

"That sucks." I yawned. Emily was always more interested in spreading the gossip than actually having a discussion, which was why I didn't feel compelled to offer any commentary of my own.

"Kenzie's on the *warpath*," she went on. "She's ready to,

like, *murder* Alexis Nichols."

That got my attention, though.

"Why?" I sat up in bed. "It's not Alexis's fault. If you want to blame somebody *other* than Kenzie or Evan, blame *Sapphire*: she's the one who dared Kenzie to do it."

"Are you serious? Alexis was the one who went and tattled on her, like a little second grader or something. If it weren't for that, she would have *totally* gotten away with it."

"I doubt it."

"Whatever. All I know is, I wouldn't want to be Alexis Nichols right now."

Kenzie, Emily had gleefully informed me, was under a social media lockdown—her dad had taken away her phone and laptop. So we had to wait for Monday morning chapel to find out what had happened after Ms. Lally grabbed her and Evan each by the elbow, shoved towels in their hands, and escorted them to Sister Dorothy's office, dripping water all the way down the Saints Corridor. I half expected not to see her at all—after all, if sneaking a boy into gym class while dressed in a see-through bikini isn't an expellable offense, what is? But there she was, sitting in her usual seat in the back pew, nonchalantly unwrapping a frosted Pop-Tart as if it was just another boring Monday at Academy of the Sacred Heart.

Before I could even sit down, Emily came crashing past me.

"Kenzie! Holy crap!" She threw herself down in an empty wooden chair. "Are you in trouble? What happened with

Evan? What did Sister Dorothy *say?*"

"God, Emily," Kenzie said, calmly biting into her breakfast. "You are a *lot* to take this early in the morning."

"But what about the Mount Carmel game?"

"What about it? It's *one* game he has to sit out for. You know how these jocks are with sports—they think football actually has a point. Besides, those college scouts will be back for the next game, anyway."

"Not if they lose," Emily said breathlessly. "It's a playoff game, single elimination. If they lose, they're out."

"They haven't lost all season," Kenzie said. "Why would they start now?"

"Um, because their star quarterback is going to be sitting on the bench?"

"Shut up, Emily," Kenzie said, taking another delicate bite of her Pop-Tart.

"What about *you?*" Sapphire demanded. "Are you in trouble? What did Sister Dorothy say?

"Ugh. That crazy old bitch. She put me on probation and gave me JUG for the rest of the week. Totally ridiculous."

"Ridiculous? You should be thanking *God* you weren't expelled!"

"Well, normally, I would've been, but Sister Dorothy said that since we're closing at the end of the year anyway, she's going to have mercy on me."

"What else did she say?"

"Sister Dorothy? Not much. It was that idiot counselor,

Ms. Bennett, who did most of the talking. About how I had 'violated the safe space' of our school, and that I needed to stop my 'attention seeking behaviors,' and that I have to start 'finding approval from within.' All Sister Dorothy said was that if I pull any more stunts before the end of the year, she will 'personally see me out the door.'"

"What about your dad?"

"Oh, the usual threats. He said that if I don't start acting like the daughter he raised, I can forget about going to Lincoln next year."

"But where would you go, besides Lincoln? What else is there?"

"There's some dump up in Eau Claire, Wisconsin, that he keeps threatening me with. Here, I have a pamphlet." She rifled through her backpack and pulled out a glossy booklet. On the cover, a circle of laughing, ponytailed girls sat on a green lawn before a large stone archway with a pile of textbooks spread before them. It all looked relatively picturesque and normal, except that they were wearing these weird starched white blouses and navy wool skirts that reached down to their ankles. CHERRYWOOD ACADEMY, it said at the top of the photo, and then, in smaller letters, "A THERAPEUTIC BOARDING SCHOOL FOR TROUBLED YOUNG WOMEN."

"Therapeutic boarding school?" I passed the booklet to Emily. "What does that mean?"

"It's where they send you when they decide that your soul needs to be crushed. The entire school is Wi-Fi disabled. You only get to leave campus twice a month, behavior contingent, and even then it has to be supervised. And you see for yourself the burlap sacks they make you wear to class."

"Jesus," Sapphire breathed. "And I thought *our* uniforms were heinous."

"If I were you, I'd watch myself from here on out," I said.

"Oh, it's just an empty threat," she said, waving me off. "He knows that I'd die before I'd let him send me there."

"Lights out at *nine o'clock*?" Emily was paging through the Cherrywood Academy pamphlet with growing horror. "Oh my *God*, Kenz. You really *would* die up there."

"But you don't want to call his bluff, either," I said. "I mean, there's a chance he could be serious."

"I know." She picked off a bit of frosting and placed it on her tongue. "And I plan on behaving myself, once I take care of one more thing."

"What's that?"

"Kicking that little snitch Alexis Nichols's teeth in."

"Kenzie, come on," I sighed. "You would've been caught anyway. If Alexis hadn't told, Marlo would've. Or Gretchen."

"You're just defending her because you two used to be besties back in elementary school."

"That's not true. I mean, look at her. She probably wouldn't even fight back."

The four of us let our gazes drift toward the front row, where Alexis was sitting quietly, waiting for prayers to begin. There was her familiar body, the body I'd known all my life, shapeless and noodle skinny, with those shy sloping shoulders and little red bumps up the backs of her arms. Her hair was tied in a messy braid, and her backpack was as dorkily overstuffed as a freshman's.

"She *is* sort of pathetic, isn't she?" Kenzie said. "But if I let her get away with tattling on me, what kind of respect will I have around this place?" She glanced around the room to check for nuns, and seeing that the coast was clear, broke off a corner of her Pop-Tart and lobbed it toward the front row. It hit Alexis directly in the back of her head, some crumbs catching in the folds of her braid. Alexis winced, then turned around. When she saw where it had come from, her mouth set itself in a firm, hard line, but I couldn't tell what she was feeling: Rage? Hatred? Annoyance? Fear?

"Maybe *I* should play quarterback next weekend," Kenzie said, smiling broadly and giving Alexis a little wave. Alexis turned immediately back around, her braid flicking. Her shoulders had gone rigid.

"Real mature, Kenz," I sighed.

"What?" She looked at me with those huge black mascara-crusted eyes, all fake innocence and pout. "It slipped." She broke off another piece of Pop-Tart and chucked it. This time, it landed perfectly on the crown of

Alexis's head. Alexis reached up and brushed it away, but this time she didn't turn around.

"*Stop,*" I said. "It's like you took a class in Bullying 101 or something. Throwing stuff at people? That's not even, like, *original.*"

"*So?*" Emily piped. "That loser almost got her sent to a therapeutic boarding school in Eau Claire, Wisconsin."

"And *you,*" I said, not even trying to hide my annoyance, "must have signed up for Toadie 101."

Before Emily could respond, the chapel lights dimmed, and we all shut up. A senior girl from Eucharistic Ministry Club walked up to the altar and began to lead the morning prayer: "In the name of the Creator, the Redeemer, and the Spirit Who Makes Us Free." We all crossed ourselves and began to murmur along. I couldn't pay attention, though. I was staring at the bits of Pop-Tart on the carpet near Alexis's feet. God, I hated how my friends could make me feel like such a coward. They put me in these situations where the choice between right and wrong was so clear, and yet I could never seem to find the courage to choose right. "Blessed are the poor in spirit," the senior girl read, "for theirs is the kingdom of Heaven. Blessed are the meek." I glanced up at the back of Alexis's braided head, remembering the gentle way she had led me down the corridors of O'Hare to the international terminal. "For they shall see God." *Blessed are the sidekicks,* I thought, *for they shall one day learn to think for*

themselves. Blessed are the bitches, for they shall be called Kenzie
and Sapphire and Emily and Wendy.

That afternoon, when we arrived to gym class, we changed
into our hideous maroon bathing suits and climbed into
the pool as usual, ready for another leisurely class period of
pretending to play water polo. But when the door to the athletic office opened, it was Sister Dorothy, not Ms. Lally, who
stepped out to greet us.

That wasn't what threw us, though. It was the fact that
Sister Dorothy, who no one had ever seen wearing anything
but her wimple and floor-length gray habit, was now standing before us in a black one-piece bathing suit and matching
swim cap, a squat round ball of flesh perched atop a pair
of milk-white bowed legs, dimpled across the thighs and
threaded along the calves with purple spider veins.

"Good afternoon, girls," she said.

No one said a word. We just sat there bobbing in the
water, gaping up at her like a herd of stunned seals.

"You act," she said, looking down at us with her fists on
her wide hips, "as if you've never seen a nun in a bathing suit
before."

Ola Kaminski raised a timid hand.

"Sister, where's Ms. Lally?"

"Ms. Lally is not here," Sister Dorothy said, her eyes flicking briefly toward Kenzie, who, perhaps under the threat of
the Cherrywood Academy pamphlet, was fully dress-code

compliant in her maroon suit and white cap. "From now on, I'll be teaching your PE class."

We glanced at one another but said nothing. Had Ms. Lally quit? Been suspended? Fired? My stomach flipped sourly with the feeling that Kenzie's little stunt had gone and ruined the only decent thing Ms. Lally had left in her life.

"Veronica! *Please* enlighten me as to *why* you aren't dressed for gym yet?"

Sister Dorothy had swiveled around to face the bleachers and was glaring at Veronica the Vegan, who was sitting in the first row, still wearing her school uniform.

"Sister, I—I have a pass from my mom," she stammered. "I'm a conscientious objector to the water polo unit. See, the ball is made of cow leather and—"

"Well, as it so happens, I don't know how to play water polo," Sister Dorothy said, cutting her off. "Or any other aquatic sport, for that matter. So today we're going to spend the remainder of the period swimming laps. No animal leather required. Now get changed."

Veronica hesitated—in addition to her political beliefs, she also had a vague medical condition that only seemed to surface when she was required to do something she didn't feel like doing—but, thinking the better of it, she stood up and disappeared into the locker room. After all, who was going to challenge a woman who'd thrown a pie at a United States senator?

We organized ourselves into the never-used swim lanes,

and when Sister Dorothy blew the whistle, we took off using whatever rudimentary swimming skills we possessed. The only swimming lesson I'd ever had was what my dad had taught me up in Crooked Lake, hurling me off the back of the pontoon boat with my life jacket clipped on tight, shouting encouragement as I doggy-paddled back to the boat. But nobody else seemed much better off than I was, partly because most of our sports programs had been cut, and while we floundered our way to the deep end and back again, doggy-paddling, hanging on to the pool edge for support, chopping up water so the entire Sister Xavieria Schmidt Memorial Swimming Facility looked like a typhoon had hit, we could hear Sister Dorothy prowling the deck, yelling at us to go faster, push harder, stop being such wimps!

"For a bunch of girls who thought they were so *cool* just last Friday, who thought the rules of Academy of the Sacred Heart existed solely to be *mocked*, you all sure seem pretty soft! Why, I know sisters in our motherhouse, octogenarians, mind you, who could run rings around you kids! That's what you get for sitting on your behinds, staring at your laptop computers all day long!"

Her voice came mockingly at us from far away above the water, and we swam until our lungs burned, until we saw black spots, until, through blurred vision, we saw the mold-covered painting of Saint Adjutor and prayed for him to bring us mercy, but Sister Dorothy was relentless. After all, we were being punished, and no one does punishment better than the Sisters of the Sacred Heart. Finally, when Veronica collapsed in the shallow end and vomited up a watery puddle of Boca Burger and fruit smoothie, Sister Dorothy blew her whistle. Coughing, wheezing, and humiliated, we dragged ourselves to the pool's edge one by one.

All of us, that is, except Kenzie.

She continued to swim, kicking confidently with her long, tan legs, a fluid blur of rhythm and athleticism, flip-turning like an Olympian every time she reached the wall, switching easily from the freestyle to the breaststroke to the butterfly and backstroke. Her pace was easy but determined, effortless. What she had was not necessarily speed, but endurance.

For maybe the first time ever, Sister Dorothy had been outmaneuvered.

She'd figured that if she made us all do laps until we barfed, then our outrage at being collectively punished for Kenzie's crime would take the queen bee down a peg or two. Unfortunately, what Sister Dorothy hadn't counted on was that Kenzie was a Red Cross–certified lifeguard. Watching her, you got the sense that she could go all day if she wanted, and into the night, and when the engineer came down here and snapped off the big flood lights in the ceiling behind their metal cages, she would keep on swimming in the cold darkness, until everyone—Alexis, Sister Dorothy, and all the rest of us—knew that she would always outlast us, and she would always win.

It was only when Sister Dorothy blew her whistle again and instructed us to change back into our uniforms before the bell rang that Kenzie glided to a stop and hoisted herself out of the pool. Her chest was heaving and her eyes were bright, but her mouth was tightly shut—she would not gasp for air, she would not show her pathetic human vulnerability. As Kenzie headed for the locker room, Sister Dorothy watched her pass, a troubled look on her soft, holy face. If I had to guess what she was thinking, it was that she should have expelled Kenzie after all.

The locker room was quiet, palpable with jangling nerves. We were too tired to talk—my arms and legs were like Jell-O; my chest muscles would ache for a week. We huddled behind our towels as we changed, steering our eyes to the floor and trying to maintain our privacy. But Kenzie peeled off her bathing suit, kicked it away, and then marched naked across the wet tiles to the big stainless steel cabinet near the showers. All of us tried not to stare as her perfect figure retreated, but how could we not? The way she swished her hips and thrust her breasts demanded that we look, demanded that we compare, demanded that we go home that night and stare at our own imperfect bodies in secluded mirrors, knowing that we'd been taught better than to care so much about the physical but still being unable to stop wishing that, just for a moment, we could know what it was like to walk around with a body like that.

Kenzie pulled out a fresh towel, wrapped her long hair with it, and pivoted to catwalk back in the direction she'd come. On her way back to her locker, her breasts bouncing authoritatively, she moved her naked hips so that she brushed up against Alexis—barely touching her, but enough that Alexis, who was perched in a one-legged flamingo stance trying to pull on her underwear while shielding the rest of her body with her too-small gym towel, stumbled, her elbow knocking into her gym locker with a metallic twanging sound and her towel falling to the floor.

As Alexis scrambled to pick up her towel, her small breasts swinging, a dark patch of ungroomed pubic hair visible through her tangled underwear, Kenzie burst into cruel laughter. And even as it happened, I knew that for the rest of my life I would always regret what the rest of us did in response: nothing.

11

SAINT MIKE'S PLAYED MOUNT CARMEL IN the Catholic League playoffs a few days before Christmas. The bare trees were covered in frost; the frigid air was brittle; the flagpoles pinged in the wind. The bleachers were just as crowded as they'd been back at the September game against Notre Dame Prep, but the atmosphere wasn't nearly as fun: the stands were almost quiet, with everybody bundled up beneath piles of coats and scarves, trying to concentrate on staying warm. Halfway through the first quarter, Saint Mike's was already losing 14–0. I could see Evan Munro shivering on the bench, looking forlorn and holding his helmet in his lap. According to the game program, the backup quarterback was a sophomore named Thomas Wilkins, who was five foot six and 125 pounds. Every time he trotted onto the field with his offense, his thin brown face was etched in terror. He fumbled a snap, threw three interceptions, and just before halftime was sacked twice in a row by one of Mount Carmel's human tank defensive ends. The second time, he took so long to get up that an even smaller and more terrified-looking freshman boy was called upon to finish the half.

"This is so *dumb* that they won't let Evan play," Sapphire protested during the halftime break, blowing into her hands to keep them warm. "I didn't think they actually took that 'academics and character before athletics' crap seriously."

"Yeah, it's ridiculous," agreed Emily. "I mean, Mount Carmel isn't even good. It's not fair to let them win like this."

"Shut up, you guys," Kenzie said viciously. "The game isn't over yet." I glanced over at her and realized it was the first time I'd ever seen her look nervous. She was licking her lips so that her electric-pink lipstick had bled to a messy puddle around her mouth, and she kept clawing her fingers through her hair so that it stood up in the cold, dry air, a mess of static and flyaways. It must have started to dawn on her that Saint Mike's probably was going to lose after all, and there would be no more college scouts for Evan this season, or maybe ever again.

By the end of the third quarter, most of the Saint Mike's crowd had given up and gone home. With fewer people left on our side of the stands to block the wind, it howled and bit at our faces. All I wanted was to go back to my apartment and curl up on the couch with some Christmas cookies, a Dr Pepper, and *Teen Mom 2*, but Kenzie had decided that, for better or worse, she had to see her man through to the end of the game, even if all he was doing was sitting with his elbows on his splayed knees and his head in his hands, a picture of despair and failure. When the fourth quarter ended and the buzzer mercifully put the game to an end, the final score was Mount Carmel, 35, Saint Mike's, 3.

After the game, the three scouts who'd been standing on the sidelines taking notes and recording video in their brightly colored collegiate windbreakers were talking excitedly to the two Mount Carmel defensive ends who'd gone on a sacking bonanza against poor Thomas Wilkins. Other Mount Carmel players were laughing and high-fiving and posing for pictures with their parents and girlfriends, who'd flooded the field after the clock ran down. Evan stood by himself on the sidelines while his teammates lined up to shake hands.

"Let's go down to the field," Kenzie said, pulling out her phone and reapplying her smeared lipstick. "I want to go make sure Evan's okay."

"Are you sure that's a good idea, Kenz?" I asked. She whipped her head around and looked at me, her breath steaming in the night air like a wild horse's.

"Why wouldn't it be?"

"I don't know." I shrugged. "His team just lost. Maybe he wants to be alone right now."

She rolled her eyes.

"This is what girlfriends *do*, Wendy. They comfort their boyfriends. You've never had one, so you wouldn't know."

She stalked off down the steps, and the three of us trailed behind her. Evan was just walking off the field when we approached.

"Tough game, baby," Kenzie said, touching his arm. "But the good news is at least we can drink it off tonight at Sully's house."

"Are you serious?" Evan shook his arm free. Kenzie stepped back in surprise.

Sully, who'd been trudging past us toward the showers, his helmet in his hands, stopped and turned to Kenzie. "Who said *you* were invited to my party?" He reeked of sweat, his hair was frozen in wet spikes, and his eyes were blue and wet. "Or you either, Munro? That little stunt you two pulled over at ASH just cost us the playoffs. I'm a senior, man. I don't get another chance." He walked away, his cleats making little squishing noises in the torn-up mud. Evan watched him go, a yearning, broken look on his face. When he turned back to Kenzie, tears were spilling down his cheeks.

"Kenzie," he said, his lower lip trembling. He wiped his eyes with the back of his enormous hand. "You seriously ruined my life."

"Evan—" she reached out to him again, but he ducked away, his body taut with disgust.

"This?" He waved a hand back and forth between their two bodies. "Over." Then he turned around and followed Sully off the field.

Kenzie stood there for a moment with her mouth open. Sapphire, Emily, and I hung back, not knowing what to say. Finally she whirled around, her dark eyes flashing beneath the glow of the stadium lights.

"Did I just get dumped?"

The three of us stood there, shifting on our feet.

"Well?" She thrust her face into Sapphire's. "Did I, Sapphire? I mean, you would know, it's happened to you plenty of times."

Sapphire's face blushed red beneath her pile of dark curls.

"Yeah," she said. "You did."

"Was Evan *crying*?"

We didn't say anything.

Kenzie let go a deep, mean laugh. The air steamed with her breath.

"What a *pussy*. Does he really think I would even *want* to go out with a boy who blubbers in public like that? Ha!" She crossed her arms tightly across her chest, and began pushing her way through the crowd toward the parking lot. She turned around once. "Well? Let's go!" As we hurried toward my car, I saw Evan, his head bowed, standing with his mother. She was hugging him while his shoulders shook and shook.

As we waited for my car to warm up, Emily ventured a question from the back seat.

"So, are we just going home, then?"

Kenzie whirled around, her hair whipping my face.

"Well, if you want to go to Sully's party, then go ahead and be a fucking traitor. *I'm* going home."

"Me too," Emily said faintly.

"Good." She plugged in her phone and turned her *PARTY-PARTYPARTY* playlist up to a deafening volume. No one sang along this time. I dropped off Sapphire, then Emily, and turned along the train tracks. We were a couple blocks from Kenzie's house when she shot forward in her seat and screamed over the pumping music, "Stop the car!"

I slammed on the brakes in the middle of Avondale; if there had been someone behind me we would have been smashed.

"Jesus! What is it?"

"Pull over." Her voice had gone soft and dangerous.

"Why?"

"Do it."

I flicked on my turn signal and pulled to the curb. As soon as I put the car in park, though, I realized what was going on, but now it was too late to correct my mistake. Kenzie had already unbuckled her seat belt, thrown open the passenger-side door, and was striding across the road to where Alexis, violin case under one arm, was walking along the train tracks, her ears obliviously wrapped in a big white pair of headphones. A fine snow had begun to fall, dusting the road and the sidewalk. Nobody was around but us.

"Kenzie, wait!" I turned off the car, and ran after her

across Avondale just as the 9:45 freight came screaming by, filling the snowy quiet with its prolonged roar. Kenzie trotted across the street and came to a halt directly in the middle of the sidewalk. Alexis, who'd been walking along staring at the ground—counting the cracks in the concrete, I guessed, like she'd done when we were kids—jolted to a surprised stop. When she saw Kenzie, it took a moment for her to register who it was. The slack, contented expression she wore whenever she listened to classical music still lingered on her face, as if she was being shaken unwillingly out of a pleasant dream.

I couldn't hear what Kenzie said because the train was still roaring past. I could only see what she did. She reached out, almost casually, and smacked Alexis's violin case from under her arm. The leather case, curved softly like a woman's body, clattered to the ground, leaving skid marks in the new snow. Before Alexis could pick it up, Kenzie had kicked it away, sending it skittering into the street. Alexis, her headphones still over her ears, chased after it, but Kenzie got there first. She snatched it up, snapped open the brass clasps, and lifted out the lovely, mahogany instrument by its neck. The last of the train cars were now vibrating away and their echo rang around in the silent air.

"Give it back," Alexis said. Her voice reverberated in the snow and the quiet street. It had a tenacious strength in it that I nearly didn't recognize.

"How much do these things cost, anyway?" Kenzie turned the violin over in her hands, examining it. "Probably more than my grandma's car, I bet. It's always the spoiled brats who play the violin, isn't it?"

"Give it back," Alexis repeated.

"Or else what—you'll tell on me?"

Alexis said nothing.

"I bet you practice this in your little pink bedroom with the pink canopy and all those frilly decorative pillows." Kenzie ran her fingers over the smooth wood. "And your Disney posters on the wall."

Alexis's cheeks reddened. When she looked at me, her face was filled with an old hurt. Kenzie could only know what Alexis's bedroom looked like because I'd told her. Because I'd made fun of it to her. It was such an intimate insult, the kind that can only be inflicted when someone betrays you. I looked away, ashamed.

"Give it to me!" Alexis said it more forcefully this time, and her eyes scanned the empty street, willing someone to come around the corner, a witness, a car full of Mount Carmel kids, anybody. But it was freezing and snowing and nobody was out.

"Kenzie," I said, stepping between them, my heart slamming in my chest. "Come on. Give it back to her. This has gone far enough."

Kenzie turned the violin over in her hands, ignoring me.

"It's a pretty cool-looking instrument," she said. "I've never really seen one up close before. I wonder what I could get for this on Craig's List."

"I'm not afraid of you, you know," Alexis said to her.

"You're not?"

"No."

"Well. I guess we'll have to change that, won't we?" And with the same grace, the same fluidity with which she'd swum up and down the length of the Sister Xavieria Schmidt Memorial Swimming Facility for forty-five solid minutes, Kenzie grabbed the lovely mahogany violin around its neck with both hands, lifted it above her head, and smashed it onto the sidewalk. It splintered down the middle, making a high, keening, almost human sound, and the lovingly polished pieces scattered down the length of the deserted street, so that all Kenzie held now was the neck, tangled with jagged pieces and broken string. "Oops," she said, tossing it, or what was left of it, to the curb.

A strangled cry emerged from Alexis's throat, as sweet and broken as the sound of her violin, and she ran to the ruined instrument. Tears had filmed over her eyes as she gathered up the neck and the broken pieces, placing them gently into the crushed velvet of the case, which lay hanging open like a broken jaw. Kenzie loomed above, all six feet of her, arms crossed, leaning her weight on one foot, smiling with satisfaction as Alexis crawled around in the whirling snow, gathering up the shards of her violin. I just stood there, frozen, numb. When Alexis finally straightened up, clicking the case shut and holding it to her chest like a wounded child, she finally spoke. Not to Kenzie, but to me.

"You know, Wendy, I feel really sorry for you," she said. "Because I know you. It must be so freaking lonely, this new life of yours. Being friends with people like this."

"Like *what*, bitch?" Kenzie called after her as Alexis began to trek down Avondale, her violin case clutched to her chest, its broken pieces jangling horribly. "Someone cool? Someone pretty? Someone *normal*?" Alexis kept walking. "Just remember, next time you decide to tattle on me about anything, I'll do the same thing to your fucking face that I just did to your violin."

Once Alexis had disappeared around the corner, Kenzie turned to me and laughed. "Oh, don't give me that look, Wendy. You know she deserved that. I *warned* you I was going to get back at her. And now it's done, okay? I'll leave her alone now. I promise."

"How could you do that?" I asked quietly.

"Oh, relax," Kenzie said, putting her arm around my shoulder and guiding me back across the abandoned street. "Girls like that make me sick. Girls who think they're so perfect. Who get straight As and violin lessons. Who have moms who probably cut the crusts off their sandwiches every day."

"Not the crusts," I murmured. "The turkey skins."

"What?"

"Nothing."

We climbed back into Red Rocket.

"You know," she said, "she'll probably thank me one day for toughening her up. As my dad likes to say, life's a shit storm. If you want to get through it, you're gonna need a pretty strong umbrella."

After I dropped Kenzie off, after I watched her disappear inside her house, after I drove home with tears streaming down my face, hating her but hating myself even more, I climbed into my bed, hiding under the worn flannel sheets, and thought to myself that if being a bully is bad, being a coward is even worse.

PART TWO

BLESSED ARE THE BITCHES

12

I KNOW IT'S NOT VERY ORIGINAL TO say this, but Christmas has always been my favorite holiday. I love the twinkling lights on houses, the snow, that annoying Mariah Carey song that takes over the radio, the red velvet top that my mom wears to holiday parties that makes her look younger and happier, almost resembling the mom I used to know. I even love Christmas Eve mass—the dimly lit church, the altar lined with fragrant boughs of pine, the wooden crèche threaded with white lights, and the warm smell of incense that settles in your clothes and hair.

When we were younger, our family would make an annual excursion to see the giant tree in Daley Plaza. On the ride downtown, my dad couldn't resist lecturing us about subway safety—how we should never sleep on the el or play with our phones; how, if someone wants to sit next to us we should always move to the aisle so they can't pin us against the window and grope or rob us; how, if we *have* to look at the station map we should do so nonchalantly so nobody thinks we're from out of town. Once we got off the el, though, he visibly relaxed. He would buy us hot cocoa at the Christkindlmarket, and at Macy's, Stevie Junior and I each got to choose one gift that would then be wrapped up and presented to us on Christmas morning. Then we'd go for burgers at Monk's, where my dad would order a tall beer and my mom would get a glass of red wine and they'd sit in the booth across from Stevie Junior and me, giggling like teenagers while Stevie and I made gagging sounds to each other, and we'd throw our peanut shells on the floor and watch all the office workers bustling up and down Lake Street, huddled in their winter coats and talking importantly into their cell phones. On Christmas Eve we'd go to the special policeman's mass at the Mercy Home for Boys and ask for a blessing from Saint Michael, the patron saint of the police, to protect our father for another year as he worked the streets of Chicago's west side.

Now all of that feels like a very long time ago. I'm older, wiser, and maybe a little more bitter, and the holiday has lost most of its magic. So this year, when my mom was offered a bonus to work the overnight Christmas Eve and Christmas Day shifts at the hospital, she ran it past me and I just shrugged.

"We could really use the money," she said apologetically.

"It's okay, Mom," I said. "I can just hang out at home and catch up on *Teen Mom 2*."

"Absolutely not. You're not spending Christmas in front of the TV. It's a day for *family*."

"Well, let's see," I said, counting on my fingers. "Stevie Junior is in the South Pacific. Uncle Jimbo and Aunt Colleen are in Rockford. Dad's in jail, Grandma's dead, and you're working. So what do you suggest I do about that?"

"You're forgetting someone."

I thought for a minute.

"Oh God," I said.

"*Yes.*" My mom smiled broadly. "I already checked with Aunt Kathy, and she is absolutely *thrilled* to have you spend Christmas with her."

"But she's *crazy*! Dad always said so."

"Well, that *crazy* woman has been footing the bill for your education for the last two years, young lady," my mom said, finally admitting what I had long suspected. "You're going to have a great time, I promise."

My aunt Kathy is a food stylist who lives downtown in a fifteenth-floor exposed brick loft overlooking Millennium Park. We don't see her all that often because she's always doing things like backpacking through China or attending meditative retreats in New Mexico, and even when she's living in Chicago, she sticks to the trendy areas. She considers the northwest side neighborhood where she grew up and where I now live a hellish backwater where you can't even get paella or a decent deep tissue massage, and avoids coming here whenever possible. She used to make an exception and show up to our family parties every once in awhile, but even that stopped after the legendary political argument she got into with my dad at my First Communion party. I don't know what they fought about—I was eight—but I *do* know that he called her a stupid liberal and she called him a fascist thug before throwing her white wine in his face and storming out of our house in a whirlwind of clacking jewelry and spicy perfume. In her free time, she goes ghost hunting.

"Go with an open mind," my mom said, draping an arm around my shoulder. "You just might surprise yourself."

So that was how I found myself, on a snowy Christmas Eve afternoon, dragging my duffel bag up the stairs of the Jackson Avenue blue-line station and scanning the snow-swirled street for my crazy aunt and her boyfriend, Simon. When she saw me she began waving furiously, the bangles on her wrists jingling like sleigh bells. While she gathered me up in a furious assault of embroidered scarves and gardenia perfume, Simon, his graying blond ponytail edged with falling snow, bowed deeply, like a butler or a Japanese karate master, and took my bag for me.

"Look at you, Wendy!" Kathy trilled, grasping my shoulders and looking with such pleasure into my face that I felt a little guilty for how badly I hadn't wanted to spend Christmas with her. "You get more and more lovely each time I see you!"

Simon, holding my duffel bag over his shoulder like a woman's purse, led us down Jackson toward Michigan Avenue.

"Now don't tell your mother," Kathy said, throwing her arm around me as well as someone wearing a large velvet cape can throw her arm around anything, "but we're going to give Christmas mass a skip this year."

I felt a twinge of disappointment, but I certainly wasn't going to tell that to Aunt Kathy.

"Fine by me." I shrugged.

We walked to a restaurant on the top floor of the Art Institute, with floor-to-ceiling views of Michigan Avenue. It had white walls, white tables, white chairs, and a white marble bar lined with opaque white containers of unlabeled liquor.

"How do they know which bottle is which?" I asked, pointing.

"Oh, honey, at this place, no one actually cares what the drinks *taste* like," Kathy explained, scanning the menu above her rhinestone-bedazzled reading glasses. "It's just the fact of being *seen* here."

I looked at the drinks list and had to do a double take. Twenty-five bucks for a glass of wine? I thought of my mom and Aunt Colleen, sitting on our little balcony drinking their cheap bottle of chardonnay from the 7-Eleven down the street. They were going to love this story. Aunt Kathy's food stylist business had taken off—who knew there was such a booming market for people who arranged french fries at just the right angle?—and she was rich, at least by our standards. One of my mom and Aunt Col's favorite topics was discussing how their younger sister spent her money, usually with a mixture of envy and disapproval. After all, they had followed all the rules, while Aunt Kathy had skipped college and marriage, choosing, after high school, to hitchhike out to North Dakota to shack up with a landscape artist and work as a line cook on a cattle ranch. Now she made more money than her two sisters combined.

"So," said Simon, after the waiter came over and I ordered a Dr Pepper, which was brought to me in a vintage green bottle along with a tall glass filled with a single ovular ice cube, "your aunt tells me that you've never been to the Art Institute before."

"We're not exactly an artsy family," I explained.

"Nonsense!" Aunt Kathy slurped loudly from her French martini. "Art has no social class or creed. You either like it or you don't. For me, it's a better religious experience than going to a damn Christmas *mass*."

"What's so bad about the Catholic church anyway, Aunt Kathy?"

"Nothing," she said, "except *everything*. Three hundred years ago, those God-fearing Christians would've called me a witch."

"Because you ghost hunt?"

"No, because I'm not married. Because I'm not a conformist. Because I'm a strong, independent female."

"She's right on that score," Simon said, squeezing her knee. "Your aunt Kathy, Wendy, is a woman who knows how to take control." And he leaned over and started kissing her, and it was gross, and I had to clear my throat to remind them that they were in public.

Aunt Kathy paid our bill, and we spent the rest of the afternoon walking from gallery to gallery so they could show me their favorite pieces of art. Simon's was a bronze sculpture of a boy's head, one shoulder lifted, eyes closed, chest frail. It was called *Suffering*. Aunt Kathy's was *Woman Before an Aquarium* by Matisse, who apparently is kind of a big deal painter considering she almost passed out when I told her I had never heard of him. The one I liked best was *The Girl at the Window* by Edvard Munch. Aunt Kathy suggested that sometimes the art that draws us in the most is the art in which we see ourselves reflected. Which made sense to me. In Munch's painting, a figure stands hunched by a window in her nightgown, and she looks so afraid. Not afraid to go outside, but afraid of the act of even lifting the curtain. *That's me*, I thought. *Afraid of my friends and afraid of my life.*

On our way out, Aunt Kathy stopped to study a Miró painting called *The Policeman*.

"Remind you of your father at all?" she asked as we stood in a row before the canvas.

"That doesn't even look like a person," I said. "It's just, like, a bunch of shapes."

"I don't know." She cocked her head. "See that thread of dark mustache? That's entirely befitting. The assertive pose, leg forward, arm out, hands splayed? Powerful and conceited . . . *that's* your father."

"It's quite impressive," Simon agreed. "I love the way Miró plays with abstraction and representation."

"That's supposed to be a leg?" I squinted at the painting. "See, this is why I don't like modern art."

"Honey, you can't dislike something until you've educated yourself about it," Kathy said. "Great art is like great literature. Or music. Once you fall in love with it—fall in love not with your senses but with your soul, I mean—you'll never be alone again." At her words, an image bubbled up into my consciousness of Alexis's face, resting, at peace in her music, just before Kenzie confronted her on the sidewalk. I shook the thought away.

We stepped down the marble staircase and into the darkening street, then entered the shiny lobby of Kathy's building and rode the plushy carpeted elevator to the fifteenth floor. Simon brought my duffel bag into the spare bedroom while Aunt Kathy started dinner and I laid out a set of stylishly mismatched cobalt plates on the low table. There were no chairs, just puffy tasseled cushions that I guessed we were expected to sit on. Sitar music began to pipe through the surround-sound speakers. Kathy opened a bottle of champagne and poured me a glass in a crystal flute, handing it to me as if it was the most natural thing in the world to serve expensive alcohol to your sixteen-year-old niece. As I took a sip of the fizzy, crisp champagne, it made perfect sense why my dad, my chain-smoking, cursing, sports-obsessed cop dad, had never gotten along with Aunt Kathy. But I was beginning to think that there was no reason why *I* couldn't get along with her.

"I hope you don't mind," Aunt Kathy called from the kitchen while I stood before a bookshelf, sipping my champagne and running my fingers along the titles—*Pulling your Own Strings: A Guide to Self-Improvement, Sexual Empowerment in your Pre-Menopausal Years, Doing You: The Journey to Finding Your Authentic Self*—"but Simon and I are on the Paleo Diet. That means dinner tonight will consist of only real, whole, unprocessed foods. The same foods that would have been available to our ancestors two hundred thousand years ago."

"You mean to tell me that the cave men drank champagne?"

She smiled. Her cheeks were flushed from the cooking, and the windows overlooking the lights of Millennium Park had gone foggy. "For champagne," she said, "we make an exception. This *is* a holiday, after all."

I helped Kathy bring dish after dish of unidentifiable food

to the table—prosciutto cups, salmon mousse on cucumber chips, carrot soufflé, and a giant, shining red lobster, arranged on a hammered copper tray and edged with lemon wedges. A line popped into my mind from our Honors Brit Lit class, a poem that we'd read just before break that I had secretly loved, even though I didn't understand a word of what it meant: "I should have been a pair of ragged claws / Scuttling across the floors of silent seas." I must have said the line aloud—the champagne had made me feel babbly and dreamy, because Kathy and Simon looked at each other, impressed and pleased.

"They're teaching T. S. Eliot at that stuffy old place?" Aunt Kathy wanted to know. "In my day, it was all religious texts and indoctrination."

"Well, I have a cool teacher, Ms. Lee," I said, embarrassed. "She teaches honors American and Brit Lit. And journalism."

"Go figure." Aunt Kathy shrugged, snapping a lobster leg in half and dragging the flakes of white meat through a smear of butter on her plate. "The place finds some enlightenment just in time to close for good."

"So, is that what you're into?" Simon asked, sipping his wine. "Poetry?"

"I'm not *into* anything. I mean, I'm into my schoolwork. Getting good grades. Getting a scholarship and getting the hell out of Chicago."

"Here's to *that*." Aunt Kathy raised her glass.

I have to admit: the paleo food, though weird, was actually

pretty good. There was music playing over the gleaming speakers, a fake fire burned in the slate-trimmed fireplace, and outside was the Bean and the Pritzker Pavilion, cold and steely in the snow, the blinking red march of cars down Lake Shore Drive, the gray line of water and then the dark nothingness of Lake Michigan's horizon. It was hard to believe that this place of culture, of sophistication, of Miró and Matisse, was the same city I'd lived in all my life. Chicago was where I was born and raised, where my parents and grandparents were born and raised, where my great-grandfathers had slaughtered pigs in the stockyards a couple miles to the southwest. This was a city that beat inside me like blood, but in that moment, looking out at the park and the street and the water, I felt like I was seeing it for the first time.

After dinner, there was dessert: little peeled crescents of clementine oranges dipped in hardened dark chocolate. In the contented silence that followed our meal, Simon and Kathy drank sherry out of these blown-glass tumblers they'd bought during a trip to Venice, and I drank my Dr Pepper and thought about things. I thought about my mom and her antidepressants and antianxieties and sleeping pills. I thought about her monthly confrontation with the laptop as she paid our bills, her face lonely and lined in the computer's glow, figuring numbers using my old graphing calculator from Algebra II class. Rent, electric, gas, cable, cell phones, car insurance, Chase, American Express. Groceries. Lawyer fees. And on and on. I thought about how she once told me that Aunt Kathy has such a sad life, because, I guess, she never married or had children. But what I couldn't figure out was where the sadness was. Aunt Kathy had money and freedom and a ponytailed boyfriend who played the sitar and designed unisex clothing, who still kissed her in a way that older people, according to my theory, aren't supposed to kiss. *Maybe she's just hiding it, this sadness,* I thought. *Because she doesn't want me to see and because it's Christmas.* But no, that wasn't right. She wasn't hiding any sadness. It wasn't there in the first place. It occurred to me, watching Aunt Kathy and Simon drinking their sherry on the couch with their feet intertwined beneath a striped chenille blanket, that there are so many more ways to live your life than I'd once thought.

"How's that friend of yours your mom is always telling me about?" Aunt Kathy wiped a bit of chocolate from her lip with a black-painted fingernail. "Kenzie, right?"

I cleared my throat. I'd been having such a nice time because everything about Aunt Kathy and Simon felt so far away from my real life. I told them about how Kenzie had snuck Evan into the pool on a dare, about her probation, and about her five tattoos. But I didn't tell them about Alexis's violin. Mischief and rebellion were one thing: Simon and Kathy understood it and approved of it. Bullying was something different.

"A real wild child, huh?" Aunt Kathy smiled. "If I were in high school, Kenzie would be my best friend, too."

"No," Simon corrected her, "you would *be* Kenzie."

"No, she wouldn't," I said a little too quickly. Aunt Kathy looked at me curiously for a moment.

"Except for the tattoo part," Aunt Kathy said. "Needles aren't my thing. It's how I managed to avoid heroin all throughout the nineties."

Kathy and Simon helped themselves to more sherry.

"What about boyfriends?" she asked. "Got any of those?"

I shook my head.

"Good for you, Wendy! I always felt sorry for the girls who anchored themselves down to boyfriends in high school. Like your mom. She married her high school boyfriend— your dad—and look how that turned out for *her*."

I concentrated on peeling the chocolate away from my orange and didn't say anything. I don't know why it bothered me, her criticizing my dad. I mean, I hated him anyway. So what difference did it make?

Later that night, after I went to bed, I settled into the thick, cotton sheets that were so crisp I was sure they'd never been slept on, and was leafing through one of the architectural magazines I'd found in a stack on the nightstand when I heard a soft knock on my door.

"Yeah?"

Aunt Kathy, dressed in a satin kimono and matching embroidered slippers, stuck her head in the door. She was holding another tumbler of sherry and a self-help book entitled *Dynamic You! Techniques for Living Your Best Life.*

"Can I come in, honey?"

"Sure," I said, putting the magazine on my lap.

"I just wanted to say I'm sorry if I hurt your feelings, what I said about your dad. I'm just so damn angry at him."

"It's cool." I shrugged.

"I just worry about your mom," she said. "How's she doing? She never talks to me. Not about important things, anyway. She thinks I'm flighty or something. That I wouldn't get it. That I don't care."

"She doesn't think that," I said, though it was probably true. Aunt Kathy stood there quietly for a moment.

"Anyway," she said, smiling, "I forgot to give you your Christmas present." She reached into the pocket of her kimono and handed me a small black Bloomingdale's box, wrapped in a thick red ribbon.

"Thanks, Aunt Kath!" I untied the ribbon and lifted the lid. It was a makeup set—lipstick in a gold tube, a blush compact shaped like a seashell, a tube of mascara, and a small vial of perfume.

"Now, I know you weren't always much of a girly girl," Aunt Kathy said as I lifted the items, turning them over in my hands, "but your mom tells me you've been wearing more makeup these days. And sometimes just knowing you have this stuff in your drawer makes you feel a little more sophisticated. Besides, every girl deserves a little Chanel."

The makeup was so beautiful—the lipstick a rich, creamy nude tapered to a perfect point, the compact a pat of pale, shimmering pink stamped with two interlocking *C*'s—that I knew I would probably never use it. But still, I loved the gift. I could put it on the sink in our tiny bathroom with the mold etched between the cracked peach-colored tiles, next to the toilet with the yellow ring that would never come clean. I could let my mom borrow it, in the event that she ever got invited out for drinks with the other cop wives again.

"Well?" she asked, hovering nervously over the bed. "Do you like it?"

"I love it." I smiled up at her. "Thank you."

"I'm glad." She watched as I uncapped the perfume and breathed in the expensive scent. "Hey, do you mind if I sit down for a minute, hon?"

"Sure." I closed the perfume and scooted over in the bed to make room. She climbed in next to me, the cool silk of her kimono rustling against the sheets.

"How are you doing, anyway?" she asked, crossing her slippered feet and leaning against the headboard. "With ASH closing and everything?"

I shrugged.

"Fine, I guess."

"If it had happened when *I* was in high school, it would have been a dream come true. I hated that place. But you, you're different than I was."

"I am?"

"Yes. Thank God."

"What were you like?"

She thought for a moment.

"Well, I was exactly like I am now, only a natural blonde with an ass that didn't sag."

I laughed. I had to admit, it was nice, sitting side by side like this with my eccentric aunt. It had been so long since I'd had someone to talk to.

"But, I mean, like, who did you hang out with? What were your friends like?"

"Oh," she waved a hand. "I was one of the misfits. You know. The type that sits in the back row reading *The Bell Jar* and piercing my ears with a safety pin."

"So you didn't ever have friends that, I don't know, were sort of . . . bitchy?"

"Wendy." She put her arm around me gently. "In this family, we believe in female empowerment. As a feminist, I would appreciate it if you didn't use that word."

I laughed. "You sound like Sister Dorothy."

"I have to say, this is the first time in my life I've ever been compared to a nun. I don't know how I feel about this."

"It's a compliment, I guess."

"How about 'unkind'? That's the meaning you're getting at, but it's gender neutral."

"Well, I don't think 'unkind' really cuts it for the type of friends *I* have, Kath."

"Is this Kenzie we're talking about here?"

"Yeah. And Emily and Sapphire, but yeah, mainly Kenzie."

"Okay. Well, what has she done that you feel has been unkind?"

"Well, let's see." I sat up and began counting on my fingers. "She dared Sapphire to steal a case of Abraham Lincoln's silverware from a party. She snuck her boyfriend into our gym class, which basically made him lose his football scholarship and got our PE teacher fired in the process. She throws Pop-Tarts at people. And, you remember the girl I was friends with in elementary school? Alexis Nichols?"

"Of course I do. What a sweetheart. How's she doing, anyway?"

"Well, probably not great. Alexis snitched on Kenzie about the gym class thing. So Kenzie took Alexis's violin and smashed it into, like, a thousand pieces."

As I sat there, rehashing the events of the past school year, Aunt Kathy's eyes grew wider and wider.

"Are you finished?" she finally asked.

I nodded.

"Well then, I've got a question for you, Miss Wendy Ann Boychuck. Why in the name of Christ are you *friends* with a bitch like that?"

"It's kind of hard to explain." I opened the compact and looked at the small oval of my face, pale and plain, in the little mirror.

"Try me."

"It's because . . ." I snapped the compact shut and looked

down at the Christmas lights twinkling on the street below, trying to figure out how to explain it. "I don't know. There's something powerful about being popular, I guess."

"Oh, come on, Wendy. Don't tell me you're one of these teenage girls who actually cares about being popular. Who's always talking about how fat she is, or how fat other people are. I can't stand those girls. They are so terribly *boring*."

"No." I shook my head. "It's not that."

"Well, then what is it?"

"It's like, popularity is this magic shield. It kind of protects me from my own last name. If I'm friends with Kenzie, no one can make fun of me or—or *worse*—just because I'm a Boychuck."

"Ah. So *that's* what this is about. Your dad."

"Well, I guess so. In a way."

She sat up straight, and examined me with her pale gray eyes.

"See, that's what the neighborhood does to you," she finally said, settling back into the pillow. "Makes you feel like it's the whole world. Everybody so insular, so obsessed with each other's business. It's like living in a small town, but with rats and muggings."

"It's not *that* bad," I laughed.

"Oh, it's *worse*. Trust me—I grew up there, too! But now I live *here*. Downtown. Do you know what the best part about living in this building is? It's that Simon and I don't know anybody who lives in it. Nobody knows my business, and nobody cares!"

I could feel the soft thumping of her heart and the up-and-down movement of her throat as she sipped her sherry.

"You know, there are other forms of protection, Wendy. Self-esteem, for one. A jujitsu class. Hell, even a religious relic is probably going to protect you better than some snotty sixteen-year-old 'friend,' and that's coming from someone who doesn't really even believe in God."

"You're right," I agreed. "It's just so hard to walk away."

"Well, what is it that you're afraid of? So what if people say your dad did some awful stuff? Guess what, honey? He *did* do some awful stuff. And now you and your mom and your brother have to live with that. It's not fair, but that's how it is. You can either let it crush you or you can let it make you tough. Your choice."

"Aunt Kathy, you don't remember what high school was *like*! It's a freaking war zone, okay?"

"Wendy, look at me." She took both my hands in hers, her long nails tickling my palms. "I wish I could make you understand just how *young* you are. But, as the saying goes, youth is wasted on the young. So here's what I'm going to tell you instead: the average life expectancy of an American woman is eighty years. And you're in high school for exactly *four* of those years. That's, what, *five percent* of your life that you spend in high school? And yet, everybody acts like it's some big goddamn deal. Like what happens to you there, who you hang out with, what your grades are, should somehow *define* you for the other *ninety-five percent* of your life. Please. It's all so silly. There are so many people you still need to meet, so many experiences you still have to live. Life is so *fun*, honey! It's so *wonderful*! And it's so *big*! It's a road that just keeps getting wider and wider. So it's just plain stupid to think that *these* are supposed to be the best years of your life."

She put her sherry on the end table, leaned back against the headboard, and closed her eyes. Even at this time of night she was perfumed and pedicured, her face dewy with night cream. She was the picture of confidence and self-possession, a woman entirely satisfied with her own widening road.

"You're going to do so many great things, Wendy," she said, her eyes still closed. "You won't believe how many great things you're going to do. And once you get out there in the world? No one is going to give the littlest *shit* who your dad was."

"You really think so?"

"I *know* so, honey. As someone who's lived plenty and always has to learn things the hard way."

We lay there, side by side in the bed, my head resting on the cool silk of her kimono. Kooky, my dad had called Aunt Kathy. Goofy. A flake. A wingnut. But who cared that she wore capes and kimonos and ate paleo and drank too much sherry on Christmas Eve? When you actually *talked* to her, she made a hell of a lot more sense than most of the other adults I knew. I'd never met someone who was so comfortable being exactly who she was. She made being true to yourself seem easy. No, more than that: she made it seem like a party.

For a minute, I thought she'd fallen asleep. I put the compact aside and lay there for a while, feeling her warmth and watching the snow and the cars zipping by in a blur of light down Lake Shore Drive. From where I sat everything was so frighteningly far away, fifteen floors down, except for the flakes of snow, which sifted against the window like little fingerprints, scratching to get into this warm, cozy space that smelled like flowers and cooking and Aunt Kathy's peppermint foot cream.

Her eyes fluttered open, as if she was startled into waking, and she leaned over to kiss me on the cheek, leaving behind a smear of her rose-scented lip balm. "Merry Christmas, honey."

"Merry Christmas, Aunt Kathy."

Before she left the room, she stopped and turned back.

"Oh, and Wendy?"

"Uh-huh?"

"Get some rest. We're going to be up early tomorrow—we're going ghost hunting."

13

I WOKE IN THE MORNING TO the rich smell of brewing coffee. A gray light had filtered through the pale pink curtains of my bedroom, and when I opened them, I saw the whole city, the frozen scallops of shoreline, the cold waves of Lake Michigan on Christmas morning. I padded out into the kitchen, where Kathy and Simon were sitting on the leather fainting couch, dressed in his-and-hers satin kimonos and reading the *New York Times*.

"Oh, you're up!" Aunt Kathy swished over and gave me a hug. "Merry Christmas! There's coffee in the pot. Sorry, though—no cream or sugar—remember, we're a paleo home, honey, but there's maple syrup if you really need to sweeten it."

It made no difference to me; I'd never drunk coffee in my life, so when I took a sip of the rich, bitter liquid, I wasn't sure whether cream and sugar would even be able to improve the situation. But I choked it down, along with a couple scrambled eggs, while Aunt Kathy hurried off to her bedroom to get ready for our ghost hunt and Simon cleaned up in the kitchen. Apparently, he did not share his girlfriend's curiosity about paranormal activity and was planning on spending his Christmas morning down at the Bikram yoga studio on the third floor of their building. When Kathy emerged from the bedroom ten minutes later, she was dressed in head-to-toe black Lycra and carrying a large metal contraption with a rubber handle and a series of dials on the side.

"What the hell," I asked, "is that thing?"

"This," she said, raising it above her head like a torch, "is a single-axis electromagnetic field meter."

"A single-axis *what*?"

"An EMF meter, for short. Standard ghost-hunting equipment."

I picked up the contraption and examined the various dials and screens.

"What does it do?"

"Oh boy," said Simon, who was standing in front of the sink in tree pose, drying off a sauté pan. "Here we go."

"Well, you see, Wendy," she began, her voice taking on the instructive singsong of a teacher, "all conscious human minds emit an electromagnetic field, okay? When you die, your body disintegrates, but *your electromagnetic field doesn't.* So what we ghost hunters do is, we carry this EMF meter around with us, and when it detects a spike in electromagnetic levels when there is no visible human presence, that's a pretty sure sign there's a ghost there. Conscious mind," she said, pointing to her temple, "just no more body."

"And you actually believe in that stuff?" I asked.

"You look incredulous."

"Well, Aunt Kathy, it does seem a little . . . out there."

"Let me ask you this," she said, snatching the EMF meter out of my hands and stuffing it into her leopard-print tote bag. "How is this any different than you going to mass and praying to a totally invisible God? Religion is one kind of faith, ghost hunting is another. At least I have my EMF for evidence. What kind of evidence do you have that there's a God?"

"I don't know," I said. "Sunsets? Mountains? Newborn babies?"

"She's got you there," Simon commented.

"Well, guess what, Wendy? One can believe in God *and* ghosts. The two are not mutually exclusive. Just go with an open mind, okay? If not for your sake, for mine. Ghosts can sense skepticism, and they don't appear to people who don't believe."

The Hotel Belvedere, a short cab ride from Kathy's condo, was a gray building with tall, narrow windows and its name advertised in big blue neon letters at the top with one of the *E*s burned out. I knew it immediately—you could see its big sign if you were driving down Lake Shore Drive—but from far away, it looked regal and posh. Up close, it was clear that the hotel had seen better days. The purple awnings were frayed along the edges and coated with a crust of salt and ice. The big revolving door was smeared with fingerprints, and a bored valet with an oversize gray uniform was slouched next to a luggage rack, scrolling through his cell phone.

Inside the black marble–floored lobby, a domed ceiling of ornate gold painted all over with fat pink angels had once probably appeared to be the height of luxury, but now it just looked sort of tacky. A skinny goateed guy, whose name tag read *Emmanuel*, smiled broadly at Aunt Kathy.

"Kathleen, baby!"

"Manny! Merry Christmas!"

He stepped out from behind the concierge desk and they hugged each other.

"All right, honey. What do you got for me?"

"Not much, Kath. A guy's alarm clock went haywire in three oh two last week. Other than that, I got nothin'."

Aunt Kathy pulled out a carefully folded bill from her wallet and palmed it to him.

"You sure?"

Manny took the money, slid it into his pocket, and smiled slyly.

"You're always so good to the little people, Kathy. I just remembered something else. There's been some *serious* activity in the Florentine Ballroom lately. Not one, not two, but *three* weddings in a row; we've gotten reports."

"The Hand of Mystery?" Aunt Kathy stopped just short

of grabbing Manny by his lapels. "The Twelfth-Floor Refugees? H. H. Holmes?" He shook his head slowly with each of these suggestions, grinning, drawing out the moment of reveal.

Aunt Kathy couldn't take it anymore. She grabbed his arm.

"Not—not Lady Clara?"

"That very one." Manny nodded triumphantly. "Not only have we had people *hearing* her, one of our maids claims to have actually *seen* her—nightgown and all."

"*No!*"

"Yep."

"Manny, we've known each other a long time—can you please, pretty please, just because it's Christmas, open up the Florentine Ballroom for us? Just for ten minutes?"

Manny sucked his teeth.

"I'd love to, Kathy, you know that. But you know hotel policy."

Kathy reached for another bill, palmed it to him again.

"Ten minutes. All we need is ten minutes."

Manny glanced down at the bill to see how large it was. He must have been happy with what he saw, because he slipped a small key card across the concierge desk.

"Ten minutes," he said. "And if anybody finds you in there, you don't know me."

"Thank you!" She leaned over the desk, planted a

red-lipsticked kiss on his cheek, then grabbed my hand and dragged me out of the lobby and down a long, narrow hallway of faded burgundy carpet. Doors stood on either side of us, framed in gold-leaf designs that were flaking off, revealing the dull wood beneath. As we walked, she told me the story of Lady Clara.

"Lady Clara was a beautiful Gilded Age debutante, the daughter of an American mother and a British father who made piles of money in the railroad industry. Not only was Clara rich, she was gorgeous—long black curls, flashing black eyes, a tiny waist, and feet so small her father had to employ a children's bootmaker to custom-make her stacked heel shoes.

"Lady Clara had everything, and she could have had any man she wanted. But like so many beautiful catches over the millennia, from Desdemona to Whitney Houston, what do you think she did?" Kathy looked at me, but didn't wait for me to answer. "She fell in love with a jagoff.

"His name," she continued, "was Cornelius Clark. What a jagoffy name, right? The wedding between Clara and Cornelius was planned, down to every beautiful detail. The date was set—a Saturday in June, 1886. The day before the wedding, all of Chicago was abuzz with anticipation. Three-foot bouquets of hydrangeas were arranged on all the tables in the Florentine Ballroom. Caviar was imported from Moscow, champagne from France, lobster tails from the coast of Maine. The trains chugged in from New York and San Francisco, on tracks her father had built, bringing all the country's powerbrokers toward the Belvedere. The wedding gown and corset—designed by House of Worth in Paris—hung in the penthouse suite where Clara and Cornelius were supposed to spend their conjugal night together. An orchestra arrived. Ice sculptures of winged horses were carved and displayed in the four corners of the ballroom.

"The night before the wedding, after the rehearsal dinner and the cognac and cigars, Cornelius kissed his bride-to-be goodnight and went up to his bedroom to get some shut-eye before the big day. When he got there, he found that someone had slipped an anonymous letter under his door. It revealed, with proof, that Lady Clara's father had lost all of his money in a series of bad financial deals—he had paid for the entire wedding on credit and his good name. Turned out, the lovely, gilded Lady Clara was almost entirely destitute.

"Now, a good man—a man who really *loved* her—would have felt a pang of disappointment, maybe, upon realizing that the spoiled life of leisure he'd been expecting was now slipping away. But after a few moments of self-pity, he would have tossed the letter aside and gone ahead and married the woman of his dreams. But not this jagoff. Nope, what this jagoff did was, he packed up his suitcase, hustled up a couple of his servants, and stole away into the hot June night for Union Station. He took a train to San Francisco, where, the story goes, he married another beautiful black-haired girl—the daughter of a gold speculator—and the two of them lived happily ever after in the golden hills of Sonoma County." She glared. "The men always have it easier, don't they?"

"But who sent the letter?" I asked. "Who had it out for poor Lady Clara?"

She waved her hand impatiently, and her bracelets clacked against one another.

"That's not the *point*. You're focusing on the wrong *thing*."

"Okay," I said, "so what happened next?"

"On the morning of the wedding," Kathy resumed, "she dressed in her gown of white bobbin lace. Her mantilla, hand-sewn with a thousand seed pearls, was pinned into her hair. She stood at the end of the aisle of Holy Name Cathedral on the arm of her father, the eyes of Chicago and New York and London society upon her, and waited. And waited and waited and waited. The women fanned themselves and the men wiped their faces with their handkerchiefs. The murmuring began after fifteen minutes had gone by and no jagoff. After thirty minutes, people began opening their collars and asking each other—where was he? And after an hour, they began to get up, one by one, and, casting a sympathetic look at the stricken bride, slipped out the doors of the church and into the hot afternoon.

"Clara's mother and a couple servants whisked her back to their hotel room. God knows what they said to her, what comfort they could give after a humiliation that complete. But whatever they said, it wasn't enough. That night, after her mother had fallen asleep, Clara slipped out the door of the hotel room and, dressed in a diaphanous nightgown—"

"Diaphanous?"

"Great word, isn't it? It means, you know, translucent."

"She was wearing a see-through nightgown in public?"

"Wendy, stay with me here!"

"Sorry!"

"She slipped out of her room dressed in a *diaphanous* nightgown and came down to the Florentine Ballroom—the grand room where her wedding reception was meant to have taken place. She climbed to the second-floor balcony overlooking the parquet dance floor—"

"And jumped?"

"Splat." Aunt Kathy nodded sadly.

"Killing yourself over a guy," I sighed. "What a cliché."

"Yes, well, here's where things get weird: When the maids found her body the next morning, all of the winged-horse ice sculptures, which had been placed in the far corners of the ballroom the day before and that weighed no less than four hundred pounds apiece, had *moved*. They now stood at each corner of the dance floor, their icy eyes frozen on Clara's poor broken body, as if they were waiting for the signal to gallop her into the afterlife."

"Yikes," I said.

"And get this: despite the oppressive June heat and the stuffiness of the closed ballroom and the lack of air-conditioning, *all of the sculptures were totally unmelted.*"

She paused dramatically, then continued. "Now this sad story is over one hundred thirty years old, but to this day, whenever events are held in the Florentine Ballroom, anyone who sits alone at a table while people are dancing may hear the nearby whispering of a woman's voice."

"What does she say?"

"Oh, various things. Sometimes fragments of poetry. Sometimes lamentations. And sometimes, according to Manny, words of wisdom, pieces of advice, things that the listener might really need to hear at that particular moment of her life."

We had reached a pair of giant gilded doors. Aunt Kathy slipped the key into the slot, and the lock clicked.

"And if you ever dance on that dance floor, you're meant to feel this—life—pulsing through you. A presence, you know? Of poor Lady Clara, who can't escape her heartbreak, even in death."

"Aunt Kathy," I said, "do you *really* believe that story?"

"See for yourself," she said. "Just tell me—*tell me*—that this place doesn't give you the creeps." With that, she flung open the door, and we stepped inside an enormous dark room, as huge as a football field. The floor was lined with a streak of dim emergency exit lights, and in the bluish gleam,

179

I could see that the walls were painted with the sad faces of cherubs and angels and mythological creatures: centaurs and Minotaurs and harpies. The royal blue carpet was so thick I wobbled in it in my winter boots. I followed Aunt Kathy as she walked toward the center of the room, across a large dance floor, smooth and shiny as an ice rink. Far above me were the golden domes of the ceiling, and the scrolled iron bars of a balcony stood all around the perimeter. I looked up.

"It's a long way to fall, isn't it?" Aunt Kathy stood next to me, our shadows reflected in the glassy surface of the dance floor.

"If you're gonna jump from there, you must *really* want to die," I murmured. Despite my skepticism, I did feel a little bit goose-bumpy. I nearly screamed when I heard a click behind me, followed by a *whooshing* sound. I whirled around and saw a glowing object—Aunt Kathy had turned on her EMF meter.

"Ideally," she said, holding the thing up in the air and scrutinizing the digital reader from behind her rhinestone-studded reading glasses, "we would walk, step by step, in a grid pattern around this entire room, but that would take ten hours, and we only have ten minutes. So what we're going to do is, we're going to concentrate on the dance floor. Smaller, more manageable, and chances are that if Lady Clara's here, she'll be haunting the place where she, as they say, gave up the ghost."

She dug into her leopard-print tote bag and handed me a notebook and a pen.

"While I operate the EMF meter, I need you to write down all my measurements. If we get a concentration of high electromagnetism: *bam*."

"Okay." I shrugged, turning to a clean page and uncapping the pen.

Kathy took a position at the far corner of the dance floor, and called out to me, "Ten point one milligauss."

I scrawled down the number.

"Is that normal?"

"Pretty much anything between nine and thirty is normal. What we're looking for is anything between a two and a seven—these low readings signify paranormal activity."

I watched her as she made her way at a glacial speed up and down the dance floor. She'd call out a number—10.2, 12.5, 15.3, and so on—and then take a big step forward, call another number, and move on. It was a little like watching a character in one of those old fashioned video games going up and down in a maze.

"Who knew ghost hunting could be so boring?" I yawned. "How much longer is this going to take?"

"Bear with me, Wendy," she said, pivoting on one foot and heading up the dance floor in the opposite direction. "Lady Clara is my spiritual soul mate. I really *feel* something in here."

"Okay, Aunt Kathy, but can you at least try to hurry up? It's kind of freezing in here." I zippered up my coat to emphasize my annoyance.

"Freezing? I'm practically overheating. It's these old radiators—they always work too well or not at all. It's got to be eighty degrees in here."

"Well, not where I'm standing. Where I'm standing, it's cold as hell."

"Wait a minute." Aunt Kathy stopped abruptly in the center of the dance floor. She ran over to me and pushed me to the side.

"Hey!"

"You're right!" she gasped, and looked at me with wide, excited eyes. "It *is* cold right here."

"Told you."

"What this means, Wendy, is that you've found a cold spot!"

"A cold spot?"

"Yes!" She grabbed me excitedly by the shoulders. "See, all ghost hunters believe that ghosts exist, obviously. But we don't know *how* they exist. Still, one thing we *do* know—one universal law of science—is that any kind of energy will alter its environment in some way. When you walk into a room, for example, the heat from your body will change the temperature of the room—imperceptibly, of course. And ghosts are no different. They need to draw energy from their environment in order to manifest themselves—hence, cold spots."

I shivered a little. It was all so weird, but Aunt Kathy's enthusiasm, and her pure faith in the process, was kind of catching. Also, it really *was* cold, and only right where I was standing. She turned on the EMF meter. It went nuts.

"Two point four! Did you see that?" She waved the metal device in my face. "Two point four!"

"Okay, so now what?"

"Lady Clara," Aunt Kathy said, closing her eyes and arranging her face into a serious, gypsy-like expression. "We know you're here. You are safe—we wish you no harm. We, too, have known heartache. We, too, have been disappointed by the men in our lives. Ex-boyfriends, in my case. A father, in my niece's." Her eyes snapped open. "Sorry, honey. You know what I mean, though." She closed her eyes again. "Show yourself to us, and we promise, we will share it with no one."

She had grabbed my hand and was holding on to it tightly as she whispered into the empty room. We stood there, nerves on edge, the painted angels watching us from the walls, waiting for the slim shape of a dark-haired girl in a diaphanous white nightgown to appear. We waited. And waited. But nothing happened.

"Come on, Aunt Kathy," I said gently. "It's been over ten minutes now. Manny could get in trouble."

She sighed, nodded. As she began to arrange her meter

and notebook back in her tote bag, I looked up to the balcony, where Lady Clara had jumped to her death. I half expected to see her brokenhearted lovely face, a pale oval in the gilded shadows. But instead, directly above our cold spot, what I saw was a large vent—and it was blowing directly down to where we stood. I opened my mouth to tell Aunt Kathy—to make a joke about our gullibility—but before I could, she'd thrown her arm around me, and her velvet cape was soft against my cheek as she pulled me toward her.

"A cold spot," she said, shaking her head. "I can't believe you found it, you lucky dog! It's the closest I've ever come to real contact. Now let's go get some lunch. My treat."

"Okay," I smiled. I mean, true faith is a hard thing to come by these days. Why ruin it for her?

That night, just as I was drifting off to sleep under those crisp sheets, the snow softly pelting my window, Aunt Kathy knocked on my bedroom door again.

"Honey?" She pulled her satin kimono around her waist. "Can I talk to you for a second?"

"Sure." I scooted over and made room for her in the bed.

"You remember yesterday, when you were asking me about what I was like in high school?"

"Uh-huh?"

"Well, I sort of lied a little bit."

"You did?"

"I mean, I *was* a misfit who sat in the back of the classroom and read Sylvia Plath and dyed my hair black. But that was only my senior year, after . . . Well, the point is, I was in the popular crowd for most of high school. So I know what kind of girls you're dealing with."

"Well, what happened? What changed?"

"It doesn't matter."

"Come on, Aunt Kathy," I said. "You can't come in here and tell me you lied to me about something, and then keep lying about it."

"Fine." She slipped into the bed next to me. "But it's going to depress you."

"I think I can handle it."

"Okay. You know those two crosses down by the railroad tracks that run along Avondale Avenue? For the two ASH girls who were hit by a train all those years ago?"

"Of course. I know all about it. Tiffany Maldonado and Sandy DiSanto. When they died, mom's painting of Our Lady of Lourdes in the Saints Corridor cried for a week. And people claim that if you say their names at midnight when there's a full moon, the streetlights explode. Why?"

She fiddled with the belt of her kimono, tying it and untying it. Outside, I could hear the cars rushing by on Monroe fifteen floors below. Finally she let out a long breath.

"Sandy and Tiffany were my best friends."

"*What?* Oh my God, Aunt Kathy. I'm so sorry."

"Oh, honey, don't say that. That's why I never tell people about it. *I'm* the one who *lived*. No need to feel sorry for me. On the night it happened, we were all at the homecoming dance after-party. Kerri O'Rourke's house. At the time, I was dating this boy, Tony Cutro. He was this Italian kid, real religious. Altar boy and everything."

"*You* dated an altar boy?"

"An altar boy who smoked unfiltered cigarettes and drove a Camaro. He wasn't a *total* saint, okay? So anyway, Tony had been to our house a couple times and had noticed the little shrine to Our Lady of Lourdes your grandpa had set up in the front room. Being the smart Italian kid that he was, Tony knew that the way to get in good with a girl was to get in good with her father. So, that night, it was our six-month anniversary, and he gave me a gift: a scapular of Our Lady of Lourdes."

"Like mine!" I exclaimed, my hand fluttering involuntarily to my naked neck as I remembered the moment after David Schmidt's graduation party when it had been torn off me.

"Just like yours. You're right. Anyway, *I* figured he was going to mark the occasion by giving me his Saint Mike's ring, or flowers, or some bracelet he'd bought at the Harlem Irving Plaza. But this scapular—it was so thoughtful and sweet, I didn't know what to do with myself. Before this night, Tony and I had kept things very PG. But when he got all shy, pulled that scapular out of his pocket, and put it around my neck? It changed everything.

"Tiffany was supposed to give me a ride home a little while later, but I was so gaga over my gift that Tony and I snuck down to the laundry room. One thing led to another, and, well, I ended up losing my virginity on a pile of the O'Rourke family's dirty towels."

"Aunt Kathy! Real classy!"

"Hey! The important thing is, we used a condom. Remember that. Anyway, I guess Tiffany had to get home—her dad was always a stickler for curfew—and she and Sandy were stumbling around the house trying to find me. But Tony and I were in the basement laundry room with the door locked and we couldn't hear what was going on upstairs and we didn't know what time it was because we were doing things together that sort of made us lose track of time, if you know what I mean."

"I don't," I admitted, "but I wish I did."

"Good. Hang on to your virginity like the prize that it is. Remember that, too. Anyway, earlier that night, Tiffany had snuck a flask of tequila into the dance in the waistband of her pantyhose. She had no business getting behind the wheel, but who was going to stop her? She was untouchable, the most beautiful, popular girl in school. So she and Sandy left without me. And, well, you know the rest."

"So you were supposed to be in that car?"

"I was supposed to be in that car. And the only reason I wasn't was because of that Our Lady of Lourdes scapular."

"That's amazing. And also horrible."

"Yeah. Well, anyway, a week or so after they died, the nuns gathered us all into the auditorium for a special memorial service. And at the end, Sister Dorothy got up and gave us this big lecture about the dangers of drunk driving, and how Sandy's and Tiffany's deaths should teach us to always behave ourselves and make good decisions. I mean, she had a point, of course. If Tiffany hadn't been drunk, they probably wouldn't have died. But at the time, I was this big festering pile of grief. I didn't appreciate Sister Dorothy standing up there and trying to teach us a lesson, to assign logic to this awful loss. I figured if God was the type of higher power who'd put two innocent girls in front of a train as some sort of elaborate public service announcement, then that wasn't a God I wanted to believe in. I don't know. Maybe it was survivor's guilt. Or maybe it was just that the world can be a terrible place, and sometimes when people try to explain it, all they do is make it worse. Whatever the case, the day Tiffany and Sandy died is the day I stopped considering myself a Catholic."

"But what about Our Lady of Lourdes?" I asked. "I mean . . . in a way, she kind of saved your life, didn't she?"

"Honey, I *said* I stopped believing in God. But Our Lady of Lourdes? She's my girl until the day I die." She reached into her kimono and fished out a faded scapular on a scrap of brown string around her neck. "Haven't taken this off in twenty-five years. It's the only part of the Catholic Church

I still believe in." She dropped it again and it disappeared into the folds of her kimono. "I don't know very much about the ways of the universe, Wendy," she said. "I don't have any answers. Except one: If you've got Our Lady of Lourdes on your side, nothing can ever hurt you."

After she left the room, I couldn't sleep. I lay there for a long time, thinking about things, and finally reached over and switched on the bedside lamp. I picked through the architectural magazines on the nightstand until, at the bottom of the pile, I found a heavy hardcover book: *Rituals of the Ancient World*. As I paged through it, listening to the blowing wind and the cars rushing by far below me, I came across a chapter titled "Tattoos and Spirituality."

Tattoos were prevalent in many cultures across the globe, dating as far back as the Neolithic period. People ornamented themselves in tattoos for a wide variety of purposes, both cosmetic and spiritual. The Pazyryk people of Siberia boasted some of the most beautiful and intricate tattoos known to the ancient world. Pazyryk mummies dating back to the third and fourth century BC, whose skin has been preserved by the permafrost, display intricate etchings of roosters, goats, tigers, panthers, and other animals.

Interestingly enough, most of these tattoos were located on the right shoulders of the mummies, a part of the body that normally would have been covered by clothing. Scientists can conclude, then, that these beautiful images were tattooed on their owners not for cosmetic purposes but for their magical powers of protection.

Magical powers of protection.

As I read those words over and over, an idea began to take shape in my mind.

It's important to remember that while today, tattoos are seen largely as a cosmetic, ornamental, or fashion statement, they have an ancient tradition of protecting their wearers from danger, and for paying homage to religious and spiritual figures.

I closed the book and drifted off to sleep, and by the time I woke in the morning, my idea had solidified into a decision.

14

AFTER I GOT BACK FROM CHRISTMAS at Aunt Kathy's, I needed to come up with a plan for avoiding my friends for the remainder of the break. The thought of confronting them directly, of just saying the words *I'm done* was too terrifying, and I needed to buy myself some time, to figure out a plan. So when Sapphire sent a group text about a Saint Mike's party that we all *COULD NOT MISS* because some boy she was obsessed with was going to be there, I made up a lie that my mom had found the bottle of cherry-flavored vodka Kenzie had gotten me to stash under my bed for her earlier that summer. *So I'm grounded,* I wrote. *Can't even go out for New Year's or anything.*

Grounded? was Kenzie's skeptical response. *Your mom doesn't really seem like the grounding type.*

Well, her dad was an alcoholic, I said, another lie flowing effortlessly across my keyboard. *So she's weird about drinking.*

Fine, came the reply. *But you better not have told her it was mine.*

I couldn't look Jayden up on Facebook because I didn't know his last name, and the only person I knew who had his phone number was Kenzie, who I wasn't about to ask. So what I did was, I just showed up at his garage one afternoon near the end of Christmas break when my mom was at work and I had the day off from the deli.

It was a nasty, freezing, windy day. The snow that had fallen at Christmas had turned dirty and slick; the sky was gray, the sun a weak yellow ball hanging low in the sky. As I trudged through the slushy alley toward Jayden's garage, I thought of the flight boards at O'Hare, sitting there with Alexis as we fanned ourselves and pretended to dig our toes into the hot sand. Honolulu. Phuket. Fiji.

"You've been to California, right?" Alexis had asked me once.

"Yeah, last summer."

"Tell me about the ocean."

I'd told her about its briny taste, the delicate crust it left on your skin that made your legs feel like warm sugar pie, about the way it curled back on itself, white and alive, when it crashed against the cliffs. That's when I fell in love with the idea of going to college out west: UC Santa Cruz. Loyola Marymount. Santa Clara. Or maybe if I did really well on the ACT and got some sort of huge scholarship—hey, if I was going to fantasize, I might as well really go for it—Stanford.

I took a deep breath and knocked on the garage door. After a moment it yawned open. Jayden stood there in a puffer vest and sweatpants, glowering into the light from the cave of his garage. I stepped inside.

"You're Kenzie's friend, right?" He pressed a button and the garage door screeched shut behind me. "Sergeant Boychuck's kid."

"Yeah, that's me."

"What can I do for you?"

"I was wondering if you could give me a tattoo," I said.

"Course I can. What do you want?"

I scrolled through my phone and found the picture of Our Lady of Lourdes that my mother had painted in the Saints Corridor, the one that had been watching over me since the day I started high school, that was the patron saint of my family, that had saved my aunt Kathy's life, and that now, I hoped, was going to save mine.

Jayden took the phone from me and squinted at the screen.

"Is that the Virgin Mary?"

"Yeah. Well, I mean, it's the Virgin Mary as she appeared to Bernadette Soubirous at the grotto in Lourdes, France, in 1858. There are, like, hundreds of different versions of the mother of Jesus in Catholicism. Our Lady of Lourdes is one. Our Lady of Knock is another. Queen of Peace, Queen of Heaven, Star of the Sea, the Blessed Mother, the Madonna, you get the idea."

"Of course I get it. I'm Mexican. You basically want Our Lady of Guadalupe, but white."

"Our principal says that the Virgin Mary transcends our ideas of race or ethnicity."

"Wow." Jayden whistled. "They teach you pretty good up at that Catholic school. So where do you want this Virgin Mary who transcends race and ethnicity, anyway?"

"Across my right shoulder. Just like the Pazyryk people."

"That some new gang I don't know about?"

"No," I laughed. "They're a tribe who lived in ancient Siberia. They wore tattoos on their right shoulders. For protection."

"Oh yeah?"

"Yeah."

"Well, thanks for the history lesson. This *is* a sacred ancient art form I practice in this garage here. Which is why I charge the big bucks. You got money?"

"Sure."

"Okay, then. You're lucky you caught me on a slow day. This is gonna take three, four hours just to do the outline. Then we wait for it to heal—which will take a couple more weeks. Then you come back and I'll fill in the color." He peered at the picture on my phone and nodded to himself. "Yeah. Two sessions. You can pay me at the end."

He had me lie facedown on the office chair, my chin hanging over the headrest so that I was looking down at the concrete floor.

"You're going to need to take your shirt off," he said. I complied, and he moved the space heater closer when the goose bumps began popping up and down my back.

"You're going to have to take your bra off, too."

"No problem." I tried to sound casual, but my heart was hammering in my chest. I reached back and unclasped the bra, feeling my breasts fall free, and I squirmed so that they wouldn't show between the cushions of the office chair. I remembered all my dad's cautionary tales about the women's bodies he'd seen, raped, beaten, strangled, dropped in rivers, and chopped up in abandoned suitcases. And here I was, in a garage with some strange man, shirtless, while not one person on earth knew where I was, and my phone was floating somewhere at the bottom of my backpack, just out of reach on the ground beside my chair. I stared at the motor oil stains on the garage floor, squeezed my bra tightly in my hands, and felt my mouth go dry with dread.

"Sorry, but I'm not gonna be able to talk to you while I work," Jayden said, adjusting his earbuds. "I need music to help me concentrate."

"That's all right," I said. "I'll just . . . zone out or something."

"Do whatever you gotta do." He brought up his music on his phone and placed it on the workbench. After he traced the design onto my back, there was a jolt as the needle buzzed to life and bored its way into my skin. At first, I had to fight the urge to flinch and squirm—I knew it would hurt, but

I hadn't realized how badly—but soon the sharp, even pain suffused from my back throughout my body, purifying my mind of fear, and I relaxed. There's something about physical pain that almost feels like relief—it's so simple, so clean; you know exactly why you have it and exactly where it came from and exactly what you need to do to make it stop. I'd take it any day over loneliness or fear or heartbreak or that weird lost feeling that had dogged me ever since the day I decided not to be Alexis's friend anymore. The harder Jayden pressed into my skin, the more it hurt, and the more it hurt, the more relief I felt, until the pain had become a part of me, beating through my body like blood. I almost couldn't remember what it was like to *not* feel it, so when the garage door groaned open again and I saw a silhouette, backlit by the snow, step into the garage, I was grateful when Jayden kept working, not even bothering to look up and see who it was.

"Wendy?" Tino squinted into the darkness of the garage. He was carrying a greasy bag from Suzy's Red Hots. "Is that you?"

Mortified, I squirmed against my chair, hoping to God that my breasts were fully covered.

"I didn't know you had tattoos."

"I don't," I said a little too defensively. "Just this one."

He craned his neck to check it out.

"What is that supposed to be?"

"It's Our Lady of Lourdes."

"Oh. Is that kinda like Our Lady of Guadalupe, but white?"

Jayden swiped off his earbuds. "The mother of Jesus transcends ideas of race and ethnicity, dude," he said in a high, urgent voice that was clearly meant to make fun of me. Then he stuffed the buds back in his ears and resumed his work.

"Does it look all right?" I asked.

Tino leaned closer.

"It's hard to tell—he's still only, like, halfway through. It's probably gonna be another hour or two."

He rolled one of the wheelie chairs over and sat next to me.

"Need someone to keep you company?"

"Sure," I said. "I feel like I've been here forever. I'm not used to just, like, lying around without my phone, you know?"

"Totally. They write you up if you use your phone at work, but kids are getting fired over it all the time. Bad habits."

"Where do you work?"

"Target." He grinned. "Didn't you notice my Red Team polo shirt? I'm just coming from there now. Today I had to break up an actual fistfight between two crazy college girls fighting over the last sequined tunic from the guest designer collection."

"An actual fistfight?"

"There was punching. And scratching. And the popping off of fake nails."

"Who got the tunic?"

"Nobody! They both got arrested."

"Sounds a lot more exciting than a day at the Europa Deli. You don't really see too many fistfights over the last batch of smoked trout."

"I *thought* you worked there!" He sat up in his chair and turned his snapback so the brim was facing forward and his eyes were cast in shadow.

"Yeah, I work there. How did you know?"

"I saw you through the window last weekend. I waved to you, but you didn't see me. You were scooping some potato salad for this old dude."

My mind traced back to the previous weekend. Had I worn makeup to work that day? Had I been wearing my hairnet? It seemed very important that I remember the answers to these questions.

"Well," I finally said, "why didn't you come in and say hi?"

"I was going to, but you were kinda busy. I was gonna buy some of that homemade dumpling soup they got. You ever had that soup?"

"Yeah. It's good."

"It's *superb*."

I laughed. "Well, it's one of our bestsellers. The old Polish ladies line up in the mornings, after mass, to buy these big tubs of it."

"What do they put in there? They got a secret ingredient or something?"

"I don't do the cooking," I explained. "I just work the deli counter. But the owners, Alice and Maria, they've got some recipes that have been passed down for, like, generations."

"Man, I could go for some of that dumpling soup right now. It's so much better than this crap." He held up a wilted french fry.

"Well, you should have told me that. I get a fifty percent discount. I could've brought you some."

"Dammit." He shook his head. "But wait. How could I have asked you to bring me dumpling soup if I don't have your number?"

Up until now, I'd been starting to relax, a new feeling for me when talking to a cute boy. But now I froze. I mean, was this him asking me for my number? Was I now supposed to offer it? Well, I was *not* going to do that. I'd been burned before.

"I guess I should just start carrying a tub of it around in my backpack, in case I run into you," I said instead. I thought for a minute that I saw his face fall, but it was hard to tell in the dim red-and-green glow of the garage and his hat pulled down low.

"Well, anyway," he said, "it may have been a shitty day at Target, but hey, now I'm sitting here having a nice conversation with a beautiful topless woman, so I guess things could be worse."

Beautiful. Did he just call me beautiful?

"Can you try to relax, Wendy?" Jayden interrupted. "You're, like, trembling all of a sudden."

"Sorry." If a person could die from blushing so hard that

all the blood in their brain rushes to their face, I would definitely no longer be alive.

"So," Tino said, spinning back and forth in his wheelie chair and knitting his fingers behind his neck, "he's a real piece of shit, isn't he?"

"What?" I looked at him, the giddiness of the previous moment immediately replaced by another, more familiar feeling. "I mean, you don't even know him. Being a cop is one of the hardest jobs—"

"What? No!" He shook his head. "I'm not talking about your *dad*. You know, paranoia is a real medical condition, Wendy. I'm *talking* about Iago."

"Iago?" I said dumbly.

"*Yeah*. Like, one of the worst characters in all of literature."

"Oh." The relief gushed out of me like a deflating balloon. "You're talking about *Othello*. Sorry."

"I mean, aside from being totally racist, he was just conniving and evil and awful. You know who he reminds me of, actually?" He turned his hat backward so that now I could finally see his eyes clearly. "That friend of yours."

"She's not my friend anymore." Even as I said it, I realized that this was only true in my head. It was going to be a lot harder to make it true in real life. It was one thing to blow off Kenzie's texts, to pretend I was grounded as an excuse for why I couldn't hang out. But I knew that once we got back to school, I would have to face her and Emily and Sapphire head on. I would have to find the courage to walk away.

"So," Tino said, "you finally saw the light?"

"I finally saw the light."

"I'm glad."

I smiled.

"Me too."

By the end of the third hour, evening had fallen and the golden purity of the pain had given way to a yellow agony that didn't clear my mind so much as muddle it. I couldn't talk to Tino anymore. I just had to focus on the pain. He went over to the couch and read his book, while I began to concentrate on not passing out or barfing. The smell of Suzy's Red Hots hung in the air, a pungent mix of au jus and fries, except now, instead of making me hungry, it was starting to make me nauseated.

"Almost done," Jayden reassured me over the buzzing needle, as if he could feel the tension through my skin. Finally, when I was at the point of abandoning my pride and flat-out begging him to stop, the pressure eased, and the needle snapped into silence. Jayden called Tino over to check out his handiwork.

"Pretty dope, huh?" he said.

Tino didn't say anything. I didn't take that as a very good sign.

Jayden took a picture of my shoulder with my phone and brought it around to show me. All I saw was an expanse of pink, swollen skin. I couldn't even get a good look at the tattoo itself because blood was seeping from my pores as quickly as he could blot it away.

"The blood and stuff is normal," Jayden said. "This is a real operation. Clean. Professional. Tell your friends."

I tried to answer him, but found that I couldn't speak. Black spots were worming across my vision, like my eyes had become lava lamps, and I sat slumped in the chair with my face pressed against the damp stickiness of the headrest, waiting for the feeling to pass.

"Hey." Tino's voice was soft and close by. "Take it easy. Let me help you." Jayden sauntered out to the alley for a cigarette while Tino took his place on the little wheelie stool. With as much gentleness as my mom's nurse's touch, he began patting the A+D Ointment onto my skin.

"I guess I'm just a wimp," I murmured.

"Nah." I felt his gentle fingers, the goodness of him, even through the aching of everything else. "The first one is always the hardest. My William Shakespeare nearly killed me."

He reached to the floor and picked up my bra.

"Lift up your arms," he instructed. "I'm not going to look, okay?"

"Okay."

Somehow, he managed to loop the bra straps around my shoulders and hook them closed over the gauze while keeping his eyes squeezed shut the whole time. Then he helped me with my shirt. Finally he stuck out his hand. I put mine in his, and he pulled me to my feet.

"Does it look all right?" I asked. "Be honest." His eyes, I noticed, were the color of brown velvet. Not flashily gorgeous, like the flinty copper of Darry's, but softer, kinder. They seemed to absorb light, not reflect it, and they had a pattern of lighter brown threaded throughout, like honeycomb.

"I'm not gonna lie to you," he said. "It's not Jay's best work ever, okay? But, I mean, it's still hard to say. You're going to have to let it heal before you can really get a sense of it. You're going to have to see the final product."

I followed him out into the alley on shaky legs.

"Hey," he said. "Why don't you let me walk you to your car?"

"Okay."

I leaned on his shoulder as we picked our way through the slushy potholes in the alleys and back out onto Fullerton Avenue. We didn't talk, but I didn't feel the need to fill our silence with nervous chatter, the way I usually did.

"So," he said when we arrived at Red Rocket.

"So," I said.

We looked at each other.

"You've gotta come back in a couple weeks and get it finished, right?"

"Right."

"Okay. So I'll probably see you then?"

"I'll see you then."

"Bye, Wendy." He brushed his hand on the arm of my coat. I wanted to say something more, but I didn't know what and I didn't know how. He put his hands in his pockets and disappeared back down the alley.

When I got home, the apartment was dark. My mom was at work as usual. She'd left a plate of cold ham and baked beans under plastic wrap on the counter. Just below me, Sonny was blasting AC/DC, the album he listened to when he was getting himself pumped for a night on the town. I left the plate of ham untouched, locked myself in the bathroom, removed my shirt, and gingerly unpeeled the bloody, sticky gauze to examine the tattoo. I craned my neck around and, when I saw it clearly in the mirror, I felt a rising panic in my gut.

The face of Our Lady of Lourdes was drawn with rough black lines, thicker in some places than others, like when I'm trying to take notes in class but my mind wanders and my pen, held in place for too long, bleeds blots of ink on my paper. Absent of color, its face looked more like that of a demon woman in serious need of an exorcism than the mother of Jesus appearing to a young French girl in a grotto. Its eyes were unnaturally large and round, pupil-less, and seeping little dots of blood through my aching pores. It watched me watch it, silent, dead-eyed, unholy.

I just barely made it to the toilet, painting the bowl with a yellowish mess of the potato pierogies I'd eaten for lunch.

Then I lay on the cool tiles, splayed on my stomach, until the nausea passed. Slowly, I rewrapped the wound with gauze and changed into a loose sweatshirt that wouldn't stick to my skin, then flopped onto my bed and opened my laptop, desperate to think about anything but the thing I'd tattooed across my shoulder. I fiddled around on social media for a little while before tapping into my email. That's when I saw something that made me want to puke all over again.

A PRISONER FROM THE FEDERAL DEPARTMENT OF CORRECTIONS HAS SENT YOU AN EMAIL. TO ACCEPT, CLICK THE LINK BELOW.
IF YOU DO NOT WISH TO BE CONTACTED BY INMATE STEPHEN BOYCHUCK, PLEASE CLICK *HERE*.

This was not shaping up to be a very good day.

My dad had sent me various cards and letters since his imprisonment, for Christmas and Valentine's Day and my birthday. Whenever I saw my name printed in those small, neat capital letters and the Nebraska postmark, I threw the mail away unopened. So I don't know why I opened the email now, even though my fingers had turned into gummy worms and my heart slammed in my chest. But I did, and there in front of me were words written by my father, the first words I was allowing him to speak to me in over two years.

Hi honey,

How's my girl?

So, they have this new program where you can email for 5 cents a minute (better type quick, I guess, haha!). If you're reading this, it means that you agreed to read my letter, and that makes me so happy. Mom says you've grown three inches, that you wear your hair down these days, that you're even wearing mascara and rouge and all that other stuff I KNOW you don't need because you're perfect just the way you are (I know, I know, that might be the most "dad" thing anyone has ever typed).

Anyway. Things here are okay, I guess. The best word I can use to describe prison is BORING. When you kids were first born, people would tell us, with a new baby in the house the years are short but the days are long. That's how prison feels. Except the years are long, too. And my babies aren't here. So I guess it's not the same at all.

One good thing, they have programs here to help us pass the time. I've started a painting class. I know what you're thinking—the only thing I've ever painted is drywall. Remember when I tried to help you paint your dollhouse? And the job I did on the shutters? Yeesh. But still, I like it. It gives me something to do. And I've been reading, too. Probably more books than I've ever read in the rest of my life combined. I'm hoping that by the time I get out of here I'll be smart, like my kids.

Well, anyway. Just thought I'd drop you a line. Remember the lyric from "Born to Run," the one we named you for? Well, Wendy, I want you to know that I still love you with all the madness in my soul. And I'll keep loving you, like the stubborn bastard I am, no matter how you feel about me. When it comes to your kids, love ain't always a two-way street, you know? It goes and goes and goes, even if there's no traffic coming in the other direction.

All my love,

Daddy

I closed my laptop, stood up, and paced around the apartment for a while. I wanted to call my mom, or Aunt Colleen, or Aunt Kathy. I wanted to call Alexis. I wanted to go out partying with Kenzie and Sapphire and Emily in something tight and skimpy, drinking beer until my stomach hurt and my head felt like a balloon. I wanted to grab Tino by the shoulders and kiss him until I forgot who I was.

But instead, I unwrapped the plate of ham and beans, warmed it up in the microwave, and ate my dinner alone at the kitchen table. When I was finished, I washed and dried my dishes, sat back in front of the laptop, and composed a very short reply to my father's email.

Don't ever contact me again. I won't respond. As far as I'm concerned, I don't have a father.

I hit send immediately, before I could change my mind.

During one of her many anti-war lectures, Sister Dorothy told us about the drone pilots whose job it is to attack targets in the Middle East from the safety of an American Air Force base. The way she described it was sort of like a video game where instead of seeing in real life the spray of blood, the torn-apart limbs, the screaming children and howling women and rubbled houses after an air strike, you watch your destruction onscreen, thousands of miles from the front lines. But, she said, the strange thing is, killing from afar doesn't prevent those soldiers from getting PTSD, because they still have the knowledge of what they've done, without the honor of having risked their own lives to do it.

On a much smaller scale, sending a hateful email must feel a little like that. All you're doing is sitting at a computer. All you're doing is moving your mouse over the send button and clicking it. You don't see the email zipping through the atmosphere. You don't see the explosion in the recipient's heart when they read what you've written. You believe that what you're doing is necessary, even good, and yet after it's done, even as *soon* as it's done, the thought of that exploded heart begins to seep into your own heart, a cold, wet drip.

After I sent my dad that email, I felt great.

Five seconds later, I burst into tears.

15

AND SO CONTINUED THE LONELIEST CHRISTMAS
break of my life. My mom was so busy working extra shifts at
the hospital that I doubt she even noticed I spent pretty much
the entire holiday either working or sitting on the couch.
When I was at home, I spent most of my time examining
my tattoo in the bathroom mirror. It seemed to get more
and more hideous every time I looked at it. And that was the
weird thing: even though just looking at it made me sick,
I couldn't *stop* looking at it. It was mesmerizingly horrible.
Still, I felt it had its own dark power, and even after it was
mostly healed I could still feel it pulsing, as if it had its own
heartbeat.

I recognized that my belief in the power of my Our Lady
of Lourdes tattoo might just be as superstitious and crazy as
Aunt Kathy's obsession with the ghost of Lady Clara. Still,
when I walked into school on the Monday morning after
Christmas break with her face hidden beneath my uniform
blouse, I felt strong. I felt protected. As I gathered my books
for my morning classes, the original Our Lady, painted above

my locker, gazed down at me with that saintly half-smile, as if to say, *Hey, I know your secret. And I've got your back.*

I had made a promise to myself on New Year's Eve, standing alone on our balcony wrapped in my thin peacoat and watching my downstairs neighbors blow off illegal fireworks in the parking lot behind our complex. High school might only make up five percent of my life, but for the next sixty-some years I had left, I was going to be better, starting right now.

How was I going to do it? My plan was pretty basic, actually. Every teenager knows that the cafeteria is the ground zero of social drama at any high school, the place where friendships bloom and die by the simple placement of a lunch tray. The first step for breaking free, I figured, was to stop sitting with Sapphire and Emily and Kenzie at lunch. It was simple, it was bold, and it was terrifying, not just because of how they would react, but because I didn't have any other friends to fall back on. I'd done the math: In the eyes of 90.5 percent of my classmates, I was a bitchy, stuck-up stranger.

So much for popularity, huh?

When the fourth-period bell rang, I went down to my locker to get my lunch, lingering below the painting of Our Lady, praying for her to give me the strength to do this one small, hard thing. I took a deep breath, walked into the cafeteria clutching my lunch bag in my fist, and, looking straight ahead, I found a table near the vending machines and sat down by myself. I pulled out my Dr Pepper and a leftover piece of strudel I'd brought from the deli and arranged it on my tray. Then I began pretending to work on my Spanish homework. I knew Alexis saw me. I could almost *sense* a tiny tunnel of hope opening in her heart that maybe I wasn't a total and complete coward and consummate asswipe. Then I heard Kenzie's voice, rich with confidence, peal across the vast linoleum plain of the half-empty cafeteria.

"Hey, Wendy! What are you, lost?"

I looked up at her. I could now feel not just Alexis, but the whole school watching me.

"I just have to catch up on some homework," I mumbled.

"Homework? We just got back from break, dork! Get your ass over here. I have a new man and you need to hear about it."

"I really have to get this Spanish project done," I told her. I bit my lip, forcing myself to look her in the eye. She sucked some Diet Coke from her pink bendy straw, staring at me over the lid of the can.

"Your loss." She shrugged finally, then turned back to her lunch table.

For the rest of the period, I ate my strudel, pretended to do my nonexistent homework, and listened to the conversations that hummed around me in the cafeteria. Girls talked about Christmas and New Year's and boyfriends and sports and music and clothes and physics homework and Ms. Lee's new pixie haircut. They traded sleeves of Oreos, bruised bananas, and ziplock bags full of Chex Mix. They worked on their math homework. They borrowed pencils and hair ties and ChapStick.

They were nice to one another.

I realized, as I sat there listening, that Academy of the Sacred Heart was full of kind, funny, genuine girls. Girls who would have accepted me no matter what my last name was. When I thought about how in five months this school would close forever and most of us would be swallowed up in the enormity of Lincoln High School and its labyrinthine hallways packed with 3,200 strangers, I felt tears spring to my eyes, mourning the losses of all the friends I'd never made. And when PE class came along, the last class of the day and the only one I shared with Kenzie, Emily, and Sapphire, I whispered to Sister Dorothy that I had period cramps and asked her if I could just have a study hall that day instead. She opened her mouth, prepared, most likely, to give me a lecture about how girls had been getting their periods since the beginning of time and if every woman felt the need to take the day off just because of a few cramps the world would cease to run. But when she saw the look on my face, the tears in my eyes, she relented and wrote me a pass to the library.

The next afternoon, I carried my tray to the same empty table and sat down, spreading out my things like it was totally normal and not at all awkward. I had barely cracked open my Dr Pepper when Kenzie called out across the cafeteria: "Let me guess: more Spanish homework?"

Alexis was sitting at her table a few rows behind me with Ola and Marlo and a couple other orchestra girls. *Don't go, Wendy,* I could feel her thinking. *Show me you can be better than them.*

Our Lady of Lourdes, I prayed, *please let me be brave. Let me be good. Let me stand up to her.* In the silence that followed while I waited for some kind of sign, Kenzie picked up her bag of cheese puffs and her Diet Coke. She shook out her hair, stood up, and walked toward me, her micro-mini uniform skirt swishing ominously. Sapphire and Emily gathered up their lunches and followed her.

When she got to my table, Kenzie yanked out an empty chair, sat down across from me, and cracked open her pop.

"Okay," she said. "If there's something wrong with that table, then we'll come to you."

"Um," I said. Then my tongue turned into paper. I'd used up the little courage I had on my long march across the cafeteria to this table for one and now I had none left. I suddenly understood what Sister Dorothy meant when she'd told us once that the right thing is always the hardest thing.

For the rest of the lunch period, it was as if nothing had changed, at least outwardly. I heard all about Kenzie's new boyfriend, an older guy named Gabe, who was a semiprofessional DJ and had his own apartment in Logan Square. I heard about the sick New Year's party he'd had there, at which Emily had vomited all over his vintage record player and Sapphire had hooked up with an Italian exchange student named Alessio who wore decorative scarves and had never eaten a hot dog.

"So, are you still grounded or what?" Kenzie finally asked.

"Um, yeah," I said, concentrating on the little air holes in my sandwich bread.

"For how much longer?"

"My mom didn't really say. At least another couple weeks."

"God, your mom's a bitch."

I winced. Tino was right: Kenzie really *was* evil. I felt like grabbing her pink bendy straw and poking her mascara-fringed eyes out with it. "Yeah," I said instead. "She really is."

16

IN THE WEEKS THAT FOLLOWED, I tried to make myself as invisible as I possibly could. I picked up extra shifts at the deli, not just for the money but to keep myself unavailable on the weekends. I turned my phone off whenever I could, and let my voice mailbox fill up so that Kenzie couldn't leave me any messages. But I couldn't pretend to be grounded for the rest of my life, and eventually I ran out of excuses for avoiding my friends. When that happened, my pathetic rebellion ended, and things returned to the way they used to be: rolling through the hallways four across with my clique, sitting together at lunch, partying together on the weekends, pretending, acting, and secretly disappointing all the people I actually cared about—Alexis, my aunt Kathy, Tino, and most of all, myself.

In March, Sister Dorothy made an announcement during homeroom that she would be canceling classes the following Monday to organize a shadow day at Lincoln. The idea was to give us all a window into what our new public school lives were going to be like. Everybody signed up except for Kenzie, whose dad had found out she was dating a twenty-three-year-old semi-professional DJ, and was now taking the day off work to drive her up to Cherrywood Academy: a Therapeutic Boarding School for Troubled Young Women just, as he said, "to check out our options."

My first taste of the new stresses of public school was choosing what to wear. Ever since kindergarten, my daily outfits had been chosen for me by the nice people at Schoolbelle's Catholic Schoolwear Company, whose eye for fashion had always been a predictable blend of plaid, pleats, and Peter Pan collars. Now, standing before my open closet, I was paralyzed with freedom. The look I was going for was cute but not cutesy, trendy but not edgy, expensive-looking but not actually expensive, sexy but not slutty. In the end, I was so overwhelmed that I ignored Sapphire's advice to go for something "timeless" like an elastic crop-top and high-waisted floral leggings, and showed up for my first day of public school in jeans and a plain black T-shirt.

Sister Dorothy had instructed us to meet in the glass lobby of Lincoln at seven a.m. sharp, to give her time to assign us our shadow partners for the day. We trickled in one by one, trying to act casual, sizing up one another's clothes. Because I'd spent most of high school with my head stuck up Kenzie's ass, I'd never hung out with most of my classmates outside of school before, so it was weird seeing them dressed in normal street clothes. One look around made it clear that I wasn't the only one who'd spent hours deciding what to wear; most of us had tried way too hard, and it showed. Veronica the Vegan was dressed in a long, shapeless hemp skirt and a crown of plastic flowers on her head; she looked like she'd made a wrong turn on her way to a folk music festival. Ola Kaminski, usually modest and sensible, had on a sweater so tight and a bra so padded she looked like she was carrying around two Nerf footballs beneath her shirt. Marlo Guthrie wore an inexplicable pair of riding breeches that gave her a bad case of camel toe. Only Sapphire and Emily looked confident in their tight jeans and high tops, except for the fact that they were wearing the exact same outfit. I was happy I'd gone the safe route, but as I looked around at the public school kids who were beginning to flood the entrance, whose fashion sense had been honed by *years* of this kind of freedom and who looked far more effortlessly cool than any of us, my confidence rapidly deflated. My hands, feeling fluttery and awkward, reached instinctively for the pockets of my ASH cardigan, but found nothing but the thin fabric of my T-shirt.

"This doesn't even feel like a *school*," Emily said, her voice soft and almost reverential as she looked around the lobby with her darting, gossip-greedy eyes. "It's like—like the *movie set* of a school."

I knew what she meant. As we milled around the sun-filled lobby in our specially chosen clothes, waiting for our guides to pick us up, we did our best not to seem amazed by Lincoln High. In addition to the total absence of religious icons, there was a set of bright green couches situated beneath the skylights. Couches! In a school! Where kids were actually allowed to sit! On one of them, a boy in ripped-up jeans was lounging, legs splayed, peering at his iPad, while a girl with long braids lay with her head on his lap, catching a little snooze before first period. Her *head* was on his *lap*. Mere inches from his package. And the yawning security guard—a *real* security guard, not just a nun with a walkie-talkie—at the front desk didn't even seem to care. It was incredible.

Sister Dorothy had handpicked a Lincoln girl for each of us to shadow, based on our extracurriculars, our class schedules, and our GPAs. But when I approached her for check-in, she informed me that my partner was out sick with the stomach flu.

"So you're going to have to double up with someone. I'm putting you with Alexis Nichols, since she's also an honors student." She peered at me over her reading glasses with those crafty old eyes. "Does that sound all right, Ms. Boychuck?"

I had no doubt in my mind that Sister Dorothy had done this on purpose. It was as if she knew, by some strange form of nun telepathy, what had gone down between me and Alexis and Kenzie. I was willing to bet that my assigned partner didn't even have the stomach flu. In fact, there probably was no assigned partner in the first place. But I knew better than to argue with a Sacred Heart nun.

One by one, ASH girls were met at the security desk by their Lincoln counterparts and walked off together chattering to one another like nervous blind dates. I felt a weight lift off my shoulders as first Emily disappeared down a hallway with her guide, then Sapphire. When they'd turned the corner, and I saw that Sister Dorothy was still eyeing me over the rim of her glasses, I walked over and sat down next to Alexis on one of the green couches. As soon as she saw me coming, she pulled on her headphones and began to blast her classical music so loudly there was no possible way she could ever hear me try to say hello.

The bell rang for first period, but Alexis and I had still not been picked up. As we sat there in the now-empty lobby, I decided that I might as well make the best of the situation. I poked her and she glared at me, plucking a headphone from her left ear.

"What?"

"Do you know that listening to music that loud damages your stereocilia?"

"My what?"

"Your stereocilia. The little hairs in your inner ear that help with hearing."

Rolling her eyes, she snapped her headphone back into place. I poked her again.

"What?"

"I'm just trying to help you out."

"I'm not deaf."

"No, not yet. But you will be, if you don't turn that crap down."

"This 'crap'"—Alexis glared—"is Tchaikovsky."

"Doesn't matter. You've been listening to those headphones nonstop since at *least* fifth grade. You're going to be deaf by the time you're forty."

She sighed, lifted off the headphones, and placed them in her lap.

"Happy?"

I smiled. "Very. You'll thank me when you're older."

Alexis, shaking her head, reached into her backpack and pulled out a Moleskine notebook. When she opened it, I saw that it wasn't lined like a regular school notebook but with musical bars. All over the page, written in light pencil, were notes and musical notations, as foreign and fascinating to me as hieroglyphics.

"Do you write music?" I asked.

"Uh-huh." She didn't look up.

"I didn't know that. I mean, I knew you played. You've always played. But I didn't know you wrote your own stuff."

"There's a lot you don't know about me anymore, Wendy."

She positioned her left arm so that I couldn't see what she was doing, and then lifted her pencil to the paper.

"Listen," I said, deciding that maybe the direct approach was best, "if you want to get through this day without it being totally awkward, you're gonna have to talk to me."

Alexis threw her pencil into the margin of the notebook and snapped it shut. "I don't think what you're feeling is awkwardness, Wendy. It's guilt."

Before I could respond, a tiny girl with red cowboy boots and an enormous bun of tight black curls came running breathlessly toward us. She was carrying an instrument case of pebbled black leather on her back.

"Sorry, you guys! It's my idiot carpool driver. Who stops at Starbucks when there's *five minutes* before the first bell? Like, do you *really* need your mocha-frappa-what*ever* so bad that it's worth a detention?" Her quick, bright eyes moved back and forth between us. "Which one of you is Alexis Nichols?"

"That's me," Alexis said.

The girl stuck out her hand. "I'm Edie. Your guide for today."

"You're a cellist?"

"I try to be," Edie said, jabbing a thumb toward the heavy case on her back. "We'll see if Juilliard agrees."

"Juilliard?" This was the closest I'd ever heard Alexis come to squealing with excitement. "Are you really auditioning for *Juilliard*?"

"Who's Juilliard?" I asked.

"It's only the best music school on the planet," Edie said, looking at me like I was a complete ignoramus. "It's like Harvard for musicians."

"Oh."

"Anyway," Edie said as she began leading us down a hallway papered with advertisements for unfathomable extracurriculars like Poetry Slam Team, Break Dancing Society, Horror Movie Club, and Gay-Straight Alliance Network, "you basically have to audition to audition. My orchestra teacher helped me submit an audio recording for the prescreening. I find out at the end of the month whether they'll invite me to New York. They only invite, like, one percent of people to even come and audition, so it's a long shot."

"What did you play for your audio recording?" Alexis asked excitedly.

"I went with Paganini's Moto Perpetuo and the Saint-Saëns cello concerto, but only the second and third movements, obviously."

"Obviously." Alexis glanced over at me. I could tell that she was enjoying the fact that I had no idea what the hell she and Edie were talking about, and I couldn't say I blamed her. It was payback for all the conversations she'd surely overheard at our lunch table over the years, with Kenzie's expert lectures about boys and blow jobs and booze.

"What about you?" Edie said, turning back to look at

me as her cowboy boots clunked across the slick linoleum. "Do you play?"

"An instrument?" I asked.

"No, varsity badminton," Edie laughed. "*Yes*, an instrument."

"I mean, I took piano lessons for a little while," I said. "I can play 'Chopsticks' and a couple Christmas carols."

"Oh." Edie looked disappointed. "Well, you're gonna be pretty bored today. I completed most of my state requirements as an underclassman. First period I have AP Lit, and fifth period is AP Bio, but other than that it's pretty much music electives all day long."

"For real?" Alexis's eyes were wide. "We only have *one* orchestra class at ASH. I'm stuck in there with freshmen who still play on training violins!"

"Well, not today you're not! I'm sure Mr. Fleming will let you play with us in Advanced Strings. Did you bring your violin?"

"I don't actually have my own violin right now," she said, her eyes flitting in my direction. "I'm using a loaner from my teacher until I get a new one."

"Well, that's no problem. We've got a couple practice ones in the band room you could borrow."

"I can't *wait* to come here next year," Alexis giggled and linked her arm through Edie's elbow. "What did you say your last name was?" And the two of them headed off down the hallway together while I trailed behind, feeling like a moron, but also grudgingly admitting to myself that I was sort of happy for her.

We walked into Edie's AP Lit class, a large, modern space with windows that overlooked a soccer field and a Smart Board hanging in the front of the room. Before I could get over my amazement that the teacher taking attendance at the front of the room was wearing *jeans*, I noticed a dark-eyed boy in sweatpants and a zip-up track jacket.

Tino.

He didn't see me at first; he was slumped over his desk and glaring into a paperback copy of *Native Son*. When he finally looked up and saw me, he seemed startled and then— but maybe I was just imagining this—happy. He tented the book on his desk, gave me a little wave, and smiled this smile that turned up only a corner of his mouth in a way that made my heart feel like a glass jar with a glowing firefly flitting around inside of it.

The class was discussing *Heart of Darkness*, which I'd never read, so it was hard to find it interesting. In fact, the most interesting thing about the class was the back of Tino's head, which I was able to stare at now that it was unobscured by a hat. I have to say, it was a very nice-looking head: proportionate, shapely ears, and neatly groomed hair that shone black in the fluorescent track lighting of the classroom. He didn't participate in the discussion, but I could tell by the tense, still way he held his shoulders that he was listening to every word. I was studying him so closely that when the bell rang and he stood up and began to walk toward me, the shock I felt was the same you might feel if you're admiring a statue in a museum and it suddenly comes to life.

"So," he said, pointing at my backpack. "You got a tub of dumpling soup in there or what?"

"Sorry," I laughed. "I didn't know I was gonna see you today."

"But that's the whole *point*, Wendy." He leaned on the desk so his body was angled irresistibly toward mine. "You're supposed to carry it around just in *case* you run into me."

"I don't think that would be very sanitary considering we're talking about a cream-based soup that requires refrigeration," I shot back. "The last thing I want to do is give you food poisoning."

"Well, in that case, I appreciate you looking out for me. I forgive you."

"You're welcome." God, I loved flirting with him.

"Anyway," he said, "I, unlike you, *have* been carrying something around in my bag just in case I were to run into you again. And luckily for you, it isn't even perishable."

Just like that, my flirty persona abandoned me and I stood in front of him, tongue-tied, staring anxiously at his backpack.

"You like to read, right?"

I hesitated for a moment before remembering that Kenzie and Sapphire and Emily weren't around, that I was standing in an AP Lit class in a high school filled with thousands of strangers. I could be as smart as I wanted to be and it didn't matter.

"I love to read." It felt so good to just say it, like a dirty secret I was finally getting off my chest.

"Good." He rummaged around in his bag and pulled out a battered copy of a paperback novel.

"You ever read Hemingway?"

I shook my head. "I mean, I've heard of him, obviously."

"You've gotta try this. *A Farewell to Arms*. It's some dark, *dark* shit. But it's some beautiful, *moving* shit."

"Cool." I took the book from him and flipped through the well-worn pages. Some of them were dog-eared, others threaded with neat underlining. "What's it about?"

"It's a love story," he said. "In Italy during World War I. There's this American guy, Lieutenant Henry. And he's in love with this English nurse named Catherine Barkley. You sort of remind me of her. The way I imagine her looking. She's got blond hair that she wears pinned up all the time, and that day I first saw you at Jayden's, you were sitting there on the couch, reading *Othello* with your blond hair all pinned up, and it made me think of Catherine Barkley." My fingers unconsciously fluttered up to my ponytail. I thought back to that day. I'd probably pinned my hair up at work because I'd forgotten my hairnet at home and Maria had made me, citing the incident when Mrs. Janek had found a long, yellow strand in her beet salad. It felt strange, knowing he'd been watching me. Good strange.

"There's this one part," he went on, "where Lieutenant Henry takes out Catherine's hairpins one by one. And then her blond hair falls down around them, and when he kisses her he says it's like being in a tent, or behind a waterfall."

"Oh," I said faintly, grabbing onto the edge of the desk. My knees seemed to have stopped working.

"Hey, Wendy," Edie said impatiently from the doorway. "We've gotta get to class."

"Coming," I said, willing my knees back into action.

"Anyway, let me know what you think sometime, okay?"

"Thanks." I smiled. "I will." I tucked the book under my arm and followed Edie out of the classroom, stepping in time to the sound of my heartbeat as I dreamed of tents and waterfalls. *No offense, Our Lady of Lourdes*, I prayed, *but I think I'm going to love public school.*

Like Edie promised, most of her other classes were music electives. There was AP Music Theory, Honors Orchestra, and Film Scoring, and that was just before lunch. In the afternoon, after a spirited discussion in AP Bio about whether genetics play a role in shaping human behavior, there was

Music Composition and finally, Advanced Strings. In this class, Mr. Fleming, the white-goateed teacher, gave Alexis one of the training violins from a cubby against the wall.

"Play me a couple lines of something," he told her, "so I can figure out how to fit you in for today."

"Okay," Alexis said. As the other kids in the class chatted or played with their phones or tuned their instruments, I watched as she placed the violin under her chin, held the bow in one hand and then this sort of stillness came over her. She closed her eyes, opened her lips, and began to play. As soon as she did, the stillness that had come over her seemed to spread out until it had entered every person in the room. The kids who'd been chatting fell silent and the ones who'd been looking at their phones let them hang, midtext, forgotten in their laps, and the ones who'd been tuning their instruments froze, and Alexis's violin became the only sound in the whole room, in the whole world.

I, too, became a part of the stillness. Just as Alexis could take that piece of wood and make it live, it seemed to touch her back in the same way. The Alexis Nichols I knew was shy and gangly, a quiet girl with a halting voice and plain, wispy hair. But the moment she moved her bow across the strings of that borrowed violin, everything about her changed. She was bold and brave, splashy and erotic. She curled over the instrument, threw her head back, thrust her hips off her seat as the bow moved faster, the notes higher, and then she collapsed back against the chair, tears squeezing from her closed eyes, as the notes grew longer, wailing, aching. I'd never heard music this way before. It was more than music. It was like she was distilling life itself into sound.

I knew nothing about classical music or violins. But she wasn't asking me to know. She was only asking me to feel. And I did, I did, I did.

I sat alongside Edie and her classmates and Mr. Fleming, who all watched her wordlessly, their jaws hanging open. Some of them had tears standing in their eyes. When she finished we all applauded, and a faint color spread on Alexis's cheeks, not of embarrassment, but of the quiet pride that comes when you possess the power to turn yourself inside out, so that just for a moment, you wear your soul on the outside.

At the end of the day, after Edie and Alexis exchanged phone numbers and promised to get together over the summer and share audio clips of their performances, I sat down next to Alexis as we waited for the bus to arrive to take us back to ASH.

"What was that you played today?" I asked.

"Oh, it was the first movement of Violin Concerto in D minor, by Jean Sibelius."

"Well, whatever it was, it was incredible."

"Thanks."

"No. You don't understand. It was, like, *incredible*."

She smiled a little. "Well, it ought to be. Violin is pretty much my whole life. And when I'm not practicing, I'm listening." She held up the headphones. "If I get into Juilliard, then a little damaged stereocilia is worth it, don't you think?"

"Forget Juilliard," I laughed. "I say you're ready for the Vienna Philharmonic."

She looked at me, a look of shared memory, of the days we'd spent dreaming up our wild futures on the benches of Terminal Five.

"I didn't know you remembered that."

"Of course I remember it."

A silence hung between us.

"Look," I finally said, "I've been wanting to say something to you. When Kenzie trashed your violin, I should have stopped her. I mean, I should have tried harder to stop her." What I wanted to say was, *I get it now. I get what music means to you. It's how you speak to the world. When she killed your violin, it was no different than if she had cut out your tongue.* But instead I only added, "So I'm sorry. I'm really, really sorry."

Alexis didn't say anything. She fiddled with the cord of her headphones.

"So, are you going to get a new one? Your birthday's next month, right?"

"Are you kidding me?" She threw the headphones back to her lap. "Do you know how much a violin costs? The one that your 'best friend' smashed into a million pieces was almost three thousand dollars. Do you really think my parents have the money to buy me a new one?"

"Did you tell them what happened?"

"No way." She shook her head. "I told them I accidentally left it on the bus."

"But why? Weren't they mad at you?"

"Oh, they were furious. But if I told them what Kenzie did, they would have freaked completely. You know my mom, how overprotective she is. She would have stormed down to Sister Dorothy's office and made a scene. Kenzie would have gotten expelled for sure."

"You protected her? Why bother, after what she did to you?"

"Wendy, you don't get it, do you?" She looked at me, her eyes steady and clear. "The night she wrecked my violin, I told her I wasn't afraid of her. But that was a lie. *Everyone's* afraid of her. Including you. If you weren't, you wouldn't be friends with her anymore."

"I *have* been trying to break away from her," I said, crossing my arms tightly across my chest. "From all of them. Kenzie and Sapphire and Emily and the whole thing. It's just harder than you'd think."

The bus finally pulled in front of the school and Alexis stood up.

"You know what I think?" she asked as she pulled her headphones over her ears and headed toward the door.

"What?"

"Try harder."

17

FOR THE REST OF THE WEEK, I couldn't sleep. Friday came, and with it rumors of a massive house party in Wildwood, but I didn't much feel like partying. I stayed home and watched *Teen Mom 2*, then climbed into bed and opened up *A Farewell to Arms*. When I turned to the first chapter, a little slip of paper fluttered out from between the pages. I picked it up and my heart quickened. Tino had written his name in neat black letters, and beneath it, his phone number. Grinning like an idiot, I programmed the number into my phone, just in case I ever worked up the nerve to actually call him. Then I picked up the book and began to read. As far as I could tell, it was just a lot of descriptions about rocks and trees and rivers and troops. There were soldiers drinking and talking about things I didn't understand. There was no mention of Catherine Barkley. I wanted to text Tino and ask, *Does it get better?* But of course I didn't have the guts. I gave up at the end of the second chapter and went to sleep. I slept for ten hours, but in the morning when my alarm went off and I dragged myself out of bed to get ready for work, I still felt exhausted. When I got to the deli, I made myself a piece of warm buttered bread with plum jam, my favorite, but could barely eat two bites. My stomach was in knots. My head pounded. My legs shook. I knew what it was: My guilt about Alexis's violin was starting to make me physically sick.

At the end of my shift, I climbed into Red Rocket, drove to the bank, and deposited my paycheck into my college savings account as I always did on payday. I got back into the car, turned on the ignition, and sat there for a minute staring at the flashing neon sign for the Vape Emporium next to the bank. It was a gray day and the sky was clogged with heavy, inert clouds, the kind that threaten rain but never deliver. The faces of the people walking down the street were washed out and exhausted, everybody dreaming of summer.

I turned off the ignition. With a determined sigh, I climbed back out of Red Rocket, retraced my steps across the parking lot, into the bank, and back up to the teller's counter.

"Did you forget something, ma'am?"

"Yes," I said. "I'd like to make a withdrawal." I filled out the withdrawal slip and slid it across the counter. The teller looked at the number, raised an eyebrow, and opened her drawer. She counted out the bills in hundreds and fifties, put them in an envelope, and handed it to me.

"Would you like our security guard to escort you out to your car?" she asked. "That's a lot of money to be carrying around with you."

"No, thanks," I said, suddenly unable to control a smile. "I got this."

I sat in front of Alexis's house with the car running and the fog steaming up the front windshield. It had been a long time since I'd been to that yellow brick bungalow on Menard Avenue, but everything was exactly as I remembered: the sour cherry tree in the middle of the front lawn, whose inedible fruit we had once picked and smashed into a red paint that we smeared into our palms because we wanted to make a blood oath of eternal friendship but were too scared to cut ourselves and draw real blood. I remembered the line of ferns that waved in the wind beneath her front window. When we played cops and robbers—I was always the cop, so I could be like my dad, and she was always the robber because it was the only role left—the ferns were always the place she hid, and when I asked her once why she didn't hide somewhere new she said, "Because I always want you to be able to find me."

I was hoping for some sort of sign that would make me change my mind. After all, what I was about to do was stupid and foolish and completely illogical. But as I sat in Red Rocket in front of Alexis's house, these flooding memories only made me more determined. At last, I took the envelope containing $3,304.75—my entire college savings—and in careful block lettering so she wouldn't recognize the handwriting, I wrote: *ALEXIS NICHOLS VIOLIN FUND* across the flap. Then, leaving the car running, I pulled my hood around my face, hurried up the walkway to her front door, dropped it in her mail slot and drove away before anyone could see me.

18

IT WAS AROUND THIS TIME THAT my tattoo started itching. It had begun to scab over in places, and one night, I dreamed that I had fallen on top of a termite nest and couldn't get up. I woke from the dream thrashing, my fingers clawing at my back and shoulder. This lasted for several unbearable days. In school, I would sit in class shifting uncomfortably in my desk, sweating, suffering, willing the bell to ring so that in the commotion of packing up backpacks and switching classes no one would notice me sticking my hands down the collar of my school blouse to scratch frantically.

Then the whole thing started to molt like snakeskin. At night, lying in bed, I would tear at it with my fingernails, accumulating a disgusting pile of scabs and skin flakes in the folds of my sheets and in the wasteland of missing socks between my bed and the wall. The scabs were colored with the top layer of my tattoo, and they came off like puzzle pieces of the face and shawl and halo of Our Lady of Lourdes. I made sure to pick them up and throw them in the outside garbage cans, not just because they were gross, but because

I knew that if my mom ever decided to clean my room, she might put the pieces together and think she was witnessing a religious miracle.

That same week, too, just when I thought we had nearly made it to spring, Chicago lapsed into a deep freeze. The wind howled, buffeting our third floor apartment. The dirty snow left over from January and February blew across the parking lot of our complex, sticking to the cars already filthy with salt, and when the new snow fell, it was so hardened by the cold that it rattled against our windows like tossed handfuls of sand.

At school, I tried to keep my head down. I arrived just before first period began and left as soon as eighth period ended. I did my homework but never raised my hand in class. I wore a thick white T-shirt under my school blouse so that when we changed for gym, no one would see the strange depiction of Our Lady of Lourdes that reigned over my right shoulder like some demonic holy queen.

Alexis had told me I needed to try harder, and she was right, but I was still too afraid to have a full-on confrontation with Kenzie and company. I knew that if I tried to stop eating lunch with them again, they would just follow me to my new table the way they'd done before. So instead, with the passive-aggressive bravery of a lifelong coward, I stopped eating lunch with my clique, abandoned the cafeteria completely, and took to eating in the school library. It was a drafty, echoing room with cracked tile flooring and shelves full of moldy, outdated textbooks, tucked away in an abandoned corner of the second-floor arts wing. Sister Catherine, the sleepy, ancient librarian who presided over the pointless circulation desk, spent her days in a squeaky chair sewing Biblical proverbs into decorative pillows or flicking through the card catalog with her thin, shaky fingers. Behind a maze of dusty shelves, I discovered a heavy wooden table where I could eat my lunch in obscure quiet, drenched in the cold sunlight that flooded through the high, arched windows and watching a pair of brown mice scurry in and out of a hole in the plaster floorboards.

I was lonely and bored and sad pretty much all the time. The only thing, really, that made me feel good was imagining Alexis finding the money I'd left her. When I went to bed at night, I lay beneath the covers, and instead of daydreaming about Tino or Stanford or the big bathtub in my old house, I'd imagine Alexis taking a break from her practicing to come downstairs for a glass of orange juice, her white headphones blasting Tchaikovsky, and accidentally kicking the envelope with her socked foot. It would skitter across the front hallway and she'd walk over to pick it up. When she saw her name on the envelope, her curiosity would get the best of her and she'd forget all about the orange juice. She'd bring the envelope back up to her room where she would sit on her bed, tear it open, and fan out the bills in wonder. She would count them in order, from the hundreds all the way down to the coins, with a building sense of disbelief and elation. She'd scrutinize the envelope for some clue as to where it came from, but lacking anything there, she'd fall back on her pink bedspread and burst out laughing, thanking Saint Anthony, the patron saint of lost and broken objects, for working in such mysterious ways.

On the weekends, I looked forward to the cozy monotony of the Europa Deli. I didn't have to think. I just had to scoop and stir and serve and ring up, and being there, amid the smell of frying onions and the conversations in Polish and Russian and Bulgarian and the constant roar of the sausage grinder, my heart felt calm and my worries about school and life felt far away. But then, one frigid Friday evening toward the end of the deep freeze, as I stood behind the counter arranging cabbage rolls in the display case, the front door chimes tinkled and Kenzie walked in.

She wore a fake fur coat and a slouchy knit hat with an enormous fuchsia pom-pom on top that matched her gloves and lipstick. The cold air had made her cheeks pink and her eyes gleam. She looked beautiful.

"Hey." She smiled.

"Hey."

"I was in the neighborhood and figured I'd stop by to grab some dinner."

A queasiness gathered in my stomach. I knew how much she hated this place. Why was she here?

"I thought you said the food here was disgusting," I said.

"When did I say that?" she asked innocently.

In a moment, I had my phone out of my apron and found the Instagram post from last fall. I held it in front of her:

Beet soup or murder scene? #EuropaDeli #nasty #worstjobever

She glanced at it for a moment and laughed lightly. "Well, you *do* have other stuff here besides beet soup, don't you? That pine nut spinach salad doesn't look totally putrid. Give me a small one of that."

"All right." I took a plastic container from a stack on top of the counter and slid open the glass door. As I began to scoop the salad with a long metal spoon, the door chime tinkled again, and this time Sapphire and Emily, dressed in variations of Kenzie's winter outfit, walked in. They stood behind her, their arms crossed, smirks painted across their faces as they watched me work. My mouth went dry.

"So," Kenzie said, watching me from the other side of the glass, "we need to talk to you."

"Right now?" I tried to make my voice sound as breezy as I could. "I'm sort of working at the moment."

"This will only take a minute."

I placed the salad on the scale, then took the printed sticker and sealed the package with it.

"Okay," I said, pushing it across the counter. "What is it?"

"Something's been up with you lately," Kenzie said. "Like

all of a sudden you've got a problem with us."

"A problem?" I played dumb, stalling for time. "What do you mean?"

"I *mean* the not sitting with us at lunch. The not answering your phone. The disappearing act on the weekends. You've never even *met* my new boyfriend."

"Yeah," Sapphire said. "Are you, like, mad at us about something?"

I swallowed.

"No," I finally said. "I mean, I don't know. It's not that I'm *mad* at anyone. I'm just . . . it's just that I—I can't . . ." I trailed off.

Kenzie opened her salad container, grabbed a plastic fork from the silverware tray next to the register, and stabbed at some spinach leaves. "Can't what?" she asked, her mouth full.

The itching of Our Lady of Lourdes started up then, all of a sudden. It took all my self-control not to shove my hands down my shirt and scratch till it bled.

"I can't be friends with you guys anymore," I heard myself say. As soon as I said it, the itching stopped.

"Can't be *friends* with us anymore?" Sapphire's voice was incredulous. The pom-pom atop her winter hat trembled indignantly.

"It's nothing, like, personal," I said. "It's just that I've sort of changed."

Sapphire's and Emily's mouths hung open in dumb fury, but Kenzie just laughed.

"Wendy, we're your *best friends*. You don't get to break up with us like we're some stupid boy you don't like anymore."

"Well, actually, I guess I do."

"It's that thing with that loser and her violin, isn't it?"

"Her name is Alexis," I said quietly.

"Alexis. Fine. Whatever. Look, Wendy, what do you want me to do? My dad's all jazzed up about Cherrywood Academy. I might end up at some loony bin in the middle of a cornfield next year, and if I do, it's *her fault*. And you think I should just let her get away with that?"

"Well, see, I don't think it's her fault." The tattoo on my back itched encouragingly. "I think it's *your* fault."

Kenzie stepped forward now, close enough that I could see her tiny, perfect, unclogged pores and smell her peachy scent.

"Okay. If this is how you want to be, fine. But just remember, Wendy, when I met you, you and your family were the enemy of this entire fucking city. High school could have been literal hell for you. It *would have been*, except that *we* came and rescued you. *We* made you. You've got a pretty fucking short memory."

"That will be three dollars and sixty-five cents," I said, meeting her eyes. "For the salad."

She took a step back, stunned that her threat seemed not to intimidate me.

"You can shove your three sixty-five," she snarled. She lifted a finger and pointed it in my face. "And never forget, when someone disrespects me, I *always* hit back harder."

Then, with a squeak of her Uggs, she turned around and headed out into the frigid street, Sapphire and Emily hurrying behind her.

I stood there, still holding the metal spoon, frozen in place until I felt a warm hand on my shoulder that for a second I believed belonged to Our Lady of Lourdes herself.

"You showed *her*," Alice said, hugging me to her pillowy body. "I'm proud of you. And don't worry about the three sixty-five, either."

"Here," Maria added, holding out a tray of apricot-filled cookies. "Have a kolaczki."

For the rest of my shift, the cold kept the customers away, and I leaned on the counter, reading *A Farewell to Arms*. Normally, this would have resulted in a scolding: If there was one thing Alice and Maria couldn't stand, it was a person not earning her keep. Just because there were no customers didn't mean I couldn't be stocking or prepping or hosing down pans. But this one time, they let me read in peace.

After I got off work, I drove straight to Jayden's. I'd been putting off finishing my tattoo because it already looked so awful I was afraid that adding color would only make it worse. But now Kenzie's threat dangled darkly in my mind. Just because I'd acted tough didn't mean I actually was. In fact, I was completely terrified. *I always hit back harder.* Maybe if I got this tattoo finished, paid Our Lady this final act of devotion, she could protect me now the way she once protected Aunt Kathy on a Homecoming night decades ago.

Even with the heat blowing full blast in Red Rocket, I couldn't stop shivering the whole way to Jayden's garage. I found some street parking, slipped and slid down the frozen alley, and was still shivering when I knocked on the door and it slowly yawned open. Tino stood before me, his hat pulled low, his hands in his pockets.

"Well, well, well," he grinned.

"Hi," I said, trying to wipe my nose as discreetly as possible.

Jayden was sitting in the middle of the velveteen couch, his legs crossed and his ankle resting on his knee, enveloped in a giant plume of smoke and enjoying the last puffs of a thin, tightly packed joint.

"I was wondering if you were ever gonna come back," Jayden said sleepily, his eyes never leaving the TV. Then, he started giggling uncontrollably. Tino rolled his eyes.

"I swear, if that dude ever needs a CAT scan, all the doctors are gonna find in his head is a big swirling cloud of smoke."

"Hey. I heard that." The joint sizzled as Jayden took another long, crackling hit.

"So," Tino said, ignoring his cousin, "did you start *A Farewell to Arms* yet?"

"I just finished Book One," I said.

"And?"

"*And*, I thought you said this was supposed to be a love story."

"Well, isn't it?"

"Not as far as I can tell. First, there's that awful scene where a guy gets his legs blown off while eating a piece of cheese, and *then* I find out that Lieutenant Henry is just another typical *player*."

"A player?"

I reached into my bag, pulled out the book, and pointed to the folded-over page. "See? You even underlined it."

He moved closer to see the page and was now standing so close to me I could feel his warm breath on my neck as he read the words over my shoulder.

> *I knew I did not love Catherine Barkley nor had any idea of loving her. This was a game, like bridge, in which you said things instead of playing cards.*

"I forgot about that part," he said.

"I mean, there's that nice scene where he's dreaming about taking her to the hotel in Milan and drinking wine with her and lying under a sheet because it's so hot. But that's only because he wants to sleep with her. Not because he loves her."

"Oh yeah?"

"Yeah." I crossed my arms.

"Just wait," he said.

Jayden, who finally seemed to remember who I was and why I was there, stubbed out his joint on a paper plate and directed me to the office chair. He and Tino stepped into the alley while I quickly undressed, pressing my chest into the fabric so they wouldn't see anything, all the while thinking how weird it was that Tino had seen my bare back, from neck to waist, and yet we had barely ever touched.

The door creaked open and the two of them returned.

"This is gonna look so great," Jayden said, squeaking over to me in his little wheelie stool. His voice was slow and his eyes were red slits. I wondered whether it was the best idea to let a guy who was stoned out of his mind come at me with a needle, but I figured that at this point it was more important to have the tattoo finished than to have it perfect. I adjusted in my seat while he pulled on his headphones.

When he lifted his needle and it bore into my skin, the pain was excruciating, white hot, unbearable, far worse than I had remembered. I buried my face in the headrest of the office chair, willing the tears to stay behind my eyes, but despite my efforts they dripped onto the concrete, blending in with the oil stains already soaked into the ground.

"What's up with you, girl?" Jayden sighed. The cloud of marijuana-chill had lifted from his voice, and he sounded aggravated. "Last time you sat for hours without so much as moving a muscle."

He was right. Something *was* up with me. Everything in

my body rebelled against his hands. I squirmed and shuddered, grimaced and gasped, and curled my toes tightly in my winter boots. It was ridiculous, a voluntary torture, like sitting before a plate of poisoned food and eating it anyway because you don't want to seem impolite.

"It hurts more than last time," I said through gritted teeth. "Is it supposed to hurt this much?"

"Go easy, man," I heard Tino say.

The needle continued its incessant waspy whine, and all the while it burned and burned. I clung to the arms of the office chair so tightly my fingernails burst through the pleather surface and plunged into the wooly stuffing beneath. I could feel the sweat pool beneath my palms and stand out along my hairline. The black waves seeped in at the edges of my vision and my mouth filled with saliva, but I knew that if I stood up to puke, I would pass out before I made it out of the garage. So I swallowed hard and squeezed my eyes shut and remembered my mom telling me that when she was a little girl and had to get a tooth drilled, the only thing that would help was lying in the dentist's chair and repeating the Hail Mary again and again in her head until it was over.

So that's what I did. *Hail, Mary. Full of grace. The Lord is with thee. Blessed are thou amongst women, and blessed is the fruit of thy womb, Jesus. Holy Mary, Mother of God, pray for us sinners, now and at the hour of our death.*

Once, I jerked so suddenly that I knocked Jayden's needle gun out of his hand and onto the sticky floor.

248

"Sit *still*," he snapped, swiping up the gun and wiping it on his shirt, "unless you want this to look like total shit!"

"You don't have to yell at her, Jay," I heard Tino say.

"Can't you do something to calm her down?"

"Hey." I felt his hand on my bare arm. "Do you want to stop?"

I shook my head into the headrest. "I can't."

"Okay. What if I read to you? You think that might help?"

"You can try," I murmured.

Tino found *A Farewell to Arms* in my bag and picked up from where I'd left off. Lieutenant Henry had been wounded, and he was recovering in a hospital in Milan. Tino began to read from the part where Catherine Barkley shows up at Lieutenant Henry's hospital bed. He had to sit close to me, his knee brushing my elbow, so that I could hear his voice over the whining of the needle. When he began to read, I could feel his breath as it stirred my hair.

> *She came in the room and over to the bed. "Hello, darling," she said. She looked fresh and young and very beautiful. I thought I had never seen anyone so beautiful.*
> *"Hello," I said. When I saw her I was in love with her. Everything turned over inside of me.*

As he read, the pain began to fade. I could still feel it, still was aware of the burning, but his voice was like cool water putting out the flames.

God knows I had not wanted to fall in love with her. I had
not wanted to fall in love with anyone. But God knows I had . . .

Eventually, the needle clicked off and Tino put the book down. Jayden set the gun next to the dye cups and sponged some warm, soapy water across my back.

"Well, it's done," he said. "I'm not gonna lie—you were moving around a lot. So, you know."

"Know what?"

I turned my head a little to look at him, but I was still sort of nauseated and it felt best to keep my eyes trained on the floor.

"Well, it's a little crooked in places. That's what happens when you jerk around like that."

"Let me see."

He picked up the hand mirror and held it up to my shoulder, while I flipped on my phone camera with shaking hands. When the picture came into focus, I saw an expanse of taut, shiny skin—as if it had been badly burned—and even though Jayden had wiped it clean with the soapy water, thin blooms of blood were already seeping out of my pores and dripping down my back. This, I guess, didn't bother me too much: I knew from experience now that the blood and the swelling would be temporary. What *did* bother me was that there was something wrong with Our Lady's face. And what bothered me even more was that I couldn't quite figure out what it was.

Maybe it was her pupils, which were so large she looked like a meth-head having a serious tweak. Or maybe it was the eyes themselves: on the wall of the Saints Corridor they were turned upward to heaven in holy contemplation, but here, they gazed straight ahead, as if staring down an approaching train. Maybe it was her mouth, which hung open—a detail that, in the original painting, made it seem like she was whispering a prayer. But in Jayden's version, she just looked like she was gathering up a scream over whatever terrible thing she was staring at with those empty aquamarine eyes.

And the background color—the light shining from the grotto behind her wasn't even close to the bold, vibrant pink I'd envisioned from the walls of the Saints Corridor, but a greasy, dead color, like pink slime or a slab of week-old salmon. I shuddered, feeling a sour taste travel up the back of my throat.

"It's different than what I thought," I said faintly.

Jayden pushed away from me on his wheelie chair.

"Well, it's the best I could do, with you squirming around like a kid with a poop stuck halfway out his butt."

"But her face . . ."

"You've gotta let the color set. You've gotta let it heal. Then you'll love it. Tell you what, I'll knock twenty-five bucks off your final price. No one ever said I wasn't reasonable."

I handed him the cash I owed him. It was the entirety of my most recent paycheck and the only money I had left.

"You gotta remember, Wendy," Jayden said, lighting a cigarette, "this is a real operation here. Clean. Professional."

"I know, I know." I waved him away in defeat. "Tell my friends."

Tino helped me get dressed, squeezing his eyes shut like last time, to give me my privacy.

"I'll walk you to your car, okay?" He helped slip my cardigan around my shoulders. "This neighborhood isn't the safest."

I pulled my coat gingerly around my shoulders and we stepped out into the cold. The alley was depressing, coated with a slick layer of gray slush. Somewhere close by, somebody was burning leaves.

"Still think Lieutenant Henry's a player?"

"No," I admitted. I wanted to say, *Is that how love happens? Creeping up on you before you even know it's there? Burning slowly but invisibly until all of a sudden, the fire catches?* "He better not break her heart, though."

"He won't. But she might break his."

He turned to me in the purple darkness. Our eyes met and his mouth opened slightly as I leaned toward him. I felt myself both bracing and melting, and my eyes fluttered closed, and the words he had read still hung in my mind like the trace of a firework after it's burned out in the sky. *Everything turned over inside of me.*

That's when the garage door swung open.

"You forgot your leftovers," Jayden said, holding up a plastic bag with a yellow smiley face on it.

"Oh," I said, stepping backward. I could actually feel the magic being sucked from the air.

"What's that?" Tino nodded at the bag.

"I—I almost forgot," I stammered, taking the bag from Jayden and thrusting it into Tino's hands. "Dumpling soup."

19

I DROVE HOME SLUMPED FORWARD SO my shoulder wouldn't graze against the car seat. My mind was empty, too overloaded with all that had just happened, and almost happened, and not happened, to process anything at all.

My mom was working overnights all weekend, and for once, I was grateful. I knew that if she was at home right now, she would take one look at me and *know* that I had done something irrevocable to myself. The woman has a talent for sniffing out bad decisions. But the apartment was quiet except for the screaming wind that rattled the windows and blew fine sheets of snow across the parking lot. I tried to watch some TV, tried to play around on my phone, tried to read some more *A Farewell to Arms*, but my back felt scorched and raw, and by midnight I'd given up on the idea of trying to sleep. I got up, padded into the kitchen, poured myself a glass of water, and swallowed two of the pain pills my mom takes for the back she's thrown out too many times to count while lifting patients in the ER. I went back to bed and lay facedown in my pajamas until my body felt like it was floating, and the screaming wind began to sound like California waves, and I slipped under them, into a dark, heavy, dreamless sleep.

I woke up in the full sunlight, my mouth gummy and foul tasting. I fumbled for my phone, cursing under my breath when I saw the time. It was 6:45 and I was supposed to be at work by seven. I'd never been late to work in my life and I wasn't about to start now. I ran to the bathroom, tore off the T-shirt I'd slept in, and it wasn't until I felt the dull ache and saw the bandages that I remembered my Our Lady of Lourdes tattoo. Her face was hidden, swaddled in the damp wrappings, which I had no time to change even though they were slimy with ointment and dried blood. Carefully, I pulled my Europa Deli polo over my head, gave my teeth a frantic brush, threw my hair up, and hurried off to the deli, head down, as sharp needles of snow began to fall, pelting my face and neck.

When I got to work, Alice and Maria were in the back, mixing batter for a batch of fruit blintzes. An enormous pot bubbled with stewed apples: the smell of them, which would seep into my hair like a beautiful shampoo, was one of my favorite things about the job.

"You're late," Alice said, stirring the apples with a long wooden spoon. "You're *never* late."

"Alice, it's seven oh five," I said. "Can you give me a break?"

"And you look like crap," Maria helpfully added. "Didn't you get no sleep last night?"

"Not really." My shoulder was on fire. It felt like it had a pulse. And my eyes felt like paperweights were sitting on their lids.

"Are you sick? Depressed? Boy trouble? Those bitchy little friends of yours giving you grief again?" Alice put down her spoon, wiped her hands on her apron, and sat down on a pallet stacked with canned beets.

"Nothing like that," I said. "I just couldn't sleep. No reason."

"Well, if all it is is nothing, then I suggest you start sautéing some mushrooms. You know Mrs. Ivanov will be here in twenty minutes wanting her cabbage rolls."

I twisted my ponytail into a hairnet and clicked the burner on the giant stovetop, swirling olive oil into a cast-iron skillet. While I waited for the oil to heat, I looked up at the little television that was mounted on the wall above the deep fryer. A reporter with a fur-lined parka fringing her face was huddled over her microphone at North Avenue Beach.

"And if you'll look behind me, you'll see that even though the storm itself hasn't landed yet, the lake is already kicking up *quite* a fuss!" The news camera zoomed past her and panned out over the gray expanse of Lake Michigan, where angry, foam-flecked waves heaved and crashed along the shore. "And the temperature feels like it's dropped about *ten* degrees even since our crews have arrived here at North Avenue!"

"This damn city," growled Maria, cracking eggs. "Why I leave Poland for this? I could've gone to Hawaii."

"I seen you in a bathing suit," Alice joked. She was pulping the stewed apples with a potato masher. "It's better for everybody you came here."

"And who you think *you* are? Kim Kardashian?"

"You're damn right I do." Maria leaned over, waving her flat, pancake ass in the air and smacking it for good measure, leaving a floured handprint on the pocket of her sweatpants.

I shook my head, smiling at their hysterical laughter as I tipped the mushrooms into the hot oil. They hissed, filling the air with their earthy smell.

"But seriously, I don't like this blizzard in March," Alice said. "Back in my town, we used to say a snowstorm in the spring is a sign of restless spirits."

"Why are you so superstitious?" Maria demanded. "It's not Christian."

"What are you talking about? In my town, we believe the saints and the ghosts exist right beside each other."

"Well, with beliefs like *that*, it's no wonder you never had a pope from *your* town." Maria's greatest pride in life was that she came from Wadowice, the city of Pope John Paul II's birth. She worked this piece of information into conversations whenever possible. The two of them began to bicker about the superiority of their hometowns back in Poland, but I had stopped listening. I was thinking about what Alice had said about saints and ghosts. Where had I heard that before?

"Wendy, wake up and stir those mushrooms." Alice was pointing her potato masher at me. "What do you think, they're gonna deglaze themselves?"

By the time I got off work, filling up the long hours with thoughts of Tino and our almost-kiss, the sky was an ominous, monochromatic sheet of iron, and the temperature had dropped well below freezing. When I got home, Sonny was in the lobby sifting through his mail, dressed in a muscle tank top that was cut out so I could see his tiny brown nipples. When he saw me, he stood up tall, flexing his chest.

"Hey," he said, "we're in for a big one tonight." I nodded and moved past him toward the stairs. Why was it that even when he tried to say normal things, they came out sounding perverted?

"Yo, Wendy!" I stopped on the stairs, took a breath, and faced him.

"Yes, Sonny."

"Make sure you leave your faucet dripping tonight. Otherwise your pipes will freeze. And then they'll burst, and I'll get *your* water dripping through *my* ceiling, right onto my brand new leather couch."

"Thanks for the tip, Sonny."

"Well, I figure, you and your mom don't got a man around

the house, you need help with this stuff." He grinned at me, showing off his unnaturally whitened teeth, and I rolled my eyes and plodded up the stairs. When I got inside the apartment, I crossed the front room, slid open the glass doors, and stepped onto the balcony. The clouds were like anvils, low and towering in the horizon, and the air, so cold it tasted metallic, was strangely still. I admitted to myself that Sonny was right: this was gonna be a big one. I shivered in my thin peacoat. Next year, I would really have to buy myself a new coat. A warmer one, with down filling and a hood. I went back into the apartment, crawled under a blanket, and flicked on the TV. The unfortunate reporter from earlier that morning was still hanging around North Avenue Beach, waiting for something to happen.

"And, now," she said, huddling with her mic as the waves crashed and receded behind her, "we'll hear from the commissioner of Streets and Sanitation about tonight's snow-removal plan."

The screen cut to a man in a mustache standing behind a podium.

"Our advice tonight," he said, "is not to leave the house unless you *absolutely have to*. I'm talking, if you're in labor. I'm talking, if your appendix bursts. The visibility is going to be *very poor*. The snow is going to be *very heavy*. And the temperature is going to fall to *life-threatening* levels."

"No problem," I told the commissioner, snuggling deeper under the blanket and grateful my mom was working twelve hours—long enough, according to the forecast, to ride out the worst of the storm. It was still a Saturday night, though, and in my old life, word would have probably spread by now of a party in Gladstone Park or Rogers Park or Lincoln Park or Lincoln Square or Noble Square or somewhere in the suburbs, and Kenzie would have rounded us up on a dog sled if that's what it took to make it there in time for the tapping of the keg. It felt good to have nowhere to go.

Eventually, I turned off the TV and decided to take a shower.

As I waited for the water to heat up, I slowly peeled off the damp gauze that crisscrossed over my shoulder and down my back. The closer I got to my skin, the wetter it became. A faint, unpleasant odor had begun to emanate from it. Holding my breath, I peeled off the layer directly covering my skin. I turned and looked over my naked shoulder and there she was.

I stood there for a moment, watching her watch me. It occurred to me that those two vacant eyes would hang across the thin, protuberant bones of my shoulder until the day I died, no, even *after* I died, after they laid my shriveled old body in a casket and buried me in the earth, Our Lady of Lourdes would stare into the unturned mud below me, for months or years or however long it takes for skin to finally decay. Unless, that is, I get buried in the permafrost like the Pazyryk people, and thousands of years from now a new civilization uncovers my body and tries to figure out just what the hell I was trying to say with that strange woman tattooed across my shoulder with her hands clasped in prayer.

I stepped into the shower and let the hot water run over me. I knew that I could stand here as long as I wanted, until I used up everything in the hot water heater and neighbors began to complain, and it would never be enough to wash her away. She wasn't like a scapular that I could take off if I wanted to. I wasn't allowed to change my mind, to grow out of needing her. She and I were forever—proof that in spite of everything, I still could call myself a believer.

After my shower, I pulled on a loose sweatshirt and leggings and found a bag of microwave popcorn in the cupboard. I put it on the counter, took a big bowl from the cabinet, and opened the fridge.

"Oh my God," I said to the empty kitchen. "We're out of Dr Pepper."

Of course, I *could* eat this nutritious dinner accompanied by a glass of water, but what sane person drinks *water* with popcorn? What's even the point? I looked outside. Snow had begun to fall, barely, more like a leak from the sky than an actual storm. Was it totally insane to run down to the 7-Eleven and buy a Super Big Gulp that would last me until the blizzard was over and the streets were cleared and/or somebody went to the grocery store? It probably was. It *definitely* was. But, then, no one was at home to stop me.

Almost as soon as I stepped out of the lobby, the trickling, anemic snow turned on full blast, blanketing the sky in swirls of white. A text came in from my mom: *Stay warm tonight, honey,* she'd written, as if she had some sort of weird mom inkling that her brainiac daughter had just decided to risk life and limb for a vat of carbonated sugar water. *I love you.* By the time I reached the bus stop at the end of my block, I couldn't even see across the street to the green awning over the karate dojo or the neon sign for Siam Palace.

Halfway to the 7-Eleven the neighborhood had already become unrecognizable. It had turned into a moonscape—white, blank, abandoned. I wrapped my scarf around my face, stuffed my hands into my coat pockets, and began to march, lifting my legs through the powdery snow, unable to see anything in front of me but the dim haze of streetlights through the whirling white sky. By the time I got to the 7-Eleven I could no longer feel my toes, and an icy layer of snot had formed inside my scarf. I imagined myself lying in a snowdrift and staring up sightlessly at the stars, the tragic victim of acute hypothermia. The list of people who would miss me that I compiled in my head was depressingly short.

Inside the fluorescent oasis of the 7-Eleven, my skin immediately prickled over and I realized how cold, wet, and hungry I was. I went over to the pop machine and filled the giant bucket-cup halfway with ice, then, as I hit the Dr Pepper button and waited for it to fill, my mind began to drift into a daydream of me and Tino sitting together in my old back-yard on the creaky swing my dad had hung on a low branch of the spreading oak tree. It was quiet back there, a sunny, warm autumn day, and the leaves above us were edged with yellow. Tino and I sat there on the swing and talked about books. Maybe we even held hands. Maybe I wore my hair pinned up and he took the pins down, one by one, until it all fell around us and he leaned in and—

"Wendy! Hey!" Govinda, my favorite 7-Eleven cashier, was calling to me from behind the cash register. "Why you wasting all my soda?" I looked down and saw that the Dr Pepper was overflowing, running down my hands and drip-ping onto the floor.

"Sorry, Govinda," I muttered, grabbing a napkin from the stack next to the lids and wiping up the mess.

I paid for my drink, took a long, glorious sip to assure myself that the trek had been worth it, and was almost out the door when a familiar voice called me back.

"Wendy?"

It was a voice I knew well from my past, from backyard barbeques and police picnics and charity softball games in Jefferson Park. My heart sank. But what could I do? I had to turn around. And there, standing before a case of endlessly rotating hot dogs, stood Terry Ryan, my dad's old friend, the one who had placed the handcuffs around his wrists. Beside him was a short, pudgy-faced young guy I assumed was his beat partner. They were standing at the coffee station filling their thermoses and stomping the snow off their black boots.

"Oh. Hi, Terry."

"What the hell you doing out in this weather?"

"We ran out of Dr Pepper."

"Oh, now *there's* a good reason to go out in the worst blizzard we've had in twenty years." He grinned at me, but I didn't much feel like smiling back.

"How's your ma?"

"Fine."

"Junior?"

"Fine."

"He's in the navy now, I hear."

"Yeah."

Terry stirred his coffee.

"I don't remember you being this chatty," he joked.

I took another sip of my Super Big Gulp and didn't say anything.

"You didn't drive here, did you?"

"No. Walked."

"Well, you're not walking home. Not in this blizzard." He glanced outside at the white wall that pounded against the glass doors of the 7-Eleven like a tsunami. "Ray and I are just going to pay for our coffee, and we'll take you the rest of the way."

"I live, like, five blocks away."

"In this kind of storm, even five blocks is dangerous."

I looked at him coldly, remembering that clean click of the handcuffs he'd snapped around my father's wrists.

"No, thanks." I put my hand on the door.

"Wendy, don't be stubborn. You're crazy if you think I'm going to let you go out in a storm like this with nothing but that thin jacket." He reached out and pinched the threadbare fabric of my peacoat.

"Don't touch me!" I twisted away from him, surprising myself at my sudden rage. The last thing I saw before I ran out into the snow was Terry Ryan standing there dumbly, holding his coffee in his hands.

I ran as fast as I could, the Dr Pepper spilling and freezing all over my ungloved hands. It was snowing so heavily I couldn't see where I was going. The snow blew at my face, icing my eyelashes, burning in my nostrils. I stumbled ahead, not knowing whether I was on the sidewalk or in the middle of the street, whether I was heading toward my apartment or away from it. Even sound had fallen away, the snow absorbing everything until all that was left was a muted swirl of silence. The endless march of planes that had been roaring across the skies of the northwest side of Chicago for my entire childhood had come to a halt, leaving the sky a white, wintry void. Every flight out of O'Hare would be canceled in a storm like this. I stopped running and stood for a minute, trying to get my bearings. My right shoulder felt like it was on fire, and the heat was spreading down my back and chest, too. It hurt so much I felt lightheaded and nauseated. Up ahead, I saw a flicker of glowing green light—I couldn't be sure, but I thought it might be the awning of Siam Palace, and I moved toward it, wading through snow so thick it felt like trying to tread through water. The closer I got, though, the dimmer the flicker got, until I was lost again in the whiteout.

I tried to ignore the tight ball of panic that was gathering at the pit of my stomach. *Just keep going*, I told myself. *This isn't the Alaskan frontier—this is Jefferson Park!* Of all the crazy things that had happened in this city, I was pretty sure no one had ever been buried in an avalanche in the middle of Milwaukee Avenue, and I sure as hell wasn't going to be the first. I pushed ahead against the wind, until at last, I came to a viaduct—the one that arched over the street where the Metra trains passed over in better weather. The snow was blowing in on either side, but the concrete arch over my head offered some protection, and I could finally see in front of me. *Okay*, I thought. *This is good. You're at a landmark.* If I could manage to head straight for one block and turn right, my apartment building would be there on the west side of the street. I looked down at my Dr Pepper, which was nearly frozen solid in my purple, frostbitten hand. I took one last valiant sip, but it was too icy to even make it up the straw. I tossed the cup aside, where it clattered against the tagged-up concrete, coming to rest in a pile of debris and fast-food wrappers.

Step on a crack, you'll break your back. That was the chant Alexis and I had sung up and down Menard Avenue when we were kids. Her block had forty squares of concrete that made up the sidewalk—forty cracks, and two steps for each square. Eighty steps in all. I wrapped my scarf tighter around my face, took a deep breath, stepped back out into the storm, and began to count.

By the time I got to step eighty, my legs were trembling. I turned my face into the wind, my stomach clenching, and vomited bile. Forty more steps and the apartment should be on my left. And sure enough, as I rounded the corner and pushed ahead—thirty-five, thirty-six, thirty-seven—I saw, hazily, as if in a dream, the tall brown brick of our complex rising up through the snow. I said a quick prayer of thanks to Our Lady, touching my hot shoulder, stepped up the walkway, and stuck my key in the door.

It didn't turn.

Shit. Had I brought the wrong set? No, these were my keys, with the big plastic sombrero keychain from Señor Frog's that Aunt Col had bought me as a souvenir from her trip to Cancun. I tried the key again, with no luck. I pressed my nose to the glass front door. That carpet didn't look right. Had it always been royal blue? I could have sworn it was a poo-hued shade of brown. Or had the landlord installed new carpet? I was confused, exhausted, and scared, and then I heard a rushing in my ears, as if an avalanche was coming. I began to see little black spots oozing across my vision like jellyfish, gelling together into a bigger spot that pulled across my eyes like a velvet stage curtain. *Wrong building*, I remember thinking to myself.

Then I fainted.

20

I WOKE UP IN WHAT AT FIRST I mistook to be a jungle. Big plants with broad, waxy leaves hung over me, and the humid air clanged with the twittering of birds. A flash of yellow flitted overhead, and a small canary swooped down and perched on the arm of the floral couch where I was lying, my boots placed neatly on the floor beside me. From far away, I heard the drone of a television and the clatter of dishes being washed. My head throbbed, and so did my shoulder. My mouth was bone dry, my tongue heavy and lolling. The chills persisted, and my teeth began to chatter so loudly that the startled canary swooped away and disappeared down a hallway.

"Hello?" My voice sounded foreign, moose-like and mournful. There were footsteps, and finally a stooped old woman appeared in the doorway, holding a ziplock bag of ice in one hand and a steaming mug in the other. I lay there, paralyzed with terror, as she leaned down close enough that I could see the big, soft, porous moles all over her face and smell the combination of rosy old-lady perfume and birdseed that drifted from the folds of her old-fashioned housecoat. She had red slippers on her feet that were so worn I could see through them to the outline of her thick, yellow toenails, and her sparse gray hair was pinned up around her head with little metal barrettes.

She came over to me, said something in Polish, then clucked at me in a universal language of grandmothers that I understood to mean that I should sit up. She leaned close, and another bird, this one bigger and gray, with a shock of red feathers mohawked across the crown of its head, zoomed through the air and landed on her shoulder, peering at me with beady, jealous eyes. The lady put the bag of ice into my hand and guided it to a spot on the back of my head where a lump had formed, the hair matted with dried blood. Then, she put the mug on the glass coffee table next to me.

"Drink." She pointed. I peered into the depths of the chipped mug. It was filled with blood and floating white fingers. Wonderful: I had escaped the clutches of the most epic snowstorm in Chicago history only to land in the hands of a serial killer and/or cannibal. The black jellyfish came oozing back. Bird Lady must have seen the fear in my face, because she sighed impatiently and held the mug to my lips.

"Is borscht," she snapped. "Beet soup." She tilted the mug so I had no choice but to open my mouth and drink it. It was bitter and earthy, like drinking sun-warmed dirt, even better than the stuff Alice and Maria made at the deli. I swallowed, and my shaking subsided a little bit. Once I realized this woman was not making me drink the blood of dead children, I was able to look around at my surroundings and gather my thoughts. The walls were lined with old-fashioned iron cages, and inside them an entire zoo's worth of exotic birds twittered and preened. The whole place smelled like birdseed, which was not unpleasant, exactly, but sort of earthy and feral, like the borscht. The coffee table and wood floors were nicely polished, but fluffs of feathers floated in the air, settling into corners in small, rainbow-colored piles.

In the largest cage, an enormous green parrot dozed. He was bigger than a crow, and so green he looked like he might glow in the dark. On the wall opposite from where I was lying stood a fireplace, but instead of logs, it housed a shrine to the Blessed Virgin, arched with Christmas lights, crisscrossed with Palm Sunday leaves, and glowing with votive candles. The mantel above this shrine was lined with icons of saints, mostly Saint Francis of Assisi, the patron saint of animals. This all made me feel a little better about my situation—if Bird Lady was a devout Catholic, she probably believed in the sixth commandment, which meant that she was probably not going to kill me.

She took the mug from my hands and placed it on the table, then heaved her squat body onto the couch and put a small, soft hand on my forehead. She peered into my face.

Her eyes were small and pale blue and almost lashless, the eyebrows scraggly and white.

"I find you on my front stoop. You lucky I keep watch out my window. Otherwise, you be dead. Frozen."

I nodded weakly.

"You very sick."

"I'm fine," I said, attempting a breezy laugh that came out more like a tubercular cough. "Just must've knocked my head when I slipped on ice. What time is it?"

"Not fine," she said, ignoring my question. She produced a thermometer from the folds of her housecoat and stuck it in my mouth. While we listened to the numbers beep upward, she squinted her doughy face at me. "You homeless?"

I opened one eye beneath her warm palm and shook my head.

"You running away?"

"I just wanted a Dr Pepper," I mumbled around the thermometer.

"Hm." She put her soft, stubby fingers to my throat, rubbing the lymph nodes. She lifted one of my arms and felt beneath the armpits. She put a palm on my chest bone and tapped with two fingers, listening. My body felt noodly, muscleless, and I sat there limply and let her poke at me. Then, she leaned me forward and tapped twice, firmly, once on my back and once on my right shoulder.

I screamed in agony.

"Aha!" she said, while the Mohawk bird ruffled its feathers

and squawked. "What's problem back here?"

"It's hard to explain," I whispered.

"Show me."

I reached behind me and lifted up my sweater as delicately as I could. I heard a gasp, then a stream of hysterical Polish, and then Bird Lady ran off into the other room. She returned a moment later with another woman—her mother, maybe— who looked at least twice as old as she was and who skated in slowly behind an aluminum walker. This woman had a humpback that reached higher than her stooped head, and the only hair she had left was a few staticky wisps standing straight up at the crown of her head. The two of them whispered to each other in awe, and then, with shining eyes, they began furiously crossing themselves again and again.

"It's just a tattoo," I said. If I'd had the energy, I would have rolled my eyes. "Not, like, a vision."

Bird Lady interrupted her signs of the cross to swat me over the head.

"I *know* is tattoo," she said, her voice hushed in wonder. "But you don't see what she does."

The older of the two ladies moaned then, cast aside her walker, and collapsed to her knees. Slowly, her knobby hands clasped together, she began to crawl across the carpet on her knees, swaying back and forth.

"*O Boze! Matka Boska placze!*" she wailed. "*To jest cud, to jest cud!*"

"Yes, Mama! Yes! Thanks be to God!" Bird Lady rejoined.

She took me by the hands, drew me up from the couch, and stood me before the big gilded mirror above the mantle.

"Look!" She lifted the hem of my sweater dramatically, as if unveiling some celebrated painting. "Ave Maria! Ave Maria!"

I peered over my shoulder into the glass and saw immediately what all the fuss was about. There was Our Lady of Lourdes, her terrible, botched face staring back at me, the dead-fish pink light glowing on my hot, feverish skin.

And she was weeping.

Tears dripped and flowed from her turquoise eyes in rivers down my back and left dark stains on the waistband of my leggings. The birds began to take up the pious howls of the old ladies, and soon the room was filled with the strange jungle sounds of birdsong and the chant of the Polish rosary. If anybody else had been around, I probably would have laughed at them, these two crazy religious nuts and their silly little beliefs. But something inside me resisted laughter. Maybe it was the way the tattoo seemed to itch whenever I was faced with a moral decision. Maybe it was Kenzie. Alexis. My dad. The ghosts of Lady Clara and Sandy DiSanto and Tiffany Maldonado. The closing of Academy of the Sacred Heart. There had never been a time in my life when I needed a sign, a miracle, as much as I did now, and here it was. I could see it with my own eyes. Maybe afterward I would feel embarrassed and sneering and cynical. But for now, I just believed. I got down on my knees and joined Bird Lady and her mother in the rosary. I let their dry, soft fingers graze my back while they keened. I let myself be swept up in the miracle, in the soft, holy light of Our Lady of Lourdes.

At their insistence, I stayed for a dinner of veal chops and boiled potatoes. We ate in a small, cluttered kitchen while a trio of parakeets hopped around at our feet waiting for crumbs. I helped the women clean up, and by the time we'd wiped dry the last dish, the whiteout had trickled to a regular snowfall. I would at least be able to see where I was going now. When I looked out the front window, I saw in the glow of the streetlights that I had overshot my location by just a block. I could see the top floor of my apartment building, a short walk back toward the viaduct.

After reassuring Bird Lady over and over again that I was okay, after accepting a long, warm coat to borrow for my walk home, the pockets filled with downy feathers and seed kernels, and after they insisted that I go around blessing everything in their house: their statues of Saint Francis, their framed pictures of the pope, their Palm Sunday leaves, bottles of water that they hurriedly filled from the tap to give out to their friends, the canned beans in their pantry, the aluminum walker, and every single one of their bird cages, I stepped back out into the moonscape, my Dr Pepper long forgotten. The two women stood huddled together in the doorway of their apartment building. Bird Lady waved at me furiously, while her mother leaned on her walker and stared at me with those blue glittery eyes gleaming in her wondering, almost child-like face, still whispering softly, *"To jest cud, to jest cud."*

Yes, I thought as I lifted my legs through the mountains of snow, wading through the night in the direction of my apartment. *It really is a miracle.*

21

IT WAS ALMOST MIDNIGHT WHEN I got home. I changed out of my wet clothes and into a tank top and cardigan sweater. I put the long-awaited bag of popcorn into the microwave, having resigned myself to the fact that there would be no Dr Pepper to wash it down with, and while I waited for it to pop, I flopped down on the couch and put my head in my arms.

When I woke up, the room reeked of burning kernels. I opened my eyes slowly, groggily, and then with a start, saw that I was eye level with my mom's hospital scrubs.

"Mom?" I turned over, squinting against the light from the balcony, where the rising sun had turned the snowy parking lot into a field of diamonds.

With her thumb and forefinger, my mom lifted the sleeve of my cardigan, which had slipped down in the night.

"What," she said quietly, "is that on your shoulder?"

Oh, shit, I thought. *ShitshitshitshitSHIT.* I'd been planning on telling her about the tattoo eventually, just not until I was, like, thirty.

"Um," I said.

"Take off your shirt."

I did as I was told.

"And your bra."

I unclasped the bra and turned away from her. My mom hadn't seen my bare chest since I was about eight years old.

"Lie down."

In a way, it actually felt good, knowing that I was in deep shit. It felt like finally, someone cared. I lay on my stomach, my face sinking into the couch cushions.

"I can't believe this." She took a paper towel she'd yanked off the roll and began dabbing at my back. "Where'd you get this done, anyway? Let me guess—somewhere that doesn't have a license on the wall."

I nodded into the cushion.

"You kids today are all so stupid," she said, dabbing angrily and with a nurse's clinical efficiency. "Piercing your faces and your nipples and even your *balls and clitorises*—yeah, I just said clitoris, young lady. Deal with it. Dying your hair all those stupid colors. *Jesus*, Wendy. But at least hair dye and piercings can be reversed. *This?* This—this *thing* is now with you for *life*."

"Mom—"

"All these years of praying to Our Lady of Lourdes." She balled up the paper towel and tossed it on the carpet. "All the holy candles. All the Mass cards. All the rosaries. All the special intentions. I thought I was instilling a real *respect* for her in you kids. A real *reverence*. And then one morning I come home from work and I see this—this—*version* of her. Is it supposed to be some sort of horribly misguided tribute? Or are you blaspheming? What *is* this, Wendy?"

"Mom—"

"You know what? I don't even *want* an explanation, young lady. I'm going to the drug store to get you some Motrin for your fever. Then I'm going to call the doctor's answering service and get you an appointment. *Jesus Christ*, Wendy." She shook her head and headed for the door.

"*Mom.*"

"*What?*"

"What about the weeping?"

"What about the *what*?"

"The weeping. Our Lady of Lourdes is *weeping*. Don't you see it?"

"Of course I see it!"

"Well, don't you think it's a miracle? Or at least some kind of sign?"

"You're goddamn right it's a sign—a sign of an infection!" She picked up the paper towel, smeared with slimy yellow stuff and dabs of blood, and waved it in front of my face. "See that? Do those look like tears to you? That's pus, young Christian soldier."

"Oh," I said.

"And let's only hope to Christ that an infection is *all* it is. Dirty needles can carry blood-borne diseases, Wendy. *That's* what you should be worried about—Hep B. Hep C. *HIV!*" She threw her hands in the air. "I swear, you never cease to amaze me. Eleven years of Catholic school and it's like pulling teeth to get you out of bed for Sunday mass, but some scumbag scribbles on you with a dirty needle and suddenly you believe in miracles!" She stormed out of the room, slamming the door behind her.

"A dirty needle?" I asked the question to the now-empty apartment.

I should have known. There were no such things as miracles. There was only science, logic, and facts. The leaky air-conditioning unit above the painting in the Saints Corridor. The air vent in the ceiling of the Florentine Ballroom. An infected tattoo. When was I going to get used to it? You can believe all you want, but life will always smack you down with the cold, hard truth.

22

ON MONDAY MORNING, I WOKE UP to a text alert that all public and private schools in Chicago were closed on account of the storm. Sighing happily, I rolled over and slept in for the first time in about three years. Around eleven I finally got up, ate some breakfast, and relocated to the couch, where I spent the rest of the day taking antibiotics and lounging under a pile of blankets. My mom was off work, and she sat on the other side of the couch from me while we watched *Teen Mom 2*. She didn't mention the tattoo, but every once in a while I'd catch her looking over at me. "What?" I'd demand, but she'd just shake her head and look away. Which is pretty much the worst thing ever. At least if your mom is screaming at you, you know she hasn't given up on you.

When I wasn't sleeping or watching terribly awesome reality TV, I was reading *A Farewell to Arms*. Catherine Barkley had gotten pregnant, and even though she and Lieutenant Henry weren't married they were still happy about it. My favorite part so far was how the two of them would try to put thoughts into each other's heads while they were in different rooms of the hospital. Could that really work, if you were in love? I closed my eyes tightly, sat up on the couch, and tried it. *I think I'm falling for you, Tino,* I thought to him. *I got the number you left in the book, but I don't want to be the one who calls first. Here's my number: call me. Call me right now. Please?* I opened my eyes and stared at my phone screen, willing it to ring.

"Wendy?" My mom said. "Are you all right?"

I opened my eyes.

"I'm fine," I said. "Sorry." I put the phone down and turned back to *Teen Mom 2*.

I hadn't heard a word from Kenzie or Emily or Sapphire since they'd shown up at the deli that Friday. Needless to say, I wasn't exactly looking forward to seeing them again at school on Tuesday. I was hoping we'd get another snow day, maybe even a couple, but that bastard Streets and Sanitation commissioner had made sure the streets were plowed in time for the schools to open as normal after just one day off.

When I walked into chapel the next morning, I glanced to the back of the room and saw the three of them sitting in their usual seats beneath the looming wooden statue of Saint Veronica. Sapphire was frantically copying someone's homework, Emily was pretending to read a copy of *1984* but really just using it as a prop to hide her phone, and Kenzie was slouched with her feet up against the chair in front of her, her hand in a bag of corn chips, the picture of queenly calm.

I hurried down the middle of the aisle and found an open seat in the social no-man's-land known as the freshman section. I sat down, bracing myself for a Pop-Tart to the back of the head.

A senior girl from Eucharistic Ministry Club stepped up to the lectern. "In the Name of the Creator, the Redeemer, and the Spirit who makes us free." We all made the sign of the cross.

She read from the Book of Luke, and I half listened while outside, icicles dripped and melted beyond the blue-green light of the stained glass windows. As I stared ahead, Our Lady of Lourdes stared behind, like literal eyes in the back of my head. She saw my old crew all the way in the last row, watching me intently as they mouthed along to the prayers. She saw Alexis studying me, waiting to see if this time I'd tried harder. And she saw the freshmen on either side of me trying not to stare, wondering what tales of upperclassmen intrigue and betrayal had cast the popular junior with the notorious last name out among their lowly ranks. I bowed my head, ignoring all their wordless chatter, and tried to concentrate on my prayers.

"And while he yet spake, behold a multitude, and he that was called Judas, one of the twelve, went before them, and drew near unto Jesus to kiss him. And Jesus said unto him,

Judas, betrayest thou the Son of man with a kiss?"

We finished our prayers and the bell rang for first period. I threw my bag over my shoulder and hurried out the door, walking fast but not *too* fast. If Kenzie, who hated weakness, could see that I was afraid, her vengeance was bound to be even more vicious. I kept my eyes trained to the floor, moving quickly from the chapel through the Saints Corridor to the main staircase, sticking to crowded thoroughfares, and turned left at the languages hallway. My Spanish classroom was within my sight when I heard the neat clacking of high-heeled boots behind me. *Maybe it's not her,* I thought, accelerating my pace as much as I dared. *Maybe it's a teacher. Teachers wear high heels. Well, some of them do.* And then I smelled it—a wave of sickly sweet peach body splash. *Here it comes.* I held my breath.

"Hey, Wendy." Kenzie fell into step beside me. "Listen, I just wanted to tell you I'm sorry about the other day."

"Um," I said. This was not what I had been expecting. Was this some kind of psychological warfare? I'd rather just get punched in the head.

"Not to get all TV movie or anything, but it was the five-year anniversary of my mom leaving. I was not 'being my best self' that day, as Ms. Bennett would say."

"Okay," I said. We had reached the door of my Spanish classroom, with its Picasso posters and scale model of Chichen Itza. Sister Agnes, who'd been writing subjunctive translations on the board, saw me hovering in the doorway.

"*¿Señorita Boychuck?*" She put a chalk-covered hand on her hip. "*¿Vas a entrar o no?*"

"*Sí, Madre Agnes.*"

I'd never been so happy to see a cranky old retired missionary who gave mountains of homework and over-pronounced her rolling *r*'s.

"I'd better go in," I said.

"Okay. But let me just say one more thing. If you don't want to be friends with us anymore, I get it, okay?"

"Okay."

"No hard feelings?" She stuck out her hand. I hesitated. It seemed too good to be true, but I couldn't figure out her angle. The bell was about to ring and Sister Agnes had commenced tapping her foot. When I shook Kenzie's hand, she drew me toward her, enveloping me in her peach scent. Then, she kissed me on the cheek.

I'd only remember that detail afterward. I have to hand it her: I had no idea she could be so poetic.

She'd betrayed me with a kiss.

It happened later that afternoon, during US History. Mr. Winters was droning on about the Gilded Age, and I was jotting down notes while also watching Veronica the Vegan covertly picking her nose.

"Pardon the interruption." Sister Dorothy's voice crackled

across the PA. "Would Wendy Boychuck please come down to the main office? Wendy Boychuck to the main office immediately, please."

Mr. Winters, annoyed that his lecture had been interrupted, glanced over at me and nodded permission. I gathered up my books. What was this about? The only other time I'd been called down to the principal's office was freshman year, when Sister Dorothy had to inform me that my tuition check had bounced. Nothing good ever happened in the principal's office; everybody knew that.

Mr. Winters's discussion of the role of railroad unions in the economic landscape of the 1870s faded as I closed the door softly behind me and stepped out into the hallway. My footsteps echoed down the Saints Corridor under the watchful gaze of all those long-dead women. Saint Maria Goretti peered out at me from behind the sheep she held clutched to her bosom. Saint Appolonia tumbled across the ceiling, frozen forever in the moment just after a Christian persecutor knocked her teeth out with a wooden club. Saint Agnes of Bohemia leered at me with her wide, red mouth. And Our Lady of Lourdes stood above my locker, the soft folds of her shawls painted by my mother's own hand, her mouth drawn downward in a look of either sorrow or pity.

When I got to the principal's office, Mrs. Lang, the receptionist, showed me to the door. I opened it and found Sister Dorothy sitting grimly at her desk beneath the giant velvet portrait of Jesus and the Sacred Heart. Sapphire, Emily, and Kenzie sat in a row in the chairs opposite her desk. And standing against the window were two police officers.

"Sit down, Wendy." Sister Dorothy indicated the remaining open chair next to her desk. She did not smile at me. I moved to the chair on shaking legs and sat down, glancing over at my former friends, but they were all staring at their laps.

"Do you know why you're here, Wendy?" Sister Dorothy was sitting up straight as a rail, her hands folded on her daily planner.

"No."

"Are you sure?"

"Yes, Sister." I tried again to make eye contact with the other girls. But Kenzie, slumped in her chair looking almost bored, was busy methodically peeling away a layer of blue nail polish while Sapphire's and Emily's eyes remained trained to the patterns of their uniform skirts.

"Okay, then. Let me give you a hint. Do you know a boy named Ned Munro?"

Ned Munro. Ned Munro. The name was sort of familiar. And then I remembered: October. The mansion on the lake. Evan's cousin with the orange hair and the shiny apple face.

"I've met him," I said. "Once. *Why?*"

One of the police officers, a young guy, not much older than my brother, with flat blond hair and pale eyebrows, raised a finger in the air.

"I'll take it from here, Sister, if you don't mind," he said.

Sister Dorothy nodded slightly, sat back in her big principal's chair and watched me.

"Ms. Boychuck, were you at a party at Ned's family home a few months ago?"

"Yeah. I think it was in October."

"Uh-huh." He wrote something on his notepad. "Well, at that party, some very valuable memorabilia was stolen. You know anything about that?"

And suddenly everything made sense. The Abraham Lincoln silverware.

I swung around and stared at Sapphire, willed her to look up. *Look at me, you fucking liar. You fucking coward.* Instead, she fiddled with her hair and stared out the window at the cars rushing past the wrought-iron gates of Academy of the Sacred Heart.

"Ms. Boychuck? Do you hear me? Do you know anything about that?"

"No."

The cops glanced at each other. The other one, older, with a belly that hung over his belt like a sack of flour, spoke up.

"A set of silverware. You don't know anything about that?"

"*No.*"

"Okay." He sighed, strummed his fingers on the windowsill. "Ms. Quintana?"

"Mm?" Kenzie looked up, sifting the piece of peeled blue

polish onto the carpet of Sister Dorothy's office.

"Show me your phone, please?"

As she handed him the phone, she finally looked at me, and her dark eyes were coldly triumphant. The cop held the phone in front of my face. There was a picture of me, sitting in the booth at Taco Burrito Queen, with a mountain of chicken nachos in front of me, holding one of the beautiful silver Abraham Lincoln forks aloft.

"Then how," he asked, "do you explain this photo?"

I didn't say anything. I couldn't.

"Well?" Sister Dorothy leaned forward in her seat. "Can you explain that photo or not?"

"Yes!" I exploded. "I was with them when *they* took it. When Kenzie dared Sapphire to do it, and then Sapphire *did* it. Remember?" I glared at Sapphire, but she continued to be fascinated by the plaid pattern of her skirt. I couldn't stand it anymore, the way she sat there like a church mouse, her lips twitching. I reached over and smacked her, hard, on the arm. *"Remember?"* She winced and shrunk away.

"That is *enough*, Wendy," Sister Dorothy roared, jumping up from her desk and nearly knocking over a jar full of pens. "I have to say, I expected more from you. An honors student. An A average. A girl who—"

"Whose father is Stephen Boychuck, the dirtiest cop in Chicago?" I interrupted. "Because that's what this is about, isn't it? That's why you believe them over me, isn't it?" I could feel hot tears pricking my eyes. *"Isn't it?"*

The blond cop looked at me with lizard-like calmness. His eyebrows were so light you could barely see them; it sort of made him look like an emoji.

"We'd like to search your locker," he said. "If you'll come with me, please."

"Fine," I said. "You want to see my physics notes? Maybe an old Dr Pepper can will crack the case? Let's go!" I was shouting now, and I could see in the stillness with which Kenzie held her body that she was trying not to laugh. The cop held me by the arm and led me out of the office, with the other one following behind.

We walked down the Saints Corridor saying nothing. Their footsteps echoed heavily, so different from the more familiar sounds of running girls and the quick, efficient steps of the nuns. The saints were silent, watching, and so were all the girls in the classrooms that lined the corridor, craning their necks to see us as we passed, popular blond-haired Wendy Boychuck being led down the hallway by the police. Even the teachers were watching, and I knew what they were thinking: *Like father, like daughter.* We reached my locker. Our Lady of Lourdes watched as I spun the numbers of my combination. 07-08-08-17—my birthday and Kenzie's birthdays combined, because she was always borrowing my locker to store her books since it was closer to her first period class, and this was the only way she could remember the combination.

Of course.

She knew my combination.

I knew even before I opened the locker that the silverware would be there. It was placed neatly on the metal shelf where I normally put my lunch and my lab goggles. The plastic case was a little banged up, several of the tines were bent, and a withered piece of ground beef still clung to one of the knives. My lunch and goggles had been thrown carelessly on top of the rest of my books at the bottom of my locker. They'd probably planted it there after chapel, while Kenzie was distracting me with her "no hard feelings" talk.

I didn't see them take out the handcuffs, but when I heard the click, I knew exactly what it was. I'd heard that sound once before.

23

THE WINNETKA POLICE STATION WAS an immaculate brick building shaded by pine trees, with peaked windows and a brick walkway that made it look more like a country club than a building for booking criminals. I half expected the holding cell to have marble floors and satin bedding, so I was a little disappointed when they escorted me into a small, dingy room with concrete floors, a dented metal bench lining the perimeter, and a high, drafty window that looked out on the gray March sky. A steel toilet stood low to the ground, surrounded by a four-foot partition and no door.

"Aren't I supposed to get a phone call?" I asked Emoji Cop as he slid the cell door shut.

"Well, somebody's been watching *Law and Order.*" He smirked. "I'm going to process your papers, and then yeah, I'll come and get you."

I stood in the middle of the empty cell and looked around. At least I was alone—I didn't much feel like making small talk. I sat down on the steel bench, feeling the coldness on the backs of my thighs below my uniform skirt.

The weirdest part about being in here, I thought, was just having to sit and think. They'd taken all my stuff, including my phone, and without that to distract me, or a laptop, or a TV, or other people, I became acutely aware of my aloneness. I had forgotten what it was like. It was strangely calming in a way. By now, I was sure word had spread far beyond the walls of ASH, to Saint Mike's, to Notre Dame Prep, to Lincoln, to Tino, who would think I was a dirty criminal, just like my dad. At least here, in this cell, I was safe from all that.

A little while later, the cop came back.

"You still want to make that phone call?"

At first, I figured I'd call my mom, because moms are the default setting whenever you're in a crisis. But she always left her phone at the nurse's station when she was working in the ER and this wasn't exactly something I could explain over voice mail. Besides, it might be nice to delay my death sentence just a little bit. After a minute's thought, I dialed Aunt Kathy's number instead.

She picked up on the second ring.

"Aunt Kathy?"

"Wendy? Is that you?"

"It's me."

"Oh God. Why is my phone telling me that you're calling from the Winnetka Police Station?"

"I got arrested."

"Jesus Christ! What the hell did you do?"

"I didn't *do* anything."

"Uh-huh. You and every other person who's ever been arrested!"

"Look, can you just come pick me up?"

"Jesus, Wendy. I'm in the middle of a shoot for *Food and Wine*. How does this work? Do I bail you out? How much money am I supposed to bring?"

"I don't know, Aunt Kathy." My voice broke. "Just come, please?"

"I'm leaving right this instant. Don't go anywhere." There was a pause. "That was a bad joke. Sorry." She hung up.

I sat in the cell, my bare legs covered in goose bumps, and waited. The way Kenzie had smiled at me as the cops had escorted me out of Sister Dorothy's office: of course she had planned it all. But the thing that bothered me more than anything else was that she'd been so *prepared*, so *calculating*, in the way she had humiliated me: as if she'd been saving it up all along. As if she'd been just waiting for me to cross her so that she could take me down so spectacularly. Why had she offered to shake my hand that morning? Now I knew: so that everything about our friendship, even the ending of it, was on her terms.

An hour passed, maybe two. It felt like forever. There was no clock and I didn't wear a watch and my phone had been confiscated. Something occurred to me that made me feel a thousand times worse: *This is my dad's whole life.* Morning, noon, and night. This.

At last, I heard, faintly, from down the hall, the hurried footsteps of my aunt Kathy.

They grew louder, accompanied by the squeak of Emoji Cop's boots, and finally she appeared at the door, dressed in a white smock and orange lipstick. I'd never been happier to see her in my life. The cop unlocked the cell, and I nearly jumped into her arms.

"You owe me, kid," she said, hugging me tightly, then put her arm around me and held me close as we followed Emoji Cop down the dull linoleum hallway and back to the main entrance.

"Go sit down while I figure this out," she said, pointing to a row of plastic chairs. There was nobody sitting in them, and I waited, straining to hear the hushed conversation at the front desk, but only getting snippets: *first offense . . . having a difficult year . . . apologize . . . stupid teenage prank.*

At last, Aunt Kathy signed a bunch of papers. The cops made a few phone calls. Finally, they handed her my cell phone and my backpack. She thanked them and walked over to me.

"Let's get out of here," she said.

"I'm only going to ask you one question about all of this, so don't lie," she said as we pulled out of the parking lot onto the main road. "Did you do it?"

"No."

She bit her lip and nodded, gripping the steering wheel a little tighter.

"Okay. I would have forgiven you if the answer was yes. But I'm still glad you said no."

"What happens now? Am I going to go to jail?"

"I talked to this Ned Munro person's mother. Eleanor. She was a pretty reasonable lady, actually. She said that if you apologized, she won't press charges."

"But I just told you I didn't do it! I'm not going to apologize for something I didn't even *do!*"

"Wendy, it's the easiest path to make this thing go away."

"Are you serious? That's some real great advice, Aunt Kathy. Give up your name and reputation just because it's *easier.*"

"Now, you listen to *me*, Wendy Boychuck." She whirled around so quick that she nearly veered into a snowbank that was jutting out into the cobblestone street. "I believe in standing up for the truth and all that. But if they press charges, you'll have to put that on your college applications. And I am *not* going to let you throw your future away over a couple of goddamn forks. Even if they're Abraham Lincoln's forks. Even if the forks belonged to Jesus Christ Himself. You're going to *make* something of your goddamn life, goddamn it!"

There was a heavy silence.

"Sorry for that extra 'goddamn it,'" she said finally. "It was probably unnecessary."

"Well, when am I supposed to make this apology?"

"No time like the present." Steering with one hand, she fished in her purse and pulled out a Post-it. "Read that address to me, would you?"

"Wait," I said. "We're going *now*?"

"Like ripping off a Band-Aid," she said.

Ned Munro's house, in the bright light of early spring, looked even more majestic than I remembered. Aunt Kathy pulled into the circular drive.

"I'll wait right here," she said. "They're expecting you."

My heart in my mouth, I walked the gallows of the driveway, hating Kenzie and Sapphire and Emily more and more with each step. I hadn't even had time to figure out what I was going to say. Which maybe was why Aunt Kathy had insisted I do this right away. No time to construct any bullshit. I rang the doorbell. *Like ripping off a Band-Aid.*

There was a pause, then the knob turned, and finally the door swung open and a goblin-thin lady about my mom's age opened the door. She had honey-blond highlights and wore a pale pink cardigan that matched her perfect nails.

"Um," I said. "Are you Mrs. Munro?"

"Yes." She looked at me, her lips pursed and flat.

"I'm Wendy. I'm here to, um, apologize to you about your Abraham Lincoln silverware."

"Not to me," she said. "To my son."

She walked away on a pair of pointy black flats, and while I waited, I contemplated myself in the huge mirror hanging on the wall next to the staircase. I saw myself as Mrs. Munro must have seen me, my long blond hair with its raggedy split ends, my smudgy black eyeliner, my uniform skirt that was three inches above the knee, the hem held up with a safety pin. Trash, she probably thought. White trash. It probably kept her awake at night, knowing that the daughter of Sergeant Stephen Boychuck had been in *her* house among *her* fine things while she'd been soaking up the rays in Cabo, blissfully unaware. And the little bitch had turned out to be a thief, but then, what would you expect, with that name?

She returned a few minutes later, with a reluctant Ned slinking behind her. He was blushing all the way from the tops of his ears to base of his throat.

"I'll leave you two alone," she said, and disappeared around the corner, most likely to eavesdrop from the cavernous dining room.

"Hi, Ned," I said.

"Hi."

"I—" I began. I watched my lips move in the mirror. "I'm sorry about your Abraham Lincoln silverware." He stared at the floor. I could see his Adam's apple moving up and down.

"I mean, just so you know, I wasn't the one who actually took it. I just need to say that. My friends, the girls I was with that night—they took it."

He looked up.

"But did you make them put it back?"

"Well, no—"

"Did you report it to anyone?"

"No."

His Adam's apple bobbed painfully. "It's like, I *get* that you didn't do anything wrong. But sometimes, doing nothing is almost, like, *worse*. You know?"

"I do," I said softly. "I'm sorry."

"I remember you from my party. You and your friends. You guys didn't even speak to me that night. Why would you go to a party at someone's house and then not even, like, talk to them?"

It was my turn to look at the floor. When I looked up, I saw that he was about to cry.

"The thing is," he said, "my dad already thinks I'm a loser. He probably would have been *happy* that I had a kegger while he was out of town. Give him a chance to relive his glory days, you know? Except then his stupid memorabilia got stolen. And then he knew that the kids who came over here, they were just using me."

There was a flurry of quick footsteps and Ned's mom, flushing pink beneath her jewelry and her makeup, stepped back into the hallway.

"Are we finished, Ned?" she said.

"Yeah," he said, wiping his eyes with the back of his fist. "We're finished."

"Good."

She opened the door for me, and I turned back once as I headed toward Aunt Kathy's car. Mrs. Munro looked small and frail in the doorframe of her gigantic house, and Ned stood just behind her, his jug ears silhouetted in the glow of the chandelier, and I really did feel like I'd committed a crime worth apologizing for: the crime of indifference, the crime of blindness, the crime of forgetting that you're not the only one who hurts.

24

WHEN I RETURNED TO SCHOOL the next day, I chose
not to eat lunch at my secret table beneath the arched windows of the empty library. Instead, I walked into the cafeteria,
found an empty table as far away from my former friends as
I could get, and sat down. Kenzie and Sapphire and Emily
didn't follow me this time, but I knew they were watching
me. Everybody was. I didn't even need my tattoo to tell me
that. At first, I was tempted to take out my books and pretend to do my homework. Or to read *A Farewell to Arms*. Or
to play around on my phone when the lunch monitors' backs
were turned. But I didn't do any of these things. I simply sat
down, unpacked my lunch, and ate it quietly. I didn't want to
hide behind anything anymore. I was a junior in high school,
and I had no friends. I had started over once at the beginning
of freshman year, and again when my dad went to jail and
we lost our house, and I was starting over again now, only
this time, I knew it was going to be okay. I had nothing to be
ashamed of, not anymore. Maybe it sounds sort of pathetic,

but that day, as I sat eating my lunch in complete solitude, I knew that when I looked back on it, I would remember this as one of my proudest moments of high school.

One morning, a couple days later, I was sitting in chapel, working on my physics homework and waiting for prayers to start when Alexis and Ola Kaminski walked past me on the way to their seats.

"Hey, Wendy," Ola said, stopping in front of me as Alexis continued down the aisle, "can I ask you a homework question?"

"Sure," I said. I was more flattered than surprised: Physics was one of my best subjects, but Ola was the smartest girl in school. Word was she'd already been offered an academic scholarship to Northwestern. She put her bag down, sat in the empty seat next to me, and pulled out her homework.

> *Desiree is riding the Giant Drop at Great America. If Desiree free falls for 2.60 seconds, what will be her final velocity and how far will she fall?*

I took out my calculator and began to explain the kinematic equation to Ola while she scribbled notes and furrowed her brow in concentration.

Once we had figured out the answer, Ola stood up.

"You know, Wendy," she said, "you could always come sit

with me and Alexis and Marlo at lunch. We usually just do homework anyway."

I could feel myself redden.

"Thanks," I said. "I'm all right, though. It's kind of nice to just, you know, relax in the middle of the day sometimes."

"Is it because of you and Alexis?" Ola leveled me with those clear, Northwestern-bound eyes.

"No," I said hurriedly. "It's just . . ."

"Because, you know, she's not like them. *We're* not like them. We forgive. We move on."

"Okay," I said. "I'll keep it in mind."

Prayers began then, but I didn't really listen.

All I could think about was the final part of the physics problem.

What will be her final velocity?
And how far will she fall?

The following Monday, I went down to lunch and sat at my usual table for one. I was just taking that first delicious fizzy sip of my Dr Pepper when I saw Ola get up from her table, pick up her tray, and walk across the cafeteria in my direction. Without so much as a hello, she put her tray down at my table, sat across from me, and bit into her spicy chicken patty as if it was totally normal to start eating lunch out of the blue with a girl you've barely spoken to in your entire life. A couple minutes later, Marlo joined us, chomping on an apple and carrying a heavily annotated copy of Kafka's *The Metamorphosis*. And finally, Alexis, my old beloved friend, stood up, crossed the cafeteria, and sat down right next to me. The three of them worked on their homework for the rest of the period and chatted among themselves as if nothing had changed. They didn't engage me in conversation, and I didn't try to talk to them.

For now it was enough that they were there.

25

IN APRIL, IT RAINED AND RAINED. Storms lashed the oak trees on ASH's front lawn and blurred the tall windows and cast our classrooms into a darkness that even the fluorescent lighting in the ceiling couldn't fully obliterate. Rumors swirled that our building had been sold—to an international school for the children of wealthy expats, to a charter network, to a museum for vintage surgical equipment. No one really knew the truth, except that ASH began to feel like it was slipping away from us, like it wasn't ours anymore. Our teachers were absent a lot, going on job interviews, and we got stuck watching lots of movies and doing busywork assigned by the ancient nuns Sister Dorothy had dragged out of retirement to be our substitute teachers. Some of the faculty, like Mr. Winters and Sister Mary Eunice, had been at ASH for thirty or forty years, and the pine cupboards built into the classroom walls were stuffed with decades of their students' projects and papers and debate trophies and old yearbooks. As the fourth quarter commenced, they began the slow, sad job of packing away their careers into big plastic crates. Outside was darkness and rain, and inside, our classrooms grew barer. We tried not to let it affect us, but every day I left school feeling sad, and the hallways were sort of hushed between passing periods, as if a death had happened. And in a way, it had.

One Sunday at the beginning of May, Alice asked me to work a double shift so she and Maria could leave early for a First Communion. It was a slow day; the endless rain kept everyone away. Closing time was eight o'clock, but by the time I'd prepped for the morning, pulled plastic wrap over the salads, and chopped the vegetables for the next day's rush, it was almost nine, and I'd been at work for nearly fourteen hours. I wasn't complaining, though. I was going to start college in sixteen months, and my savings account was practically empty.

I locked up, put on my dad's old police windbreaker—the only waterproof jacket I could find in our apartment—pulled the hood around my face, and stepped out into the rain. Red Rocket was in the shop, but despite the miserable weather, I didn't really mind walking home. The rain was cold, but the air was warm and misty, and it smelled like mud and wet grass. Lilies of the valley had begun to bloom in people's gardens, the tiny white petals almost glowing on the dark lawns. Spring, at last, had arrived.

I was about halfway home when the rain darkened into a deluge, a real thunderstorm. Jagged flashes of lightning seamed across the sky, followed by the echoing boom of close-by thunder.

I remembered when I was a kid, my dad told me that if you counted the seconds between the flash of lightning and the roar of the thunder, that would tell you how many miles away the lightning was striking. Out of habit, I still counted every time there was a thunderstorm, and I still felt this weird excitement when the numbers grew closer and closer, especially when I was watching a storm from the safety of my apartment building. Now, a brightness forked across the sky, and I began to count. *One . . . two . . . three . . . four . . . CRASH!* Four miles away. I shivered and walked quicker, passing all the familiar landmarks of our neighborhood: the empty storefront where the Lebanese men's club gathered to sit at card tables smoking and watching soccer, Stan's Pizza with its giant oven and its gruff Sicilian owner standing watch at the window in his flour-dusted apron, the floodlit parking lot of the 7-Eleven, the sprawling stone steps and heavy wooden doors of Queen of Heaven parish church, and Dairy Hut, its windows nailed over with plywood until its Memorial Day grand opening.

My windbreaker was just a sodden plastic bag at this point, and water was in my shoes. Another flash of lightning and I began to count: *One . . . two . . . three—CRASH!* It was getting closer. I broke into a run, sidestepping the buses that lurched in and out of the Jefferson Park terminal, belching clouds of noxious smoke.

The sky lit up. *One . . . two . . . CRASH!* Shaking hard now, I ducked for shelter in the strip mall with the big green awning. It had a nail salon called NAILS, a dry cleaner called CLEANERS, a liquor store called LIQUOR, and a gyros joint with no name but which everybody called Niko's, after the owner. Clutching my windbreaker around my face and breathing hard, I huddled under the awning while the rain fell in curtains over the mostly empty parking lot. I wasn't scared. I felt giddy, exhilarated, so wonderfully small and unimportant in this big, strange, crashing world.

The lightning began to grow a little fainter. I counted four seconds between thunder bursts, then five, then six. At seven, I stepped back out into the downpour and continued down the street that runs along the tracks toward my apartment. The storm had cleared the streets and nobody was around, but when I got within a few blocks of home, I saw a girl hurrying toward me, crouched beneath a wind-battered umbrella. As she got closer, I recognized the shapeless coat, the limp brown hair, the high, white forehead, and the giant, ever-present headphones. When we met in the middle of the sidewalk, we both stopped.

She pulled her headphones around her neck. The rain drummed on her umbrella.

"Hey, Alexis," I said.

"Hey, Wendy."

"What are you doing out here?"

"Coming home from a violin lesson," she said. "You?"

"Coming home from work."

"Oh. You don't have an umbrella?"

I held out my sodden arms to the sky.

"What's the point? You're not much drier than I am."

"Fair enough," she laughed, looking down at her soaked jeans.

"So, you got a new violin?" I nodded at the leather case under her arm.

"Yeah. The umbrella is more to keep this dry than me."

"That's good. You can start practicing for Juilliard now."

"Yeah." She looked at me for a long moment. "Hey, Wendy?"

"Yeah?"

"I know it was you."

My cheeks went hot, and I was grateful for the darkness.

"What do you mean?"

"The money. For my violin," she said. "My mom saw you walking away from our house the day you put it in the mail slot."

I just stood there. I wanted to say something, but my tongue felt heavy and words had flown away. I really hadn't wanted Alexis to know it was me. I thought she would see right through the seeming generosity of the gesture, see me for the coward I was, someone who would rather give away her life's savings than stand up to Kenzie.

"It's nothing," I said.

"It's not nothing." She shook her head. "It's everything." And she reached out across the rain and hugged me. I'd totally forgotten that about Alexis: she gave the best hugs.

"I'll see you in school, okay?"

"Okay."

She slipped her headphones back over her ears, gave me a little wave, and continued on her way.

I ran toward home along the tracks, soaked to my skin but with a huge smile plastered across my face. If anyone were to pass me, I'm sure they'd think I'd lost my mind. When I got as far as the two white crosses at the site of Tiffany and Sandy's deadly crash, I stopped for a moment. I knelt down in the mud to fix the drooping display of wilting carnations. These two girls had been my aunt Kathy's best friends. It was the first time I imagined them as real people and not just ghostly legends in the lore of my neighborhood—girls with moms and dads and sisters and friends, messy bedrooms and homework, crushes and dreams and fears. I remembered that one night back in September, when Darry had said that if you whisper their names when there's a full moon, the streetlights would burn out. I looked up at the sky and saw that the moon, stationary and glowing behind the shifting rainclouds, was perfectly full, as round and shimmering as a pearl. *Tiffany*, I whispered. *Sandy.*

Nothing happened, of course. The streetlight beaming down on the crosses continued its monotonous, insect-like buzzing. I turned away to head home, a little disappointed and a little relieved that Darry's superstition had turned out to be as untrue as every other superstition I'd ever heard, when, just behind me, I heard a small noise, like a soft sigh. When I turned back around, the streetlight flickered for a frantic moment, and then with a *pfft*, burned out into darkness. All of the lights up and down the street followed suit, block after block, until the entire neighborhood as far as I could see had gone black.

I ran. I splashed through puddles and streaked past houses where, in the windows, I could see the wobbly strobe of flashlights as people fumbled around for their matches and candles. When I got home, I found my mom sitting at the kitchen table in the faint glow of her Our Lady of Lourdes holy candles, talking on the phone to Aunt Colleen.

"Goddamn electric company," she was complaining. "Third goddamn power outage this year. Doesn't anyone care that this is the season finale of *Teen Mom 2*? I need to see if Leah gets out of rehab!"

I slipped off my windbreaker, kicked off my wet shoes, and breathed, trying to control my seizing, pounding heart.

"I don't know!" she was yelling now. "What do I look like, an electrician? Probably the wind from this goddamn storm must have snapped something. Maybe if someone called the goddamn—" There was a buzzing throughout the apartment, and the lights came on again.

"You back on?" She peered out the window at the storm. "Yeah, yeah. I'll talk to you tomorrow."

After I had showered and put ointment on my still-scabbing tattoo, I got into bed and picked up *A Farewell to Arms*. While the thunder boomed outside and the trees thrashed in the wind, I stayed up late into the night, knowing, but not caring, that I would be exhausted in the morning. Great books are like great parties: you don't care about how you'll pay for it the next day, just so long as it doesn't end.

I finally put the book down at the part where Catherine and Lieutenant Henry flee from Stresa in the dead of night and row a boat all the way to Switzerland. Would I have had the courage to do such a thing? *Of course you wouldn't*, I told myself. Maybe it wasn't entirely my fault, though. Back in World War I Europe, people had all sorts of chances to show their courage. But this was Chicago in the twenty-first century. Here, you didn't need courage to survive. You just needed to be tough, which wasn't the same thing.

26

IN THE MORNING, AT THE RISK of being late for chapel, I stopped at Dunkin' Donuts for a large hot chocolate with extra whipped cream and a chocolate cake donut with red, white, and blue sprinkles. We had just over one month of school left. One more month at Academy of the Sacred Heart. We still didn't know what was going to happen to the building, but we'd all noticed that the nuns had been holding closed-door meetings with various groups of business-looking people in black pinstripe suits. We didn't bother asking our teachers who they were because we knew they would never tell us. I'd already received my schedule from Lincoln High School. Instead of plain old English IV, I had been placed in AP Language and Composition—a class ASH didn't even offer, a class that might give me college credit and save me money in college tuition, a class that Tino— I couldn't help myself from hoping—might sign up for, too. In place of Topics in Catholic Social Justice, I had signed up for Introduction to Ceramics and Wheel Throwing, which made me feel both excited and sad at the same time.

Still, I was feeling pretty good. My mom had let me borrow her car, and compared to Red Rocket, her Toyota Camry was like driving to school in a luxury vehicle. Alexis didn't hate me anymore. My tattoo was healing. I was free of Kenzie and Sapphire and Emily. And Catherine Barkley and Lieutenant Henry had escaped to Switzerland in a rowboat. I was sitting in a pink plastic booth, waiting for my hot chocolate to brew and watching the sleepy-looking construction workers and teachers who stood in line for their early morning coffee when my phone rang.

"Wendy?"

Over the course of a person's lifetime, you hear your mother say your name thousands, maybe millions of times. And each time there is a tone—of love, annoyance, impatience, affection, disappointment. But there's a special tone that all mothers reserve for the worst things, and even though, if you're lucky, she only has to use it once or twice, you still know it immediately when you hear it. Up until that phone call at the Dunkin' Donuts, I'd only heard it once before: when my mom sat down at the kitchen table with Stevie Junior and me to tell us that our dad's arrest hadn't been a mistake. She didn't even use it when my grandma died, because my grandma had had cancer for a long time and we'd been expecting it.

"Wendy," my mother said again. There was a rustling on the other end of the phone, as if she was wiping her nose. "There's been an accident."

I couldn't say anything. I was struck dumb by that tone. I waited.

"At the train crossing."

She told me, then, as I sat in a booth at the Dunkin' Donuts, waiting for my hot chocolate and my donut with patriotic sprinkles, about the thunderstorm. About how it had knocked out the city power grid, so that last night, when Alexis was walking home from her violin lesson, there was no red flash of warning lights and no guard rail going down. There was only the urgent, hysterical clang of the 9:45 freight train bound for Kettleman City, California, washed out by the soaring beauty of Jean Sibelius's Violin Concerto in D minor blasting out of her headphones. About how this train, weighted with its thousands of tons of coal, had struck her clean out of her jacket and shoes and thrown her into a nearby ditch of scrub grass scattered with beer bottles and dotted with mud puddles. About how her body had remained in that ditch for over an hour, eyes open and collecting rain, oblivious to the wind and the cold and the airplanes that descended one by one onto the runways of O'Hare Airport. About her violin case, which the police found lying in the middle of Avondale Avenue a few feet from her body. About how, eventually, the head beam of another approaching train illuminated her and the driver of a car waiting at the crossing saw the slash of her dark hair in the white lights, saw her leg that was turned at that horrible angle, an angle that made him tell his son to wait in the car because he knew that whatever was down there in that ditch was something that he didn't want his child to see.

Accidents. Coincidences. Miracles. Tragedies. Signs. The train lights had been down, I would later learn, for three minutes and twenty-two seconds—a length of time shorter than a high school passing period.

It's nothing. It's everything.

I don't remember what I said to my mom before I hung up the phone. The pink and brown walls in the Dunkin' Donuts blurred together and I felt like I was walking through a tunnel that just got narrower and darker the farther you walked in it and the Dunkin' Donuts lady had to yell at me three times before I heard her and went over to the counter to collect the breakfast I could no longer eat.

I stepped out into the drizzle, which continued to fall like a hangover from the previous night's storm, and walked across the parking lot. I climbed into my mom's car, turned on the ignition, and just sat there, not exactly crying, but breathing in this uneven, gasping way.

I'd gotten home last night just before the credits of *Teen Mom 2*, which ended at 10:00.

Alexis had been killed by the 9:45 freight train.

I was the last person to see Alexis alive.

Or was I? After all, I didn't know the exact time I had run into her on the sidewalk. Probably 9:30 or 9:35. But what if it was 9:46? Or 9:50? Or 9:55? What had Aunt Kathy once said? That you can believe in God and ghosts at the same time? Alexis had been walking alone down that dark street, and when we had stopped in the middle of the sidewalk to talk, there was nobody else around. The cold spots—I'd shivered—the cold spots. Maybe, when she'd looked at me with those wide, true brown eyes of hers and said, *I know it was you*, maybe the train had already struck and she was now crossing to the other side, her waving hand a final sign of farewell before she vanished forever into the company of all the rest of our invisible saints.

PART THREE

WHALE WATCHING

27

I DON'T EVEN WANT TO TALK ABOUT Alexis's wake.

I don't want to talk about her little sister, slumped on a chair in the back of the funeral home, twisting Alexis's violin bow between her shuddering hands, twelve years old and three days into her new life as an only child.

I don't want to talk about her dad, who stood in the receiving line, dutifully shaking hand after hand, but whose legs were trembling so hard it was like he was willing himself not to run out the door and keep running forever.

I don't want to talk about her mom, the wet circle her tears left on my shoulder after she hugged me; how she thanked me for the violin money; how even in her grief she was kind enough to pretend that I had *always* been good to her daughter, that the past three years I'd abandoned her had never happened.

I don't want to talk about the line that snaked out the door of the funeral home into the parking lot, and all the kids from elementary school who were there, kids who'd gone nine years sitting alongside Alexis in class without ever exchanging a word with her and who now would never get the chance.

I don't want to talk about the twenty retired Sacred Heart nuns, the ones who made the long journey by Greyhound bus all the way from the mother house in Kentucky, some with walkers, some in wheelchairs, to pray over a girl they'd never met simply because she was an ASH girl, and one of their own.

I don't want to talk about how beautiful a day it was when they buried her, the sunshine so tastelessly bright, the flowers rudely blooming, the mockery of the chirping birds. Or the park we passed on the way to the cemetery, where mothers pushed their young children on swings and the children laughed, throwing their heads back and drinking in the sun. How dare they laugh? Didn't they know what had happened? Didn't they care?

And I don't want to talk about how much it all hurt, because even an honors English girl like me doesn't have the language.

A couple days after the funeral, I came home from school to find my mom sitting at the kitchen table with her hands around a mug of coffee.

"Honey?" she said. "Can we talk?"

I sat down.

"It's been a hard week for you," she said, putting a

mug-warmed hand on top of mine. "A hard couple years."

"It is what it is." In the days since I'd heard the awful news, stupid little clichés like these—the enemy of journalism, Ms. Lee had taught us—were all I could think of to say. It was like, the darker and wilder my thoughts grew, the emptier my spoken words became.

"I was thinking," my mom continued. "I don't want to make anything harder for you than it already is. But, well, did you know Dad's birthday is next Wednesday? He's going to be forty-five."

"I know."

"I'm going to go to Nebraska for a few days. It's a long drive. I could use some company. And it's been almost three years now since you've seen him. He misses you like crazy, Wendy. No matter what he did, he *is* still your dad."

"As far as I'm concerned," I said, echoing the words of the email I had sent him back in December, "I don't have a father."

My mom sat back in her chair. The color rose in her cheeks as if she'd been slapped.

"He will *always* be your father, like it or not," she said sharply. "That's what a family *is*."

"Can't I just stay with Aunt Kathy while you're gone? Or Aunt Col?"

My mom shook her head. "You know Aunt Kathy—she and Simon are swanning off to Palm Springs tomorrow for the rest of the week. And Aunt Col is working overnights.

And before you even ask, I am *not* letting you stay home by yourself. I don't want you to be alone after all that's happened."

I picked at a piece of egg that was crusted onto the tablecloth from breakfast.

"You'll get to miss a couple days of school," my mom said hopefully. "Might be good for you just to get away for a while, try to process everything that's happened?"

I knew that she was right at least about that—I really could use a few days to get my head right. Someone had already placed a little white cross near the tracks at the place where Alexis had been killed. She was really gone, and soon enough, the people who had actually known her would grow older and move out of the neighborhood, and she would become just like Sandy DiSanto or Tiffany Maldonado, a ghost, a superstition, a cautionary tale instead of a real human being whose life had ended and who I had loved. Slumber parties would begin to buzz with new Alexis-related superstitions: If you listened to classical music during a rainstorm, little girls huddled beneath their sleeping bags would whisper, she would appear to you. Bored teenagers would dare one another to stand on the tracks and call her name. Parents would use her as a warning when their kids stepped out the door with their headphones stuffed over their ears. I couldn't stand it. I couldn't stand the thought of any of it.

"Honey?" my mom said gently. "What do you think?"

"If I say yes," I said finally, my eyes trained on the smear of egg, "I reserve the right not to talk to him or let him hug me."

"Fair enough." She swallowed the last of her coffee and stood up. "Does this anti-hugging policy also apply to your mother?"

"You're different."

Her arms around me were like putting a blanket over a fire—they smothered away the hot pain, at least for a little while.

28

THE SUMMER BEFORE MY DAD WAS arrested, we took a family vacation to the West Coast, driving up the 101 from Monterrey to Crescent City, California. I spent the whole week staring out the window of the rental car at craggy cliffs, dense forests, and the glinting sapphire ocean. It was my first time out of the Midwest and I felt like a foreigner in my own country, my head spinning with all this new, exotic beauty.

Of all the little hotels and motels we stayed at along the way, my favorite was a little inn on the Yurok Reservation in Klamath, California. One morning, while mom and Stevie Junior slept in, me and my dad went whale watching along the promenade behind our hotel. It was misty that morning, and the sky smelled like the sea. They didn't make mornings like this in Chicago. Together we leaned over the fence at the top of the cliff, our faces damp with mist, and suddenly my dad cried out, pointing to a black speck out on the water, "I see one! I see one!" As I craned my neck to look, a member of the Yurok tribe who was fishing with his kid nearby laughed.

"That's just a big old rock!" he said, and handed us his binoculars.

"Shit, man! I could've *sworn* that was a whale!" Dad squinted through the binoculars at the waves that crashed against a black boulder.

The man told us that if we heard dogs howling at night it was probably because a bear or some other large mammal was lurking around, and Dad told him about the time when a cougar—"a fucking *mountain lion*—thing weighed almost two hundred pounds!"—wandered down into the city from somewhere in Northern Wisconsin and ended up strolling down the middle of Hoyne Avenue in the twenty-sixth district "like it owned the place," and how the cops hadn't known what to do with it, "so we just shot the fuckin' thing. Gangbangers, we can handle. Drug dealers, child molesters, murderers—no problem. But a cougar?" He had laughed. "We shot first and asked questions later."

The Yurok man shook his head.

"No wonder you can't tell the difference between a whale and a rock," he said, and turned back to the water.

I thought about the Yurok man's words now as my mom and I drove west through the endless beige and cloudless blue of the American prairie. The drive from Chicago to Clay County, Nebraska, takes over nine hours, eleven when my mother and her pea-sized bladder are at the wheel. We'd left at sunrise on a cool morning near the end of May and had barely merged onto I-88 before I fell back asleep. I awoke again in the full light of the day when we stopped for gas in a little farm town near the Iowa border. My mom went inside to pee, and as I got out of the car to stretch, looking over the flat plains rising with new corn, what struck me as weird, as totally unbelievable, was not that my father was spending the next decade or two of his life in prison but that he lived in Clay County, Nebraska. After all, Steve Boychuck *was* Chicago: corrupt, brash, proud, thick-wristed and dark-mustached, full of quick anger and fierce love in equal measure. How could he survive out here in this quiet, polite, decent stretch of America? How could he even make sense?

It was dark by the time we arrived in Clay County, and the sky above the Roadside Inn parking lot was scattered with prairie stars. We checked in, dragged our bags up the metal staircase to our room on the second floor, and walked to the Cracker Barrel for dinner, our jackets whipping in the wind. We were close enough to the highway that we could hear the never-ending whoosh of cars driving back and forth across America. I ordered a grilled cheese; my mom got the meatloaf, but neither of us ate much. When we got back to the hotel, we changed into our pajamas, climbed into our side-by-side beds, and my mom clicked off the light on the nightstand.

"Good night, honey," she murmured.

"Good night, Mom."

"Tomorrow is going to be just fine, okay? It's going to be good."

"Okay."

I lay there for a long time, blinking up into the darkness, pretending to sleep and knowing, by the tense stillness emanating from my mom's bed just a few feet away that she was doing the same thing. Eventually, though, I must have fallen asleep, lulled by the soft moaning of the highway and the wind outside the window.

In the morning, I got dressed in the outfit I'd picked out as appropriate visiting-my-dad-in-jail attire: a plain black blouse, jeans, and a pair of black flats. I wanted him to see that I'd grown up—no pink, no florals, no glitter—but I didn't want to wear anything too stylish or memorable—nothing that would reveal very much about the person I had become. After I finished getting ready, I lounged on the bed, flipping through the TV channels, while my mom took forever in the bathroom. When she finally emerged, reeking of the jasmine perfume that she barely ever wore anymore, I saw that there was a visiting-my-husband-in-jail outfit, too, and it consisted of tight pants, a bright red top with lipstick to match, and curled, teased hair.

"Are we going to a prison or a salsa dancing class?" I asked, looking her over skeptically.

"I try to dress happy when I visit Daddy," she snapped,

her carefully done-up face collapsing into a pile of hurt. "I think it helps."

The first thing I learned about prison visits is that everything happens at least an hour after they say it's going to happen. If you make your visiting appointment for ten a.m., for example, you probably won't get through security until at least eleven. It was late morning before we got our visitors' passes, and my mom's curled hair was already starting to wilt. We had to lock up our purses in a metal cubby, then get patted down, sent through a metal detector, and branded with an invisible stamp on the underside of our wrists. Finally, we were escorted into a green-painted cinder-block room with shiny linoleum floors and a lingering odor of disinfectant and bad breath. We settled down at a table with our approved belongings in front of us: a clear plastic bag of quarters for the vending machines, our IDs, and a harmonica, which the CO had allowed my mom to bring in as Dad's birthday present only after holding it in the air and shaking it, as if he expected a snowfall of contraband drugs to sift out of the chamber. As we waited quietly for my dad to come out, I passed the time by listening to the nervous chatter of the other inmates' families and reading the signs posted all over the walls that said things like "KEEP HANDS IN PLAIN VIEW AT ALL TIMES" and "ALL VISITORS MUST REMAIN SEATED" and my personal favorite, "FEMALE VISITORS MUST WEAR BRA AND PANTIES."

We sat there for about half an hour before Dad finally appeared in the doorway. He was freshly showered—his hair was still damp—and when he stepped toward us, I could smell the harsh detergent of prison soap.

"Wendy," he said, and the sound of his voice saying my name summoned tears to my eyes. I was wiping them away when he hugged me, which is why I wasn't able to properly stop him, though it was more of a letting-him-hug-me situation than a mutual hug, and I hoped he could tell the difference.

"You look great, honey," Mom said brightly, wrapping him in a hug brief enough not to violate prison policy. This was a chipper, well-meaning lie. He did not look great. His arms and shoulders were so bulked up with muscle they strained at the faded orange of his prison shirt, but his face was like one of my English papers after Ms. Lee finished marking it up—scribbles of purple veins across his cheeks, brackets springing out around his gray eyes, deep wrinkles of parentheses enclosing his mouth. How was it possible for him to have puffed up his muscles to the size of a bodybuilder's, and yet still seem smaller and much, much older? And his hair: Could it really have turned gray like that in a couple years' time? Could it really have receded that much, revealing a new strip of shiny skin across the crown of his head?

"I'm so sorry about Alexis, Wendy," Dad began. "I really am. What a goddamn thing, huh?"

"It is what it is," I said. I wouldn't look at him.

"She was always a real nice girl."

"May she rest in peace," my mom nodded, making a quick sign of the cross.

"Now, see, Bernie," he said, "I've always had an issue with that phrase: 'Rest in peace.'"

"What are you talking about?" she demanded. "How could anyone have a problem with 'rest in peace'?" I had to admit it: It was sort of nice to hear the two of them bickering. It reminded me of the before, when our lives were normal.

"Well, it's fine if someone old dies. Like your mother. Or my mother. They both suffered from cancer for years. They *had* no peace. They were both almost eighty. But when a young person like Alexis dies? Think about it, Bernie. What sixteen-year-old ever wanted *rest*? Or *peace*, for that matter? Sixteen-year-olds want to grab the world by the balls. They want to dance in the goddamn rain. That's what *they* want. Do you know what I'm saying, Wendy?"

I bit my lip and concentrated on the patterns in the Formica table. He was right, of course, though I would never give him the satisfaction of agreeing. Alexis had wanted to make her violin sing for the Vienna Philharmonic. She had wanted to see *Carmen* at the Royal Opera House in London. She had not wanted eternal rest. She had wanted Juilliard and New York and life and life and life.

"I guess I see your point." Mom pushed the harmonica toward him. "This is for you. Happy birthday, Steve."

Dad picked up the harmonica and stared at it, wide-eyed,

like Mom had just brought him the crown jewels of England or something.

"You always said you wanted to learn," she said shyly. "And now you have the time."

"There's a guy I know in here used to play in a blues band," he said, turning the instrument over in the palm of his hand. The meaty skin just under his fingers was white with calluses from all the weightlifting he'd been doing. "I wonder if he can teach me 'Thunder Road.'" He held the harmonica to his lips, puffed out his cheeks, and blew into it, emitting an off-key bleat like a defective party horn.

"Inmate!" boomed a guard, who in two strides made it across the visiting room and hovered at our table, the brown fabric of his crotch level with our eyes.

Dad put down the harmonica and lifted his hands.

"Sorry, pal."

The guard sauntered back to his position against the wall.

"Jagoff," he muttered. He grinned at us, revealing his teeth, which were still strong and straight and white. "They don't let you have much fun in here, these guys."

I got up and bought us some treats from the vending machine: Oreos, Fritos, Starburst, and a couple cans of Dr Pepper. Dad tore open the Oreos and stuffed one in his mouth.

"I'm pretending that I'm sitting in our kitchen," he said, spewing little bits of black cookie dust into the air, "and that this is your mother's homemade Christmas stuffing."

We don't have that kitchen anymore, I thought. *We lost it because of you.* But I didn't say anything. I just stared out the barred windows at the highway and the flat blue sky. Maybe, *maybe*, if I ever visited him again, I'd actually talk to him. But for now, my physical presence was all I was willing to give. If I talked, he might think I'd forgiven him. So I just sat there and pretended I wasn't even listening while he and my mom chattered away about safe topics—registering me for my senior year at Lincoln, my mom's job at the hospital, Stevie Junior's shore leave in Cambodia—as if it really was just another family dinner at our kitchen table. Eventually, when they'd run out of things to say to each other, and an awkward silence had settled around the little table, Dad broke out the standard clueless-parent question.

"So Wendy," he said, smiling at me, "how's school?"

I shrugged, hunching my shoulders to pick at a shred of dried skin on my thumbnail.

"Grades good?"

I shrugged again.

"Wendy's in all honors classes this year," my mom piped in, her voice as full of fake sugar as the perfume she'd doused herself with earlier that morning. "She even signed up for a couple AP classes at Lincoln next year!"

"AP, huh?" my dad boomed proudly. "Those are those college classes, aren't they?"

"College?" I looked up, meeting his eyes for the first time since we'd arrived.

"Yeah—they give you credits, don't they? I think I remember Stevie taking one of those at Saint Mike's."

"You think I'm still going to college?" My voice was hard, flinty—I almost didn't recognize it as mine.

"Well, sure, hon," my dad said, blinking. "I've always dreamed that for you."

"With what *money*? The money's all gone now. We used it on you. On this." I waved a disgusted hand at our surroundings, at the cinder-block walls and prowling guards and vending machines.

My dad looked down at his big hands, stretched them so the knuckles cracked hollowly.

"You have every right to be pissed off as hell," he said. "I won't sit here and say you don't."

I caught the hangnail between my teeth and yanked, tasting the blood as it welled. I stared past him, out the window at the prairie sun. He looked at me for a moment longer, his gaze a painful pressure, until my mom, desperate to keep the peace, drew him back into conversation with some petty news about the neighborhood. Soon enough, though, one of the guards announced a five-minute warning, and as I started to get up, relieved that our visit was almost over, my dad leaned down to pull a rolled-up piece of paper from his pant leg.

"Wendy, I don't know if you'll even want this, but I brought a present for you just in case," he said, pushing the paper across the Formica table. I looked down, considering whether I should open it. This wasn't like all the cards he mailed that I just threw away. He was here, sitting across from me, and I could feel his eyes, the tense coil of his muscles, wanting and needing me to accept his gift. I picked it up.

"There's this art class they give once a week," he said quickly as I began to unroll the paper. "I know it's probably a crap version of the original, but, you know, I'm still learning. How to work with the watercolors and whatnot."

In the painting I held before me, a yellow-haired girl sat on the back of a pontoon boat, her face raised to the sun, one leg folded beneath her and the other stretched out, the toes reaching for the water. I only knew that the girl was me because I was familiar with the original photograph, taken up in Crooked Lake when I was ten or eleven. It used to hang in a frame in our basement TV room. "Sad thing is," he continued, "I did about twenty of these, and this was the best of the bunch." His voice was doubting, humble, almost shy, and I had to look up to make sure it was really my dad who was speaking.

As far as I knew, Sergeant Stephen Boychuck had never been an artistic man, and his prison painting class had not brought out any secret talents. If he had submitted this painting in Sister Attracta's Art I class, he probably would have gotten a C or a C-. My face, which was blurry and marked with water spots, was composed of generic, amateur features that could have belonged to anyone. The bathing suit was painted in sloppy strokes of red and green stripes, the legs disproportionately long. The sun was a lopsided ball in the center of the sky above me, and the waves of the lake were painted in sharp ninety-degree angles, like teeth. There were spots here and there of heavy paint, where he'd tried to cover up his mistakes.

The thing was, though, if the painting had been beautiful, I might not ever have been able to forgive him. But the way that he was looking at me now, anxious and full of hope, while I examined the thick paper and tried to come up with something nice to say . . . I guess I had what Sister Dorothy might call a moment of grace. It made me think about how maybe the art class had become something he looked forward to all week—the bright spot in the endless march of mealtimes and showers and roll call and rec time in the concrete square that stood under the harsh glow of the treeless Nebraska sun. What was it like, a prison art class? I pictured a bunch of thugs with easels, sitting in a cinder-block room like this one, taught by some do-gooder art teacher with brassy hair and breezy tunics, the kind of lady Dad would rip on mercilessly in his real life, his Chicago life. She would stroll around the easels with her hands behind her back, commenting, correcting, and when she reached my dad, she would ask him what he was painting and he would tell her it was his daughter, basking in the sun on the family pontoon up in Crooked Lake, Wisconsin.

"I'm painting my old life," he would say. Then he would return to his composition, his thick fingers around the paintbrush, clumsily, lovingly, trying to bring the old life back.

"It's really good," I lied. "Thanks, Dad."

"Wendy," he said, his voice catching, "I'm sorry for everything I put you through. I'm sorry for what I did to those people. I'm just—I'm so sorry."

Apology was as foreign to him as Nebraska, as clumsy on his lips as a paintbrush in his hands. Even though I knew he meant what he said, he still stumbled over his words.

A buzzer sounded then, and the visiting hour was over. When he reached across the table and tried to hug me, I meant to push him away, to show him that he deserved the collective hatred of our city, that the widening ripples of pain he'd inflicted could never be undone. But instead, I was struck by a feeling that was both fierce and uncomplicated. He was my dad, and I loved him. That was all. Even if he deserved my hatred, I was still going to love him anyway.

I hugged him back, burying my head in his thick, familiar chest, and my mom reached over and sandwiched me between them, and we didn't let go of one another until the guard yelled "That's enough, inmate!"—which was probably for the best because if the guard hadn't stepped in, we'd probably still be there now, clinging to one another while the skies over Nebraska went dark. I understood now that forgiveness was like letting go of a deep, long-held breath, or like stepping out into the city on the coldest day of the year. It didn't make you feel better. It just made you feel alive.

29

I RETURNED TO SCHOOL ON A STUNNING morning that stirred the curtains of my open window with warm, breezy light and woke me slowly and peacefully, the way humans were meant to wake up, before school bells and alarm clocks came in and destroyed everything. I got up, stretched, and flicked open the curtains. It was so nice out that even the parking lot behind our complex looked kind of pretty, and as I ran my fingers along the scaly scars of Our Lady of Lourdes along my shoulder, I wondered if Alexis's soul or spirit or whatever you wanted to call it was enjoying this day somehow, too. But these kinds of thoughts were too heavy for six thirty a.m. I closed the curtains again and got ready for school.

When I stepped through the scrolling iron gates of Academy of the Sacred Heart, I saw Ola and Marlo siting underneath the giant beech tree on the front lawn and went and joined them. They had their books out in front of them, but they weren't studying. They were just enjoying the breeze, the mix of sun and shade, the way you always do after a long winter, but I knew that they were thinking about Alexis, too. I'd often seen the three of them sitting beneath the tree at the beginning of the school year and well into the fall, when the leaves were edged in red, and even after that, when they began to fall and dry into dust on the grass.

As I sat, I watched Kenzie and Emily and Sapphire walk together into school. When I saw them, I didn't feel any anger. All that pettiness was gone now, after Alexis. We'd all agreed, our whole school, to be kinder to one another. It was something unspoken, but palpable. Kenzie gave me a nod, but her eyes were shaded by a large pair of cat-eye sunglasses. She was the only girl in our class who hadn't gone to Alexis's wake or funeral. People whispered about how awful this was, that even in death, she couldn't bring herself to be nice to Alexis. But I didn't read it that way. I thought Kenzie was doing it as a sign of respect. How could she take part in the ritual of saying good-bye when the only times she'd acknowledged Alexis were to torment her? You could say a lot of things about Kenzie. But you could never say that she was a hypocrite.

The Saints Corridor is especially beautiful on sunny mornings like this one, when the light from the main entrance filters down the hall, glinting off the millions of swirls of paint color all the way down to the auditorium, so you feel like you're walking down the cylinder of a kaleidoscope.

But when Ola, Marlo, and I had gathered up our stuff and walked into school for chapel that morning, the first thing I noticed when we turned past the main doors to head to our lockers was the strange way the quality of light had changed. There was no more kaleidoscope: Everything was white and one-dimensional, and it took me a moment to figure out why. I stood there, sort of perplexed, uncomprehending, until the movement of a man at the other end of the empty hallway snapped me back into reality. I couldn't see his features, only his profile against the light, and the rhythmic movement of his paintbrush.

"Oh my God," I whispered. "What have they done?"

"Didn't you hear?" Marlo's voice was bright—the over-achiever in her loved being the first to share news. "They sold the building to a developer. They're converting it into luxury condos. 'Vintage elegance in the heart of the city.' Can you believe it? That there are going to be people who pay big money to actually *live* at Academy of the Sacred Heart?"

"Well, those are some pretty dumb people," Ola laughed. "Considering that it's not vintage, it's not elegant, and it's not in the heart of the city."

They continued to joke back and forth, but I was no longer listening. I looked to my left, where Saint Rita, Patron Saint of Impossible Causes, had been gazing down at us for three long years. She was gone. I whirled to my right. Saint Rose of Lima: gone. Saint Catherine of Alexandria's red robes, faded from all the hands that had touched them for good luck before semester exams: gone. Saint Teresa of Avila, Saint Catherine of Siena, and Our Lady of Knock; Saint Appolonia, Saint Agatha, and Saint Anne: all gone, all replaced with a clean coating of white. The painting crews must have arrived the night before, while we were all sitting in our bedrooms obliviously doing our homework, and just like that, over a century of stories and superstitions and saints had all been washed away.

"It seems kind of heartless to do this now," I heard Ola say, grazing her fingers along the wall of still-damp white. "Couldn't they have at least waited until we were gone?"

She looked at me, but I didn't answer. I had already started to walk toward the man and his paint roller at the far end of the hallway, slowly at first, and then faster.

"Stop." The word bubbled up from a place deep inside of me, and I broke into a run. "*Stop!*" And then I was on top of him, pouncing, an animal, knocking the paint roller right out of his hand so that it clattered on the ground and left a white smear across the linoleum floor. I began to hit him with my open hands, wildly, limply, until I tripped on his drop cloth, pulling him to the ground and feeling a gush of cold wetness as a can of white paint spilled all down my school uniform. The painter struggled to his feet, cursing, but my rage had deserted me as quickly as it had come. All I could do now was lie on the floor in a widening pool of paint, curled into a ball and sobbing.

"Wendy! Wendy!" Ola's voice was somewhere above me.

"Wendy, what's *wrong*?"

"Should we get a teacher?"

"Should we call your mom?"

I heard them discussing what to do with me, but it was too late. It didn't matter. Before I had managed to knock him over, the painter had almost finished smothering Our Lady of Lourdes in white paint. Her sad blue eyes were all that was left.

Ola knelt down and looked in my face. It was hard to see her, or even to breathe, because paint was clumping my eyelashes together in white spikes and coming apart in long white threads every time I opened my mouth to gather breath for another sob.

"It's all right," she said gently. "Whatever it is, it's all right."

"No." I shook my head. "It's not." I scrambled to my feet, turned away, and ran, my paint-soaked shoes squeaking across the linoleum. I didn't even know where I was going, but I had only gotten as far as the blank space where Saint Anne, the mother of Mary, had once stood, when I crashed into a wall of gray wool. I stumbled backward and saw that Sister Dorothy was blocking my path.

She reached out and put a steadying arm around my waist, smearing her habit with white paint in the process.

"Girls, go to chapel," she commanded Ola and Marlo. "Wendy, you come with me."

I didn't protest, but sagged against her as she half walked, half dragged me to her office. Mrs. Lang, the reception-ist, stood up, shocked, when we walked through the door. The paint had already started to dry in a thick, hard shell, encasing my hair and face so that I was sure I resembled a statue dug up from the ruins of Pompeii, frozen forever in a moment of horror.

Once we were inside Sister Dorothy's office, she closed the door softly behind her, opened a drawer in her desk, and took out a comb and a travel-size bottle of shampoo. She led me into a small white-tiled bathroom connected to her office that held a toilet and a tiny sink. She turned on the water, testing the warmth with the underside of her wrist, then dragged one of the spare chairs from her office into the bathroom and placed it in front of the sink.

"Sit down," she ordered.

I did as I was told. She leaned my head back and began rinsing my hair in the warm water. She poured some sham-poo into her palm—it was pasty and odorless, exactly the kind of no-frills beauty product you'd expect from a nun—and scrubbed my hair from scalp to ends with her strong, gentle fingers. When she'd rinsed all the paint off, she rubbed my hair with a towel and combed it through, taking her time, until it was clean and untangled.

"Okay," she said. It was the first time she'd spoken since she'd begun to wash my hair. "You can sit up now."

I sat in the chair with the towel around my shoulders,

my hair dripping, and she disappeared back into her office, returning a minute later with a clean, folded school blouse and uniform skirt.

"The skirt might be a bit big on you," she said. "But it will do for the rest of the day." She handed me a plastic grocery bag. "You can put your dirty clothes in here."

She went back into her office again, closing the bathroom door behind her. Because I really didn't have any other choice, I stepped out of my paint-spattered uniform, balled it up into the grocery bag, and put on the spare one that Sister Dorothy had given me. Once I was dressed, I opened the door. Sister Dorothy was sitting in her big chair, and on her desk was a cold can of Dr Pepper. She pushed it toward me and motioned for me to sit down.

"Here," she said. "Have some of your precious sugar water. Then we'll talk."

I wanted to ask her how she knew that Dr Pepper was my drink, but I realized it was a stupid question: Sister Dorothy knew everything.

"Thanks," I said quietly. I picked up the can and took a long sip.

"So," she said at last, studying me across the desk, "what was that all about?"

I looked at the floor. "I don't know."

"Alexis Nichols used to be your best friend, didn't she?"

"Used to," I mumbled. "Not since eighth grade."

"Well, you must be upset about her death."

"I know what you're gonna say." I held up my hand. "Don't. Please don't."

"I wasn't sure what I was going to say next," Sister Dorothy said. "Could you enlighten me?"

I sighed. "You were going to tell me that everything happens for a reason and that God has a plan. You were going to try to teach me a lesson."

"What lesson was I going to try and teach you?" She sounded genuinely curious. It pissed me off.

"That I should never wear headphones at night. Or that I shouldn't walk by the train tracks by myself. You were going to try to *explain* it to me. Just like you did when Sandy DiSanto and Tiffany Maldonado died."

"Ah." Sister Dorothy sat back in her chair. "I see. Well, I admit that when Tiffany and Sandy died, I didn't handle it the right way. I know that now. I was still pretty new to teaching, and I thought my girls expected answers from me. Now I know that they only expected support. And love." She cleared her throat. "I don't believe God takes the lives of children to teach the rest of us a lesson."

"Well, then why?" I could feel the tears coming again. "Why did she have to die?"

"I don't know, Wendy."

"Maybe it's because God doesn't care. Or maybe it's that God isn't real. Just a big phony fantasy. A superstition. A fucking ghost."

"Maybe." Sister Dorothy shrugged. If my cursing and blasphemy had shocked her, she sure didn't show it.

"I hear that you went to visit your father," she said, folding her hands on her desk. "How did you come to that decision?"

"Who told you *that*?"

"It's not important."

"Yeah, I visited him. So?"

"So, I think that was very courageous of you. Choosing forgiveness. Choosing love."

"Whatever." I sipped my Dr Pepper and stared out the window at the sun shining through the branches of the beech tree on the front lawn.

"You know, Wendy," she said, "believe it or not, you're not the first teenager I've ever come across who has questioned her faith. I know you're hurting right now. And I'm not asking you to believe in God. All I'm asking is that you believe in love. I know that you already do. Alexis knew, too. I'm quite sure that when she died, she died knowing that you loved her."

I stared down at my hands, at the dried paint caked under my fingernails.

"But how do you know that?" I whispered.

"Because," she said, reaching across the desk and squeezing my hand, "I've been around a long time."

30

IN THE MORNING, STUDENT COUNCIL MADE an announcement during chapel that this year's prom was being opened up to all grade levels, not just seniors, because it was the only way they could sell enough tickets to afford a ball-room. The entire chapel collapsed into a frenzy: this meant we underclassmen had one week to find dates and buy dresses and make hair appointments and order boutonnieres and rent limos. Of course my mind immediately went to Tino, to the phone number he'd left in *A Farewell to Arms*, but how could I just call him up out of the blue and ask him to my prom when I hadn't seen him in over two months? What if he'd already forgotten about me? What if he had a girlfriend? The thought of inviting more hurt upon myself at the end of such a crazy, awful school year was unthinkable. I'd rather just not go at all.

The second announcement was that the dance was being held in the Florentine Ballroom at the Hotel Belvedere. When I called Aunt Kathy to share this news, she actually shrieked into the phone.

"Did you say June sixth? That just so happens to be the *anniversary* of Lady Clara's wedding day! Please tell me I can be a chaperone! I promise I'll be discreet with my ghost hunting equipment!"

"Save your excitement," I said, laughing. "I'm not going."

"Not *going*? To *prom*? And just why the hell not?"

"I don't have a date!"

"*Spare* me," Aunt Kathy yelled. "Even *I* went to my prom. It's a high school rite of passage."

"I can go next year when I'm at Lincoln, Aunt Kath. I'm still a junior, remember?"

"Oh, phooey," she said. "I swear I don't know what's wrong with you girls today."

Later that same week, Sister Dorothy told us we didn't need to dress for gym class. Instead, she brought us down to the Sister Xavieria Schmidt Memorial Swimming Facility. At first we thought she was going to brutalize us one last time with an impromptu lap session. But instead, she just told us to sit down in a circle on the moldy tiles and "bear witness" as a crew of workmen drained the pool. I don't know what was so sad about it—we *hated* that pool—but as our class sat in the clammy dimness with the painting of Saint Adjutor glaring down at us and the big drain gulping down the water, lower and lower until that notorious pool was nothing but a tile-lined hole in the middle of the room, we put our arms around one another and cried. Only Kenzie remained dry-eyed, standing at a distance from the rest of us with her arms crossed tightly, her face pinched in annoyance—if there was one thing she hated, it was these kinds of cheesy emotional displays—but when the bell rang and I headed toward the locker room door, I turned back and saw that she was still standing there, looking down at the empty pool and blinking and blinking.

I went home that night and finally finished *A Farewell to Arms*. When I read the last line, I was so angry I threw the book against the wall, and my mom had to knock on my bedroom door and ask if I was all right.

Too upset to be nervous anymore, I scrolled through my phone's contact list, found Tino's number, and fired off a text message.

> **I can't believe you made me read that book. Why did Catherine and the baby have to die?**
> **Why did you make me read that? Don't you know that people die in real life? Why would I want to read about it in books, too?**

I went into the kitchen and poured myself a glass of lemonade to try and calm down. I drank it standing in front of the refrigerator because our third-floor apartment was already so hot that my tank top stuck to my skin, even though it was only the beginning of June. By the time I got back to my bedroom, he'd already called me three times.

We talked for hours. First about the book, but then about other things. I told him about Alexis. I told him about how I'd gone to visit my dad in prison, and about how the Saints Corridor had been erased with thick white paint to make way for vintage elegance in the heart of the city. When the time came for us to hang up, all I wanted to do was talk to him some more. Which is how I think I ended up asking him to prom.

I found a last-minute dress at Marshalls. It wasn't exactly my dream gown, but it was a pretty shade of lavender, had a high neckline that covered up my tattoo, and was on clearance for $29.99. The dance was held on a beautiful blue June day, and in the afternoon Aunt Colleen came over armed with a tote bag full of styling tools, sat me on the toilet, and wrangled my long hair into a complicated updo while my mom ran around the apartment, aggressively vacuuming and tidying in preparation for the arrival of the mysterious Tino. I did my makeup with the Chanel stuff Aunt Kathy had given me for Christmas, and afterward, when I put on my dress and heels and earrings and stepped out of my bedroom into the front room, my mom and Aunt Col both got sort of emotional.

"Look at you," Aunt Col croaked, holding my hands in hers. "How dare you go and grow up on us like that?"

"I wish Daddy was here to see you," my mom said before

bursting into tears and hugging me for so long I had to gently peel her off me when the doorbell rang. I buzzed Tino up, my stomach a tight ball of nerves. He was wearing a lavender tuxedo to match my dress, accessorized with a shimmery silver tie and pointy white patent-leather shoes. If any other guy had shown up at my door dressed like that, I'd think he was either a circus ringleader or a pimp. But all I thought when I saw Tino was, *God, he's so adorable* and *God, purple really is his color.* Which, of course, made me realize how much I liked him.

"Wow, Wendy," he said when I opened the door, two spots of color rising on his cheeks. "You look really beautiful." The sincerity of his words, so different from the fake compliments Kenzie and Sapphire and Emily and I used to hurl at one another, sort of made my heart explode.

The Florentine Ballroom didn't feel nearly as haunted when it was filled with girls in bright-colored dresses and a DJ was blasting hip-hop from the balcony where Lady Clara had spent her last moments.

I had agreed to let Aunt Kathy chaperone the dance, and when she saw Tino and me walk in, she waved furiously. She hugged me, then held me out by the arms so she could examine me.

"Stunning," she said approvingly. "Are you wearing your Chanel?"

"Of course," I grinned, extending a perfumed wrist for her to sniff.

"Excellent. And who's this dashing fellow?"

"Aunt Kathy," I said, "this is my friend Tino."

"You're a vision in purple," she said, shaking his hand.

"Thanks," he said. "I like your outfit, too."

"Do you?" She spun around, showing off the tassels along the sleeves of her tunic. "They say that brocade is a winter fabric, but I say rules are made to be broken."

"I couldn't agree more," Tino said solemnly. When we walked away to find our place cards, he leaned over and asked, "What the hell is brocade?" We both found this question hysterical and laughed all the way to our table.

Kenzie walked in just as a gaggle of waiters burst out of the kitchen, staggering under the weight of their enormous silver trays. She wore a gold strapless mermaid gown and a dangly pair of earrings that caught the light from the chandeliers overhead. Her skin was golden, her black hair piled up on top of her head, her eyes framed in thick faux lashes, and her signature pink lipstick perfectly in place. The guy she was with was no one I'd seen before. He was predictably gorgeous, older, wearing an immaculate black tuxedo with a coat and tails. They both looked like movie stars. But I didn't feel awed or intimidated or even jealous. Marlo had informed me that Kenzie's dad was making her go to Cherrywood Academy for her senior year. Rumor was, she hadn't even fought him on it. Maybe Alexis's death had sucked some of the venom from her heart. Whatever it was, I didn't have the energy to hate her. In spite of everything, I wished her well.

Just before the waiters opened the lids of their huge silver trays, Tino reached out a warm hand under the table and placed it over mine. He kept it there until they served the salads, when he had to let go to pour his dressing. This was probably the first time in human history that a girl has been jealous of a cup of ranch.

After dinner, Tino got up to use the bathroom, and the DJ began to play the big summer song. The dance floor filled up, but I stayed put at our empty table. I hadn't danced with anyone since Josh Gonzalez had taught me how to salsa at David Schmidt's eighth-grade graduation party, and I wasn't about to start now. I sat and picked at my ice cream while trying to ignore Aunt Kathy, who was stooping around the perimeter of the dance floor with her EMF meter, the tassels of her tunic dragging along the carpet. As I watched my classmates whirl around the parquet, I thought about all those unimaginable cities on the flight boards at O'Hare. I thought about where I'd go to college. What I'd learn there. Who I'd meet. I thought of my dad, painting his way through those long, flat, Nebraska prison days. And I thought of Alexis, which led me, as it always did now, to think about God. About whether He existed. And if He did, how could He deny her all those years ahead, the years where she was meant to play her violin in the Vienna Philharmonic, and fall in love, and dance in the goddamn rain? *God is not a 'He'*, I heard Sister Dorothy saying in my head. *God transcends gender.* Okay, I thought. Not

He. Not She. You. And then my thoughts shaped themselves into a prayer. *How could You take that away from her? How could You take her away from me? What have You done with my only ever friend?* I sat there through that stupid pop song, trying not to cry, and it was just as Ola Kaminski began organizing the girls from our Honors English class into polka lines that I felt the faintest, faintest wind stirring my hair.

I turned around and no one was there. Then I remembered what Aunt Kathy had said about what happens when you sit alone at a table in the Florentine Room. And so, when it came stirring again as I sat watching my classmates on the dance floor, I wasn't surprised. *It's no Sibelius*, I heard Alexis say. *But I still think you should dance.*

By the time Tino returned, I was on the dance floor, sweaty and laughing and trying to keep up with Ola's polka steps. I ran out, grabbed him by the hand, and pulled him onto the dance floor with me. It was as if the self-consciousness had fallen away from me like a coat that didn't fit. I finally understood that it was possible for contradictory feelings to exist side by side in the same heart. I could feel hopeful about the future while still aching about the past. I could feel deep happiness while still harboring deep sadness. I could move on and still miss someone forever.

Prom had turned into one big dance party. And I mean a *dance party*: Sister Dorothy doing a two-step with Sister Mary-of-the-Snows. Sister Paulette lifting up the skirts of her habit to do the Irish Jig. Veronica the Vegan twirling in circles, the tulle of her homemade gown spreading around her waist. Even Kenzie and Sapphire and Emily were grinding and twerking and shaking it like their lives depended on it. Everyone was laughing and hugging, all forty-two members of the junior class, and the seniors and freshmen and sophomores, too. We were dancing our last moments as ASH girls, dancing because Alexis couldn't, dancing with our memories, dancing alongside the invisible ghosts. By the end of it all we were soaked in sweat and our faces hurt from laughing and even Aunt Kathy was so taken by the joy that had filled the room that she stood smiling against the wall, her EMF meter hanging forgotten by her side.

After it was over, Tino and I drove back to the neighborhood.

"Hey," I said suddenly. "Do you want to see my old house?"

I directed him through the quiet streets. The cicadas were buzzing in the trees and we drove with all the windows open, the damp heat of early summer soft on our faces. When we pulled up to the house, I saw it: a FOR SALE sign.

"Looks sort of abandoned," Tino said.

"Let's go look in the windows," I suggested, and we parked at the curb and got out of the car, closing the doors softly. We went through the gangway to the side of the house and peeked in. There was no furniture anywhere, and the whole place had been completely redone. The buyers must have gut rehabbed it to flip it for a profit. The cluttered, cozy front room of my memory was now clean and modern and barely recognizable, which was sort of a relief. I couldn't feel nostalgic for something that was so different from what it had once been.

We went through the back gate, closing it carefully behind us—it still squeaked on its hinges just as it used to. But when we stepped into the backyard, the small square of lawn where we'd barbequed and played beanbags had been transformed, taken up almost completely by a huge octagonal above-ground pool.

"They cut down my tree," I murmured. "With my tree swing."

The reflection of the alley streetlights floated in the middle of the pool's surface, lighting up the blue inner walls.

"Care for a dip?" Tino raised an eyebrow at me, and the pool light reflected in his brown eyes.

"Are you serious?"

"Why not? Doesn't look like anybody even lives here." He had a point. The house was dark and mute, emptied of furniture. A thick nylon cover, dusted with leaves and debris, was pulled over the gas grill on the deck.

"You go first."

"Okay." He shrugged out of his lavender tuxedo, unbuttoned his shirt, and loosened his tie, folding each piece carefully and placing them in the grass. In the light from the alley I could see the faint ladder of his backbone, the wings of his shoulder blades, the neat hairline where his dark hair ended and his smooth neck began. William Shakespeare and

Michael Jordan gazed at me from their perches on his chest. A strange, lovely ache bubbled up inside of me as he unzipped his pants and stepped out of them, leaving them in a pool in the grass next to his shirt. He climbed up the steps in his boxer shorts, which had red-and-white checks on them, looked down at me and winked, then slipped quietly into the water, coming up a moment later with his hair slicked to his head.

"You coming in?"

"Turn around," I commanded, and Tino shot me a thumbs-up, took a huge breath, and plunged underwater, while I hastily shimmied out of my prom dress, leaving it in a pile next to his clothes, and hurried up the ladder in my underwear and into the water.

The pool water was sun-warmed, almost no cooler than the air, and now that we were both in it, we were suddenly shy with each other. We kept our distance, swimming by ourselves along the edges of the pool, asking each other polite, formal questions—"So, what classes are you taking next year?" "What's the best book you've ever read besides *A Farewell to Arms*?" "How many brothers and sisters do you have?"—as if this was a normal conversation between two teenagers who just so happened to be floating in an abandoned pool wearing nothing but their saturated underwear.

But eventually, after so much time had passed that our fingers had gone prune-y, we began to circle closer, letting our legs brush up against each other beneath the surface of the water, then pushing away again, both of us pretending it was an accident. Finally, I let my legs drift toward him underwater, tangling with his, except this time neither of us pulled away. I breathed deeply, trying to remember everything— the blooming lilacs on the bushes, the charred smell of a smoldering grill somewhere close, the cicadas, the sky. I was face-to-face with Tino, and his dark hair was slicked back like an otter's, and his eyes were two gloaming stars before me. I wanted him to kiss me but then I didn't, because I knew that the moment he did, it would forever be something that happened to me in the past and not something that was happening now, not something to look forward to with delicious anticipation. Maybe he felt the same way, because we stood there in the middle of the pool, submerged up to our shoulders, just looking at each other, not speaking, not laughing, waiting, and finally when he moved closer I closed my eyes and told myself to remember this, to remember everything, and all the shyness of a few moments ago was entirely forgotten. He reached his hands out of the water and gently began to take the pins out of my hair, one by one, until it fell first in pieces and then all at once around my shoulders, and we floated there, kissing beneath the waterfall of my hair. It was like we had discovered an opening in the fabric of the everyday and found beneath it a secret world that was ours alone, and I wondered if this secret world was what people meant when they talked about love.

Clouds gathered, blotting out the moon. The air began

to shift; soon it would collapse under the weight of itself, and the sky smelled like rain. We could see forks of heat lightning flashing in the sky beyond the trees and garages and houses. Thunder rumbled low, from far away, lightning snapped across the air above us—*one . . . two . . . three . . . four . . . CRASH!*—and then the rain swept in, pinging off the gutters and blacktop roofs and needling the water all around us. It was prom night and I was here in my old backyard with a boy named Tino and the raindrops pelted the pool water, dappling our faces with cold drops while our bodies were immersed in warm, still water, and I prayed Alexis was here with me somehow, feeling two kinds of water at the same time, one cold and moving and fresh and one warm and still, but both clean.

I thought to myself, floating there with Tino, that maybe it was time I revised my opinion about kissing. Kissing, I had now decided, is not overrated.

In fact, kissing is a miracle.

There's something I forgot to say about that last family vacation out to California, something that I've never told anyone. We'd spent the afternoon sightseeing down the 101 from Klamath to Fortuna, stopping for dinner at a brewery in McKinleyville. On the drive back to the hotel, as my dad sang along to the Tom Petty song on the radio and my mom fiddled with the GPS, Stevie Junior and I sat in the back seat looking out the window at the gray Pacific. The sky was spreading in gradations of twilight and the ocean was calm and shimmering when I saw the puff of vapor about a half mile out from shore. Then, a spinning dark shape rose from the water, turning like a screw, and the gray whale breached into the purpling sky. By the time I had fumbled for my phone to take its picture, the whale was gone, leaving no proof of itself but the rocking waves. I opened my mouth to tell everyone what I had just seen, but then my mom started talking about how fresh the avocado in her Cobb salad was, and Dad said the waitress kind of reminded him of that actress with all the DUIs, and Stevie Junior started laughing like crazy at some stupid video his frat buddy Meatwagon had sent him, and by the time I had a chance to say something, I had convinced myself that maybe all I'd seen was just another boulder.

But of course it had been real. A small, extraordinary moment, the kind that dots the path of each of our lives every now and again like a smooth, shining bead, placed there, I guess, to remind you that even if you're just an ordinary neighborhood girl, there is no such thing as an ordinary life.

ACKNOWLEDGMENTS

A special thank-you to Barry Goldblatt, for believing in this book based on fifty rough pages and for helping me to figure out what it was. Deep gratitude to Alexandra Cooper, for the love and attention you bestowed on every single word of this manuscript, and to everyone on the incredible team at HarperCollins, particularly Rosemary Brosnan and Alyssa Miele, and to David Curtis for the beautiful cover.

Thank you to Kaylee Kreutz, Katie Whitman, Samantha Heneghan, Sidney Burns, Meg Duggan, Kasia McCormick, Marty McGivern, Michelle Hynes, Elizabeth Brogan, Paula Jops, Alicia Pilarski, Theresa Cowen, Tim Padar, Sean Driskill, and Bridget Quinlan, for sharing your friendship and expertise with me on a host of random matters that made their way into this novel. A special thank-you to Don DeGrazia and Matt Martin, who gave my writing an audience through their reading series, Come Home Chicago, and whose feedback on the first few chapters of this book was invaluable.

Thank you to Dr. Kathy Burke, who gave me my first-ever

publishing credit for a short story I wrote in her creative writing elective (despite its questionable literary merit). You were exactly the teacher I needed when I was seventeen.

Thank you to the 1,000+ students I had the privilege of teaching during my years at Loyola Academy and Taft High School. I could never write books for young adults had it not been for the time I spent with each of you. And thank you to my amazing colleagues at both of these schools, from whom I learned so much (and shared many a spicy chicken patty). Teacher friends are the best kind of friends (Katie Seeberg and Colleen Walsh, I'm looking at you).

Unending gratitude to my family—the Morrisons, Brennans, and Gillespies, all those generations of Chicago Catholic school kids without whom I could never have imagined this book. Love most of all to Dan, Nora, Mom, and Dad. All the good that's in me comes from you.

To my three daughters, who are goodness distilled, you are my greatest pride. And to Denis, my love: I have spread my dreams under your feet. Everything is possible because of you.

Turn the page for a sneak peek at
SORRY FOR YOUR LOSS,
Jessie Ann Foley's tragicomic novel about a teen who
tries to find his place in the world following
the devastating loss of his brother.

1

LATE ONE FRIDAY NIGHT AT the beginning of May, Pup Flanagan sat slouched in one corner of the couch in Izzy Douglass's basement, staring with great concentration at the cracked screen of his phone and trying to ignore the slurpy tongue-on-tongue sounds coming from underneath the striped blanket in the other corner.

Pup wanted to leave, obviously. But he couldn't. After watching a piece on the *Today* show about teenage sexuality, Mr. and Mrs. Douglass had announced to Izzy that she and her horrible boyfriend, Brody, were no longer allowed to be in the basement alone together. A third party—someone who was honest, trustworthy, and had nothing better to do on a Friday night—must be present at all times. Pup fit all three of these descriptions; plus, Izzy had the kind of power over him that made him incapable of refusing her a favor, even one he dreaded.

"But how will your parents know we're not having a threesome down here?" Pup had asked. "I mean, I'm *also* a hormonal, sex-crazed teen, aren't I?"

"They're not going to worry about us having a three-some."

"How do you know?"

"*Because*, Pup," Izzy had said. "I mean—no offense—but it's *you*."

Which stung. Though she had a point.

Born when his mom was forty-nine and his dad fifty-five, he was Pup the Surprise if you asked his mother, Pup the Accident if you asked his seven older siblings. He was almost seventeen and had finally, his pediatrician thought, stopped growing. He stood six feet three inches tall and weighed 142 pounds, even in a sweat suit and Nikes with a Taco Bell Triple Double Crunchwrap sitting in his stomach. This height-to-weight ratio made him look less like a human being and more like a redheaded, buck-toothed praying mantis; in other words, not the kind of boy you had to worry could tempt your daughter into having a threesome.

A hand had wormed its way out of the blanket and was now feeling around the couch for something to grab; it landed on Pup's outstretched leg and began gently caressing the knuckly bones of his ankle.

"Hey!" Pup gave a kick, and Brody's hand slithered back inside. "Sorry, dude," came the muffled apology. "Wrong leg."

Pup pressed himself into as small a package as he could manage, folding his limbs beneath him like he was disassembling a tent, and squinted more intently at his phone. A trill of giggles broke his concentration, followed by a soft moan. Pup sighed loudly, as a pink-and-red-checked bra was tossed from beneath the squirming mound of blanket and landed at his feet.

"Okay," he said, kicking the bra away from where its strap had looped around the toe of his Nike. "I'm leaving."

"Wait!"

Izzy's flushed face, framed by a pile of tousled hair, emerged. Her naked shoulders were dusted in a constellation of pale freckles.

"Just give us ten more minutes. Please?"

"No." Pup shook his head, averting his eyes from her bare shoulders. "This is gross, and anyway, I should already be in bed by now. I have to be up super early tomorrow."

Brody's head emerged now, also flushed and tousled.

"With those artsy chicks, right?"

"Yeah."

"You trying to hit any of that? That girl Maya Ulrich was in my French class last year. She's *hot*, bro."

"Hey." Izzy smacked his arm, but not nearly hard enough, in Pup's opinion.

"What?" Brody said innocently. "I didn't mean she was as hot as *you*, Iz." He leaned over to start kissing her again.

"*Anyway*," Pup interrupted. "I'm not trying to *hit* anything. I'm just taking some pictures with them so I don't fail art."

"You're getting your ass out of bed at five a.m. to watch the sun rise with a bunch of girls, and you're telling me you're not even working any angles? Sunrise is when the *magic* happens, baby. The *romance*."

"I think that's actually sun*set*," Pup pointed out.

"Sunrise, sunset, what difference does it make?" Brody shook his head sadly and worked up a loud belch from his diaphragm. "The problem is that you have no game."

"What can I say, Brody? I guess I just don't have your charisma."

"Can't you stay just a *little* bit longer, Pup?" Izzy had gathered the blanket around her shoulders and was watching him hopefully.

"No." Pup avoided her gaze. "School's out in a couple weeks and I need this grade." He stuck his phone in his pocket, stood up, and hurried up the basement stairs without turning around and risking becoming ensnared in those green-flecked eyes that could make him do anything. He slipped past Izzy's parents, who were sitting across the kitchen table from one another, typing away furiously in the glow of their separate laptops. Pup wondered whether the Douglasses had seen any specials on the *Today* show about the negative effect of workaholic parents on their teenage children, but thought it best not to ask.

On the short walk back to his house, Pup took his phone from his pocket and called his sister Annemarie. It was almost midnight, but he knew she'd pick up. Annemarie always answered Pup's calls, even if she was at work, even if she was out with Sal, even if she was in bed and half asleep. In big families like the Flanagans, everyone pretends like they all love each other equally, but of course that isn't true. Pup loved Annemarie the best, and he liked to think that she felt the same way.

"How bad was it?" she said, picking up on the second ring. Pup could hear papers being shuffled around in the background.

"Are you still at *work*?"

"I'm *always* at work these days," she said. "Do you have any idea how much flower arrangements cost?"

Annemarie was getting married in the fall, and Pup, after having been a ring bearer about eight thousand times, was finally moving up in the world: he'd been promoted to groomsman. Sal, Annemarie's fiancée, was cool and all, but Pup still worried that after they got married, things would change between him and his sister. Then what? Each of the eight siblings in the Flanagan family had his or her role, and each role had its complementary partner: Patrick was the saint and Luke the sinner; Mary the practical-minded, no-nonsense paramedic and Jeanine the highlighted, manicured former sorority girl; and Elizabeth and Noreen, who were both too good-looking to understand the struggles of normal people. Though there were thirteen years between them, Pup and Annemarie were the two Flanagan children who no one really knew what to *do* with; Pup was the quiet afterthought of a sibling, seven years younger than the next-youngest child, and even though Annemarie was a successful corporate lawyer, she was also covered in tattoos and had renounced organized religion before she'd even graduated high school. She and Pup were the two outcasts of the family, and outcasts needed to stick together.

"So how *bad* was it?" Annemarie repeated now.

"Well, you called it."

"They hooked up right in front of you?"

"Under a blanket. I couldn't see anything. But I could hear stuff. And I could *imagine*."

"Oh, Pup."

He sighed. "I just don't *get* it."

"I'm sorry," she said. "I don't get it either."

When Izzy and Brody Krueger had first started dating, Annemarie had predicted it would last a month, two, tops. She was usually right about stuff like this, but Brody and Izzy were now going on month seven of their relationship, with no sign of it letting up anytime soon. Pup still couldn't believe Izzy could *like* a guy like Brody. Sure, he played the drums, so he had that going for him, but his grades were even worse than Pup's, he always had Dorito breath, and he talked with a fake California accent. He used words like "gnarly" and "rad," and pronounced "taco" like "taw-go." Not only that, he had long, dirty fingernails, evidence that he was a secret slob, like that guy from *The Catcher in the Rye*, one of the few English-class books that Pup had actually read (almost) all the way through.

But there was no point attempting to explain all of this to Izzy. Her attraction to Brody was an enigma wrapped in a puzzle, wrapped in one of those shrink-wrapped plastic covers they put around video games that are practically impossible to open without using your teeth.

"Pup," Annemarie began gently, "you're not going to like what I'm about to say."

"Please don't tell me to move on." He turned up the path to his house.

"It's just, how much longer are you going to *wait*? She *knows* you, Pup. And if someone *knows* you and still doesn't *want* you . . ."

"Wow. Harsh."

"Look, I'm sorry, kid." On the other end of the line, Pup could hear more papers moving around. He pictured Annemarie in her big-shot office on the twenty-third floor of the Aon building, stockinged feet kicked up on the desk, pinstriped blazer covering the tattoos that snaked up both of her arms. Flowers. Mermaids. Sal's name around one wrist, Patrick's name around the other. The Flanagan family tree, twenty-eight names and counting, blooming across the entirety of her back. She liked to joke it was a good thing she was on the chubby side, otherwise she'd already have run out of space. "I'm just tired. Listen. I love you, okay? So it's just hard for me to comprehend how somebody else doesn't."

"Doesn't *yet*."

"Right. Yet. Good night, Pup Squeak."

"Don't call me that. Good night."

He turned the key in the lock and tiptoed into the front room. As usual, his parents had dozed off on the couch in front of their favorite program, *Antiques Roadshow*. As images of a Chinese enamel porcelain vase—valued at $4,000!—flickered over their faces, Pup unfolded the worn green quilt that hung over the radiator and placed it gently across their knees. He picked up the empty teacup that was balanced precariously next to his mom's elbow on the rounded arm of the couch, then crossed the room to switch off the television. In the kitchen, he rinsed the cup in the sink, wiped away the grease from his mother's ChapStick, and put it away in the cabinet. Before heading upstairs to bed, Pup opened the fridge, chugged some milk from the gallon, and stood for a moment in the quiet stillness of the house. White light from the full moon poured through the window above the sink, illuminating the faded yellow tiles of the floor. Pup sometimes felt, in moments like these, that late-night silences held secrets, and that if he only listened hard enough the secrets would reveal themselves. He stood in the middle of the kitchen, listening, the milk handle cold in his hand. But then, from the front room, his dad let out a loud, burbling snore, and the mysterious stillness was shattered. He put the milk away and headed to bed.

Powerful and poignant coming-of-age stories by
JESSIE ANN FOLEY

Read the latest from this Printz Honor-winning author

JOIN THE

Epic Reads

COMMUNITY

THE ULTIMATE YA DESTINATION

◄ DISCOVER ►
your next favorite read

◄ MEET ►
new authors to love

◄ WIN ►
free books

◄ SHARE ►
infographics, playlists, quizzes, and more

◄ WATCH ►
the latest videos

www.epicreads.com